FOGS OF TIME

By: R.M. Almonte

Library of Congress Control Number: 2025947257
ISBN-10: 1969108002
ISBN-13: 978-1969108006

Publisher: R.M. Almonte Publishing
Publication Date: January 17, 2026
Edition: 1
Language: English
Print Length: 404 pages
Dimensions: 6 x 9 x 1.01 inches
Item Weight: 16.8 oz

Printer: Walsworth
Distributor: Pathway Book Service
Headquarters: 34 Production Ave, Keene, New Hampshire, 03431
Phone: (603) 357-0236
Website: www.pathwaybook.com

First Printing: January 17, 2026

www.rmalmonte.com

Printed in the United States of America

Acknowledgements

I would like to extend my heartfelt gratitude to everyone who helped bring this book to life. A special thanks to my manager, Samuel Hamodey, whose guidance and dedication made it possible to bring all the pieces together. I am also deeply grateful to Pathway Book Service for their support in distributing this work, and to Cynthia Hagen at Walsworth for her expertise and assistance in the printing process.

To The Reader

Thank you so much for reading this book. If you could take a moment to leave a review on Amazon or Goodreads, it truly makes a difference.

Getting to this point in my life hasn't been easy. I've been knocked down, broken, and tested—but I relied on my superpower.

What superpower?

The power to improve.

That's what I want you to take with you. Whatever your goals, whatever your dreams, your greatest strength is your willingness to improve. To get better every single day.

I don't care where you come from or what kind of shithole you had to crawl out of. If you give something everything you've got—and you refus to give up, you will improve. And when you improve, you change your life.
That's a promise.
So I'll leave you with this:

"Turn red tape into runways."

Because every obstacle can either trip you—or launch you. The choice is yours.

Thank you

PROLOGUE

Prologue

The wind climbed up 164th Street from the Hudson, carrying a few cold droplets. Caña pulled his hood tighter, shivering as his eyes swept the street. A rat darted under a car.

"Coño, is it going to rain?" He asked his co-worker, who was tucking himself under the building's arches, shoulders jammed into the corner.

He took out his money and counted it for the fifth time. "I hope not." He said, putting it away and looking around for more customers. "We haven't seen one custie since ten p.m." He checked his beeper, then walked to the middle of the street. "Damn, not even a car. Why don't you head home? I got this." Plancha said with a smile.

Caña turned to him, scrunching up his face. "Yeah, aight, I need to make this cheddar for my seed, nahmean?" He pointed at himself.

Plancha relaxed his shoulders. "I feel you. We're all out here for a reason."

He raised his head to look over the cars. "Here comes a custie." He rubbed his hands together. "Dimelo, papi… watchu need?"

A man in his mid-thirties approached, shifting his feet like he was slushing through snow. His pupils were dilated, his jaw twitching as he scanned the street.

"You know, papi, I need thamedicina," he muttered.

"I'm your doctor." Caña clapped his hands, arms spread wide and confidence dripping.

"Let me get an eightball." The excitement grew in his eyes as the words left his mouth.

Caña stuck out his hand. The guy reached into his pocket, then shook it. Caña turned around to count the money, then nodded toward his partner.

Plancha walked toward a gate between the buildings that led to wooden stairs that creaked every time you stepped on them. He lifted a chain made to look like the gate was locked. The cold metal made him want to shove his hand back into his pocket. The orange streetlamp only lit the way until the gate. He disappeared into the abyss of the stairs. Neither of them said a word.

The man ground his teeth, looking at every corner as he scratched his jaw and neck. Caña pulled back and wiped his hand on his jeans. He took out a picture, kissed it, and put it back in his wallet. He closed his eyes. “I’m just trying to feed my seed, God. Give me a better avenue to make a living. I can’t see a better way. Please forgive me and give my child the opportunities I never gave myself.”

His thoughts were interrupted by the screeching of the gate. His partner shook the man’s hand, who now smiled from ear to ear.

“Now, I can get this monkey off my back.” He stuffed it into his underwear.

“Don’t finish it all in one shot,” Plancha called, his face twisted in disgust as the man walked away.

“I don’t make any promises.” The man went through the parked cars, looked both ways, then headed toward Broadway.

“Just a couple more custies, and my pockets will be

full," His partner said.

"Yo, Plancha, what's your plan?" He asked.

"Make this paper." He gestured with his fingers.

"No, stupid, I mean life plan. Or do you plan to hustle for the rest of your life?" He said, questioning him.

"Nah, fam, I'm going to figure out how to start moving weight out of state. That's where the real cheddar is at, nahmean?" He put his arms up like he was posing for a picture.

Out of the corner of his eye, something moved. He swung his foot like he was playing kickball and connected with a rat almost the size of a Chihuahua. It took flight and hit a parked car with a thud, then scurried back into the safety of darkness.

"Home run… If it wasn't for that parked car, he would've made it across the street." Plancha jumped up and down, arms raised.

Caña gave him a side look.

"Bro, what's up with you today?" Plancha tilted his head to one side and squinted at him.

"Are you blind? Look around you, at us, at the kind of tecatos we deal with every day." His hands flailed.

"What? I'm not sniffing that shit. That's their problem. If they wanna hand over paper for some bling, that's on them." Plancha said defensively.

"That's my point. We're not any better than them. If anything, we are worse." His voice grew with irritation.

"Then you tell me—how else can we eat? My mom busts her ass everyday cleaning offices for the last twenty years and barely has enough to pay the rent. We arrived to this country with nothing. So I'm gonna make it big or die on these streets. You feel me?" He pointed to the ground.

"Exactly. Don't you think we can be better?" Caña gestured with his hands. "After tonight, I'm done. I might struggle, but I'm going to figure it out. There has to be something better than this." He pointed to the ground as well.

"You do you, but I'm going to make nine figures by any means necessary." Plancha tapped his belt buckle, clinking it with his gold ring.

From the corner, a woman watched him. Something about her felt familiar, but darkness kept her face concealed.

Tires screeched. Caña turned his head. Plancha ran toward the alley, lost his footing, and rolled down the steps.

Caña reached for his piece, but before he could grab it, he saw a flicker come from the car window. He grabbed his chest, dropping his piece. The sound of the clink on the cement echoed in his ear. He gasped for air. "I'm sorry I failed you as a father…" A tear trailed down his cheek.

A scream came from across the street. Several more shots reverberated throughout the block. His vision blurred as the darkness grew closer.

He saw a woman by a spaceship. She turned. "It's her… she grew up beautifully." He reached out—not for the strange woman, who was now kneeling beside him—but for someone who wasn't there.

As he coughed up some blood, the strange woman picked up his head and placed it on her lap.

"What woman? Wait, wait! Rodolfo, don't die…"

The voice of the strange woman was now fading as he breathed his last breath.

CHAPTER 1

Quisqueya
FOOD
BASICS
COLD BEE
MEAT
Quisqueya
SUPER MARKET
COLD BEER | FRUIT &
807

Chapter 1

Two Years Earlier

Maria lay on her stomach with a book in he hand. There was a knock on the door. "Come in." She said, looking up from her book.

"Reading again?" Rodolfo leaned against the doorframe. "Do you do anything else but read?" Her brother asked.

"Yes, Rodolfo. I study and do homework." She answered with a blank look.

"I know that." He said, rolling his eyes. "Come on, we have to go to papi's bodega."

"Ok, let me finish this last paragraph." She said.

He leaned against the wall with his arms crossed.

"Ok, I'm finished." She put her bookmark on the last page she read, got up, and put her book on the bookshelf.

"Don't you think you got too many books?" He ran a finger along the spines.

"Nope." Maria said. "Mami promised me ten more when I finish this one."

"With all the books you have, you could have some really fly clothes." He said, coming closer and giving her a kiss on her head.

"Why would I need all those clothes? I prefer books." She said plainly.

"Never mind." He shook his head and opened the door.

They walked out of the building. The sky was clear and sunny, with kids her age playing on the sidewalk. She glanced at them, looked down, and then turned her eyes toward the corner of Broadway.

"Dimelo, Caña." A guy with a Yankees cap tilted to the side called him.

"Hold on, sis, be right back," He said, putting his hand on her shoulder.

Maria crossed her arms and tapped her foot. She looked up and saw older women in the windows, pillows under their elbows—the CCTVs of this era. One of the women smiled and blew Maria a kiss. She waved back. But the woman's smile soured when her eyes landed on Rodolfo. She shook it off when she noticed Maria was watching her.

Maria wondered why, but brought her focus back down to her brother, who had slipped right out of earshot.

They spoke for a few minutes. Plancha glanced over his shoulder twice, scanning the street before leaning closer to Rodolfo.

"I got you, Plancha. I'll be back later this evening. I have to go see this girl first." Rodolfo said, grinning wide.

They walked to the corner where a small diner sat—one of the few places that had stood since long before Maria's family arrived from the Dominican Republic in the late 70s, when she was only two.

Before turning the corner, the sharp crack of music hit her ears. The rich sound of **El Zafiro** spilled into the street from a nearby radio. Maria's lips curled faintly. Her mother played the same song while cooking, forcing her to dance in the kitchen. She still hated it.

"¡La botella tá vacía!" One man shouted, waving an

empty bottle of Barcelo.

Four men sat on milk crates, a worn plywood board balanced across their knees as a makeshift domino table. Others stood around with coffee cups in hand, watching intently as the pieces clacked like gunfire against the wood.

"Then go get another one!" Another man barked, pointing his lips toward Maria's father's bodega. "You've been drinking for free all week. It's payday, don't tell me you're broke."

Laughter rippled through the group as the first man walked off. A moment later, one of the players slammed his domino hard onto the board. "**Capicúa!**" He shouted, throwing both hands in the air.

Maria glanced curiously at them, tugging Rodolfo's shirt. "What does *capicúa* mean?"

Rodolfo tilted his head with a grin. "For a girl who reads so much, you don't know the simplest of things?"

"I don't read about Washington Heights culture." She replied flatly.

He rolled his eyes and nodded toward the game. "In domino, when you win on both ends, you get extra points.

That's *capicúa*."

"Oh." She smiled softly. "Thank you."

They stepped into her father's bodega, the small bells on the door jingling as it swung shut behind them.

"One forty-nine," Her father said to a man handing him two crumpled dollar bills. He slipped a cold Heineken into a paper bag and handed it over. Alex Bueno was playing from the radio behind the counter; it was so loud Maria could barely make out his words.

"Oh, excuse me, señorita." The man said, smiling as he shifting his bag.

"Sorry." She said softly, stepping aside. He reached for the wall, where an old bottle opener was nailed above an empty Bustelo can.

Her father turned sharply to Rodolfo, his face stern. "This is the time you show up?"

Rodolfo shrugged, his shoulders sinking. "I had to wait for her to finish reading." He muttered.

"La bendición, papi," Maria said gently.

His whole expression softened into a wide smile. "Dios

te bendiga, mi amor." She slipped behind the counter.

A man walked in, resting his hand on the counter. "Dame una chata."

Her father looked out the window, reached down, and grabbed a small bottle of Barceló, sliding it into a brown bag. He set it on the Plexiglas counter where all the candies were neatly stacked, then counted out change for the man.

Without looking up, he turned back to Rodolfo. "There's a bunch of boxes in the basement. Bring them up and put them in the fridge."

"I can't, papi. I have to go to the Bronx." Rodolfo said pleadingly.

Her father threw up his hands, frustration in his voice. "This new generation... nunca tienen tiempo pa' trabajar. Look, I built this store with these hands, and everything you have came from the sweat off my forehead." He wiped his brow with his palm, showing the proof.

"I know, papi." Rodolfo said, staring at the ceiling.

"¿Tú sabes? You know nothing until you have your own family. Then you'll understand."

Rodolfo stood quietly, lips pressed tight.

“Está bien, go.” Her father finally waved him toward the door.

“Gracias, papi.” Rodolfo opened the door just as a customer stepped in, brushing past him.

“Pon le veinte peso’ ahi’ siete con el catoirse. The man said in a strong Cibaeño accent, handing over a twenty-dollar bill. “Hopefully, God gives me a little luck.”

Her father jotted the numbers down in his worn notebook. “La Virgen doesn’t stay behind the door every day,” He chuckled.

“One can only hope.” The man sighed, taking his receipt before heading out.

Maria tilted her head, watching her father. “Papi... why are you so hard on Rodolfo?” She asked, her voice soft, almost pleading.

He glanced down at her, brushing his fingers through her hair before kissing her forehead. “Mi amor, he has no discipline, unlike you. You study, you read, you get good grades. Him?” He shook his head. “He barely shows up to school. The teachers say he might not graduate, and he skips most of his classes. You see the problem."

"I know, but—" She stopped when another customer walked in, the door chimes ringing again.

***

Rodolfo got off the bus, looked to the left and right, and gripped the knife that was in his pocket. A group of guys walked by him blasting Big Daddy Kane on their boombox. They gave him a quick glance, then kept walking.

He walked for a few minutes and reached a brown building that was five stories tall. He skipped up three steps that opened up into the courtyard. He reached the front door and buzzed. A few moments later, the window slid open. The afternoon light spilled across her caramel skin and curly hair. "Dímelo, mi negro chulo." She said affectionately in Spanish.

His heart skipped a beat, and he rose to salute her. "I've missed you." He said.

"Then come up and show me." She tucked her head in and closed the window. A minute later, the buzzer rang, and he ran up a few flights of stairs. The door flung open, and she jumped on him. Their lips locked as he closed the door.

***

He was looking at the ceiling with a big smile on his face. He turned to her and kissed her cheek. His hand drifted up to her chest, but she caught it with both hands. She squeezed his hand, then kissed it and held it against her cheek. She gazed out into space. Her breathing slowed, fingers twisting the blanket.

"What's wrong, babe?" He asked, sliding an arm under her neck.

"Um..." A tear rolled down her face.

He sat up. "Did I do something wrong, Carmensita?"

She sat to meet his gaze, covering her breast with the blanket. "No, no, no." She said, shaking her head. "It's just that..."

"Is someone bothering you at school, because you know I—"

"No, that's not it." She said, cutting him off. "I'm..."

"You're what?" He said, raising his voice with concern.

"I'm pregnant." She stared at him, waiting.

For a second, everything went silent, only his heartbeat in his ears. “What?” He lay there with a blank look.

A few more tears rolled down her face.

“Wepa.” He shot out of bed, ran to her side of the bed, and grabbed her hand. “I’m going to be a dad?” He said kneeling next to her kissing her hand.

She wiped her face. “You mean... you’re happy that I’m pregnant?”

He held her hands and kissed them several times. “Of course. I couldn’t be happier.”

“When are you going to tell your parents?” She asked, and he lost his smile.

He got up, walked to the window, and stared at the sky for several seconds. He turned his head to look at her. “I know my sister will be so excited.”

“And your mother?” She put her feet on the ground.

He smiled. “Are you kidding? She can’t wait to be a grandmother. The problem will be keeping her from spoiling the child.” He chuckled.

“So, the problem is your father? Isn’t it?” She frowned.

"Yup! I can hear his voice now. 'You can't even clean your own ass right, and you're going to have a baby? Don't think I'm going to raise the baby.' Those are the exact words he would use. I think it's best we keep it quiet for now." He turned his head to look at her.

Her eyes dropped to her lap as her finger played with the sheet.

He ran over to her. "I got this. I will do whatever it takes to take care of you and the baby. We will do this together." He kissed her stomach.

She ran her fingers over his head. "Yes, we will, and we will give her the things we didn't have growing up."

He looked up. "What about your mother? I know she is in D.R."

"Oh, she will be excited. It's my aunt who I live with. She will be worried, naturally, but she will come around." She reassured herself.

He looked at the clock on her nightstand. "I have to get going, but I have three hundred dollars. I will bring you more money so we can start saving for our child. You still have the shoe box that you keep your money in?"

"Yes, it's right there." She pointed at her closet on the top shelf.

He brought the box to the bed, grabbed his jeans, pulled out the cash, and placed it inside the box. "As the money flows in from hustling, I will stash it here."

"I don't like you being out there. What if..." Her voice cracked, tears pooling in her eyes.

He sat next to her on the bed. "I know, I don't like it either. But I will do this only for a short time while we save enough money, and then..." He stood up and put his pants on. "Maybe we will start a business or something. You're almost done with school, so you will graduate before the baby is born."

"Be careful out there. We need you more than ever." She rubbed her belly, stood up, and kissed him.

"Always." He gave her another. "I will be back tomorrow."

CHAPTER 2

Chapter 2

A Few Months Later

Maria sat on her bed with a book in hand. The soft cooing of pigeons on the windowsill mingled with the flutter of wings, carrying off as the neighbor's voice scolded one of her kids. The door opened. "Mi amor." A voice called to her.

She looked up. "La bendición, mami."

"God bless you, my love." She walked into the room. "Today is Friday, why aren't you outside playing with the other children? It's such a nice day."

"I like reading, and I finished all my homework." She said, lifting her chin as if stating a fact.

Her mother put her arm around her daughter and kissed her head. "La vecina is having a birthday party in the basement down the block do you want to go?"

"No, mami, I'd rather stay at home. I really want to finish this book." She closed it and showed it to her.

"Ok, sweetie, if you need me, you can come to the basement. I left moro and your favorite carne guisada on the stove. Just stick it in the microwave."

"Yes, mom. Have fun. I know how much you love to dance, but you know papi won't be happy." Maria glanced out her door, lowering her voice, as if she didn't want her father to hear.

She waved her hand as she stood up. "He's like an old mule who doesn't know how to enjoy life. I do." She walked toward the door. "Remember, don't let anyone in, and make sure to leave some food for your brother."

"I will, mom." Maria watched her mother leave, the sound of two older women gossiping drifting up from the first floor.

***

Altagracia walked in. She took a swig of her beer and closed the door behind her. She finished her beer in one gulp before walking into the kitchen. Her face was flushed, and her shoulders still swayed slightly to the rhythm stuck in her head.

She threw away her beer in the bin, opened the fridge, and took out another beer. She grabbed the bottle opener off the fridge. She dropped it on the floor, then bent over with a slight groan and picked it up, opened her beer up, and placed it back on the fridge. She walked towards the living room.

"Is this the time you show up?" Pablo asked, turning off the tv.

"Today is Friday, and I worked all week. I need to burn off a little steam." She took another swig of beer and plopped down onto the couch.

He picked up his tea off the coffee table and took a sip. "Why did you leave our daughter alone in the house?" His voice was low, tight, like he'd been waiting for this fight.

She took off her dancing shoes. "She's ten, and you know she doesn't like parties. She prefers to read with her free time." She put her feet up on the coffee table.

Pablo sat back and lifted his legs on the La-Z-Boy. "What about our son? Do you know where he's at?"

"He's probably hanging out with his friends." She said, relaxing her shoulders.

"Friends? There just a bunch of tígueres. Is that what we are raising, a hoodlum?"

"You ride him too hard. If you tried to get to know him, he might just open up to you." She drank half the bottle and placed it on the table.

He scoffed at her. "He doesn't need a friend. What he needs is a father who will teach him discipline." He drank his tea and stared at her.

"Tú sí jode." She gave him a dirty look.

"I don't bother. Why do you protect him so much?" He leaned forward in his chair.

"Because he came out of my crica." She said sharply, grabbing her crotch.

He stared at her. "He's my son too, and I'm trying to make sure he doesn't end up in jail or dead. Do you know what people are saying about him?" He tightened his mouth.

She sat straight up and picked up her beer. "You're going to listen to those chimosos?"

"It's not just gossip. They are saying that he's selling that shit out there." The room went silent for a beat, the street noise faint through the window.

She took a deep breath. “I’ll talk to him, alright.” Her tone was sharp, but her hand trembled slightly as she grabbed the bottle. “I’m going to bed.” She left towards the bathroom.

***

Merengue spilled from the little radio on top of the fridge, matching Altagracia’s swaying hips as she opened the cabinet and grabbed the salt. Pour a little bit into her hand, took the lid off the pot of boiling water and dropped it in. Then she did another turn showing off her skill.

“La bendicion mami.”

She looked over and smiled. “Good morning, and may god bless you. Did you sleep well?”

Maria walked over and gave her a kiss on her cheek. “What are you cooking?” She glanced at the sizzling pot, steam rising.

“Your favorite, mangu with the three golpes. How do you want your eggs?” She said rubbing her belly.

“Scrambled,” Maria said, going into the fridge and grabbed milk.

"Here is a cup." She grabbed a cup from the cupboard over the sink.

"Thank you, mami."

"You're welcome, my love. Can you wake up your brother and let him know that I'm making breakfast?"

"Yes, mom." She turned around and left the kitchen.

Altagracia went into the fridge, grabbed plantains, salchichon, frying cheese, and the carton of eggs. She placed them on the counter and grabbed the cutting board that was hanging the wall. She opened the drawer and took out a knife. She began by cutting the ends off the plantain. The knife tapped against the cutting board, quick and steady, her hips still swaying with the music.

"La bendicion, mami." Rodolfo came over and kissed her on the cheeks.

"God bless you."

He looked at the counter. "Oh, you making mangu?"

"Of course, this meal will make you strong." She pumped her arm and started slicing the plantain and peeling the skin off the plantain in one shot. He giggled and then reached for a cup. He walked over to the fridge and got some orange juice. "Siéntate ahí, por favor." She pointed to the kitchen table with her lips.

"What's wrong, mami?" He said, pulling out the chair and sitting down.

"People are saying that you are selling that mierda on the streets. Is that true?" Her voice was calm.

He looked down at the table and fumbled his thumbs over the handle.

"Well, is it?" She took the skins and threw them into the bin.

He looked up at her. "No, mami."

She cut the plantains into quarters, dumped them into the water, and covered them, then turned and leaned one hand on the counter. She softened her face. "Because you know everything I have belongs to my children, and nothing is more important to me than taking care of both of you. I will go to war with any person who comes between the well-being of my children. You know that, right?" She stopped to stare at him.

His heart pounded as he thought of his own child on

the way. He swallowed hard, keeping it buried. *You don't know how true that is, mom*." He thought to himself. "No, mom, I'm fine. I don't need any money."

She grabbed the salchichon and peeled the plastic off it. "You know that life only leads to two paths. Dead or in jail. Don't end up like my cousin, who was shot in the head execution-style when you were only five years old. We couldn't even have an open casket for him because it was so bad." Her voice cracked on the last word." To this date, tia mourns him, and if something happened to you, they are going to have to kill me as well."

"Mami, don't worry. I'm ok."

She scanned him over for a few seconds. "I'm not your father, you know you can talk to me. Whatever it is, we go through it together. You know why?" She paused for few seconds to let him think about it. "Because in these veins is the same blood. But you will understand when you have your own children." The words landed heavier on Rodolfo now than she realized.

He stood up and grabbed both her shoulders. "I'm ok, mom. No need to worry."

"If you say so." She looked down. He kissed her on the cheek.

Three Weeks Later

Rodolfo climbed up the stairs to his apartment. His legs felt heavy, like he was carrying more than just his own weight. He took out a wad of money and began counting it. *Once I have enough money, I will start a bodega or some sort of business. Just need to keep this up for another year or so,* he thought to himself as he stood in front of his door.

The door swung open. Rodolfo held his breath. Pablo looked at his hand. "You see, coño, this is what I'm talking about." Pablo's voice echoed in the hallway, deep and sharp, cutting through the walls. "Tato, you want to be a man, then be a man. Grab your shit and lárgate de mi casa."

Rodolfo's face fell to the ground. "Wait, papi." He reached out with his arm.

It was too late, Pablo left him at the door and flew into his room, crashing the door open and turning on the lights. He grabbed a bag from his closet and started stuffing clothes into the bag. "Papi, what's going on?" Maria sat up on her bed, rubbing her eyes. She blinked against the light, confusion creeping across her face.

"Nothing, my love, go back to bed." He opened his drawers and continued to put clothes inside of it. Rodolfo sat next to his sister, hugging her and kissing her on the head.

"¿Qué carajo tá pasando??" Altagracia said, adjusting her robe.

"Ask your son to show you all the money he had in his hand. If he wants to be a man, then let him, but he's not putting this house in danger."

"Are you going crazy? You can't kick our son out onto the streets at this time of night." She tried to take the clothes from him. Her jaw clenched, body shaking, holding herself back from lunging at Pablo.

Rodolfo stood up and held his mother, who looked like she was going to bite her husband. "Mami, he's right. I should go."

"No! No way. This is your house too."

"I'm eighteen already, and I have to find my own way in life." He held both her hands and kissed them. "It's ok, mami, I will be fine."

Maria ran over and almost knocked him down. She squeezed him so tight that he had to breathe out. "Don't leave! I need my older hermano." Her little hands clawed at his shirt, her voice breaking between sobs.

He knelt down in front of her. "It's ok, sis, I will still come around and see you." He looked up at his dad, who put the bag down and left the room. He put his attention back on his sister.

"It's not the same." She dug her face into his shoulder and began to sob.

His mother took a deep breath and wiped her tears. She ran towards her room. Pablo was sitting in his chair with his face in his hands. He looked up and wiped his eyes. She gave him a dirty look and continued to her room. When she got to the hallway, Maria was trying to pull her brother back into the house. "Don't leave. Don't leave." She pleaded.

He stood strong enough not to be moved by her, but just stared out the door. He looked at his mother with tears streaming down his face and eyes red.

"My love, he has to go, but he will be back to visit."

She tugged at her lightly. She wouldn't let go of him, gripping harder around his waist. He began to sob. Altagracia hugged both of them. She knelt down next to her and looked at both of them. "I love you guys more than I love my own life. If you want to stay, you can. I will deal with your father."

He wiped his face. "No, mami, he is right. I have to be on my own for now."

She wiped her face. "Ok, my love. Here." She passed him some cash.

"No, mami. I got this." He refused. "You need the money to buy Maria books." They both giggled, but Maria was still holding on. He knelt down next to Maria. "I will pick you up from school, and we will go to the park tomorrow. Would you like that?"

He picked her face up. "Yes." She said in between her crying. He kissed her on the cheeks and then left.

The door clicked shut. Maria collapsed to the floor, her small body shaking as she held onto her mother. Altagracia wrapped her arms around her daughter, but couldn't hold back her own sobs this time. Pablo stood frozen in the hallway, his back to them, rubbing his face with both hands, his chest rising heavy.

The apartment fell silent except for Maria's muffled cries tangled with her mother's, the sound spilling into every corner of the house.

Two Years Later

Bang! Maria sat up in her bed. Her heart was pounding in her chest. "Was that a gun shot?" She asked herself. Her feet recoiled when they touched the surface of the floor. She fumbled around, looking for slippers. She got on all fours and, in the darkness, felt around for them. She grabbed them, slipped them on, and shuffled her feet towards the door.

She turned on the lights in the hall and squinted her eyes. She walked past the bathroom and kitchen and reached the living room. She felt a little dizzy, stumbled, and sat on the floor. The room shifted, gently but impossibly. She placed both her hands on the ground to stable herself.

She looked up and saw a darkness growing on the ceiling. Twinkles of stars began to appear and surrounded her, transforming the entire living room. The air thickened, humming like something alive. Every hair on her arms stood on end. Maria's body floated up, and a green fog began to form around her. She looked at her skin and saw blue sparkles coming from it. With every passing second, the fog grew thicker until it engulfed her.

Then everything went dark.

Her father's voice tore through the darkness like a blade.

"Maria, Maria." A voice called out to her. She felt her body being picked up. "Mija, are you ok? What's wrong?"

"Oh, my god, what happened to our daughter?" She made out her mother's voice. Altagracia's voice trembled, caught between prayer and scream.

The door rang. "Who could that be at this time of night?" Pablo said. "Go and answer it. I will stay with her."

Maria felt a hand over her cheek. She groaned. "Where am I?" She blinked a few times before she could make out her father's face.

Then a scream came from the front. "Ay, dios mio! No."

"Tell one of the medics to come upstairs." Pablo heard the voice of a man. "Ma'am, calm down."

Pablo rushed to the hallway with his daughter in hand. He saw three police officers were attending to his wife. Behind them, muffled voices on the radio crackled words he couldn't process—"drive-by... one suspect... male victim down."

"What's happening?" He called out to them.

A female officer and a detective walked forward. "We need to talk to you." He tried to walk past them.

"What's wrong with mami?" She now was fully aware of her surroundings.

"She will be ok." The female officer reached out with her arms to grab Maria. Pablo stared at his wife, who was wailing and thrashing her body on the floor. "She shouldn't be seeing this. Where is her room?" The female officer cradled her. "Do you have an older daughter?"

Pablo was so focused on his wife that he didn't hear her question. Maria looked at her mother and cried out for her.

She walked into Maria's room with her and closed the door behind her.

Pablo tried to walk towards his wife, but the detective stopped him. "I'm sorry, sir, I really need to ask you some questions. The medics will take care of her, I promise. Please walk with me to the living room." He looked at her for few seconds with tears swelling up in his eyes.

He wiped his face and walked towards the living room. The detective and Pablo sat down, and he broke the news: that Pablo's only son, Rodolfo, had been killed in a drive-by shooting. Pablo's chest tightened, like the air had been ripped out of him. After about ten minutes of him trying to find out information from Pablo between his sobbing, the detective got a call on his radio. He called another officer. "I'm sorry, Mr. Del Camino. Officer Mc Cormick will take the rest of your statement. I will come back as soon as I can." Pablo nodded, put his face in his hands, and sobbed.

Down the hall, in her room with the female officer, Maria heard her mother's sobs through the thin walls. She pressed her hands over her ears, but the sound still seeped in, wrapping around her like a weight she couldn't escape. The officer crouched next to her, rubbing her back gently, whispering soft words, but Maria couldn't hear over the crying.

The detective stepped outside in front of their building, where police had already roped off the area. "Go for Detective Peterson." He adjusted his earpiece. "What do you mean, she was taken from the ambulance by a gang?" His free hand clenched as he turned toward the flashing lights, scanning the chaos. "I don't care if you have to put roadblocks up in the entire Washington Heights. Find her. She is the only witness we have to this murder."

A car pulled up to the scene, and two young detectives came out with their heads hung low. "What the hell happened?" He said raising his voice.

A Nuyorican officer looked at him. "Jefe... she's not just in shock. She's frozen. Catatonic. Whatever she saw... it broke something in her. She's just sittin' there, starin' past us, like we're not even in the room. So, we were sending her to Columbia Presbyterian to have her evaluated and then take her statement later when she calmed down. We had no idea it was this type of case."

Peterson took a few breaths and paced in front of the steps. "You're thinking the same thing as me, aren't you?"

The black detective stepped closer to him. "This is starting to look like a professional hit." His jaw tightened. He lowered his voice so only the two detectives could hear. "The only witness disappears, and no one can find the group that took her. Reports say a black female, a white male, three Hispanics, and one Native American male."

"That doesn't sound like the typical drug dealers in this area." Peterson said.

Several Days Later

Maria was sitting in the back of the funeral home. She couldn't understand why they did an open casket. The face in the box looked like a stranger wearing her brother's skin. It looked nothing like her brother, and it just made everyone feel worse. From her angle, she couldn't see her brother, and her face muscles hurt from crying. Her mother was sitting in the front, being held by neighbors and family members. Each time her mother screamed, Maria's legs twitched, like her body wanted to run—but she stayed frozen. People passed by and talked to her, like if nothing was wrong.

She turned her face and saw a young woman with a stroller. Her eyes wandered toward the stroller. The little girl stared back, wide-eyed, like she was trying to study her. A strange pull twisted in Maria's chest, something she didn't understand. Without thinking, she walked over. The lady stood in a corner, sobbing. "Your daughter is beautiful." She said to her.

The lady wiped her face and smiled. But when she looked at the casket, she began to sob again.

Maria crouched down and covered her face, playing peekaboo. The baby giggled softly, but her gaze stayed locked on Maria's steadily, almost knowing, like she recognized something inside her. Maria smiled, though it left her unsettled. The lady looked back down at them and smiled. "How did you know my brother?" Maria asked with a smile.

Her eyes opened wide. "He's your brother... then you must be Maria." Carmensita yelped, and her hand shot up to cover her mouth. Her eyes darted to the baby, then back to Maria, panic flashing before she turned away. "I'm sorry... I have to go." She turned the stroller, almost hitting Maria, and took off.

Maria stood frozen, staring at the doorway as the stroller disappeared. Her chest felt tight, the baby's steady gaze still burned into her mind. She didn't know why, but she felt connected to her—like a thread she couldn't see, but couldn't shake.

Her thoughts shattered as her mother collapsed onto

Rodolfo's empty shell of a body, the polished casket creaking under her weight. Surrounded by lilies that could not mask the sourness of death, she clawed at his suit, sobbing his name, her shrieks ripping through the silence of the room like glass shattering on marble. The mourners froze, eyes lowered, but Maria couldn't look away. Each ragged cry carved into her chest, dragging her into the brutal truth— the casket didn't cradle a stranger; it cradled her brother. That she no longer had. Her body gave out, and the light drained from the world.

Several Days Later—After the Funeral

Maria was sitting on the bench during recess in the school yard. Kids yelled and laughed around her, but the noise felt far away, like she was underwater. Her shoulders were slumped forward, and she was frowning and staring at the floor.

"Mrs. Gonzales, you should go talk to her. She's been like this since her brother tragically died." Vice Principal Peterson tapped her on the shoulder.

"My god, it's so heart breaking to hear of a youth passing such a way." Mrs. Gonzales held her chest.

"I know, and the worst part is that he was one of my students when I used to teach second grade. I can't imagine what she is going through."

"No one, let alone a child, should experience that." They both wiped their eyes.

"It's the realities of teaching in Washington Heights. I wish it wasn't." Vice Principal Peterson said.

"I will go talk to her." The Vice Principal got distracted by some kids misbehaving, and Mrs. Gonzales walked over with a smile on her face. "Hi, Maria." She sat next to her and gave her a hug from the side.

"Hi, Mrs. Gonzales."

"Why don't you have a book in your hands?"

"I'm too sad to read."

"I understand. If you ever need to talk about it, you know I'm here, right? You have my number, and you can call me day or night." She tried to look at Maria's eyes.

Maria continued to stare at the floor. "I know." She said, looking up.

Mrs. Gonzales' attention was drawn elsewhere when she saw two boys arguing over a ball. "I'm sorry, Maria. I have to go, but please come see me anytime you need me." She dashed off to break them up.

Maria continued to stare at the floor. A shadow fell over her.

Maria looked up and saw a chubby boy towering above her, about twice her size. He stood grinning, cruel and smug, blocking out the sun.

"Bang! Bitch!" He jabbed his fingers like a gun straight at her face, his smirk wide and ugly. *"Is that how your brother died?"*

Something inside her **snapped**.

The world went silent except for the pounding in her ears. Heat roared up her neck, fire burning behind her eyes. She shot up from the bench and lunged forward, her forehead slamming into his nose with a sharp crack.

He screamed, stumbling back, but Maria was already moving—faster than she thought possible. Her elbow crashed into the side of his head. He staggered, dazed, trying to balance, but Maria grabbed his wrist, planted her foot, and threw him clean over her hip.

He hit the pavement with a heavy thud.

Maria landed on top of him, fists hammering down, one after the other, until her knuckles burned. Screams rose around her, but she couldn't hear them—only her ragged breath, loud in her skull.

Hands grabbed her under the arms, yanking her up, but she kicked and thrashed, desperate to break free. The crowd's shouts blurred into a single roar, muffled and distant.

Then, suddenly, it stopped.

Her chest heaved. Sweat stung her eyes. Her whole body trembled. She stared down at her fists—scraped, red, and raw—and her breath broke into sobs she didn't even feel coming.

The vice principal ran towards the boy who now was crying. The bridge of his nose was now bruised, and his lip was busted with trickles of blood coming down. Another teacher came with tissue to wipe his face.

Mrs. Gonzales placed her on the ground. "Maria." She yelled out to get her attention. She stared at her hands, trembling. She didn't remember half of what she just did. The teacher ushered Maria towards the school.

***

Maria was sitting with the secretary, reading a book. She looked up and saw her mother fly in through the office door. Maria went to get up, but the secretary placed a hand on her shoulder. “Your mother and the vice principal need to talk.”

“Ok.” She sat back down and continued reading.

The vice principal led Altagracia into her office. “Thank you for coming.”

“What happened?” She looked out of the office to where her daughter was sitting.

“Please sit down, and I will tell you.” She pointed with her hand.

She reluctantly sat and folded her hands on her lap. “Did something happen to my daughter?”

“Well...” She looked towards Maria. Then she looked back at Altagracia. “She...” Her attention wondered off.

“What happened?” Altagracia placed her hand on the desk.

“She got into a fight.”

“Fight?” She raised her voice a bit. “Maria doesn’t even like stepping on bugs. To my knowledge, she has never got into a fight. You mean someone is bullying her." She said defensively.

"You're right, we've never had a problem with your daughter. If not, it's been quite the opposite. She is an exceptional student. Maria has the best grades and is the top reader in the entire school, and possibly even the entire district."

"What happened?"

"If I didn't see it, I wouldn't believe it either. We are all surprised as well. Well..." She looked at her desk for a second. "She beat up a boy badly. He's in the hospital now, but nothing serious."

"Maria?" Her voice got caught in her throat. "That little girl out there?" She pointed toward the office door, shaking her head in disbelief." She pointed. "She weighs sixty-five pounds."

"I know, and I agree with you." She placed her hand on her chest. "From my understanding, the boy said. "'Bang! Bitch! Is that how your brother died?'"

"Ay, dios mio." She did the form of a cross, and her eyes got watery.

"I know, that is extremely mean. She then headbutted

him, elbowed him in the head, flipped him over her waist, and got on top of him and started punching him."

"Maria did that?" The corner of her mouth twitched into the smallest smile before she forced it away, folding her hands tightly in her lap.

"I didn't know Maria practiced martial arts."

Altagracia focused her eyes on the principle. "She never has. She finds it too violent. She doesn't even train the thought."

"I've trained in martial arts since college, and let me tell you, what I saw is more advanced than me. For her to flip someone twice her size like that..." She paused, lowering her voice. "Honestly, it didn't look normal. Her movements were too fast... too clean. She seems like an advanced martial artist."

"Really, I can't believe it. I can understand my daughter losing her temper to hear something so nasty about her brother. I mean, she is human."

"Me and her teacher Mrs. Gonzales were dumbfounded. We were shocked. It took me a minute to register what we saw. Normally, an incident like this would mean immediate expulsion—no questions asked."

CHAPTER 3

Chapter 3

Six Years Later

Pablo opened the door and looked at the sky as the dawn light streaked across the horizon. He picked up both pieces of luggage and held a bag under his arm. With his leg, he held the door open for his daughter.

"Thank you, papi."

"You're welcome, my love." She did the same for her mother.

They got to her car parked in front of the building. He put the luggage down and opened the trunk.

"Did you fill up the gas tank?" Altagracia asked, hand on her hip, eyebrow raised—like she already knew the answer.

"Do you think I'm going to send my daughter on a road trip without filling up the tank? I also took it in for a tune-up, washed it, *and* filled the tank, but no, nobody notices Pablo."

He looked at her while he put Maria's stuff into the trunk and closed it.

"I'm just checking. You're becoming a viejo, so I have to make sure." She said, tightening up her lips. "Why you closed it? I have more stuff to put in."

"I closed it because it's full and the back seats are completely empty." He glared at her.

"Then be a gentleman and open it for me, or do I have to reteach you how to be a gentleman?" She looked at him up and down.

"I got it, mami," Maria said, cutting into their bickering.

"At least one person is useful in the family." She smiled at her daughter.

Pablo side-eyed her, pretending to be annoyed, but his gaze shifted back to Maria, softening instantly. "I'm proud of you, mi amor. First in the family going to college... you're making history."

"Thank you, papi." She hugged him, and he held her tight.

"The house won't be the same without you." He

squeezed her again.

"No, it won't be. You will be highly missed. Did you give her the calling card?" She looked at her husband and pushed him out of the way to give her a hug.

"I was just about to do that." He said reaching into his back pocket. "Here, call anytime you need anything." He took out his wallet and gave her a wad of cash.

"What's this for?"

"In case you need to buy anything."

Her mother reached into her bra and gave her another wad. "Ay, mija... I'm so proud, but I'm gonna miss you more than you'll ever know." Tears rolled down her cheeks.

"Mami, don't cry. Then you're going to make me cry as well." She said wiping her mothers tears.

"By the way we got you a gift," Her father said, handing her a box.

"What is it?" She wore a huge smile.

"Open it." Altagracia put an arm around her.

Maria gasped, put a hand over her mouth, and started

sobbing. "Ay, mami and papi, it's beautiful."

Her dad took it from her hand and put it around her neck. "It looks great on you."

Her mom wiped her own face. "Now, Rodolfo will always be close to you."

It was a picture of Maria and Rodolfo playing on the swings. Maria wiped her face, closed the locket, and placed it inside her shirt. Pablo hugged her, and her mother came in as well for a family hug. "Ok, I think I should get going."

Her father looked at his watch. "Yeah, so you can make good time. Try not to stay in Philadelphia too long so you don't get stuck in their traffic."

"Mijita, please take care of yourself, and remember, if you need anything, just call." She gave her another hug. Then Altagracia did the sign of the cross over Maria's front then back. She kissed her father and got in her car, turned on the engine, and pulled out.

Her parents walked to Broadway as she turned the corner heading north towards George Washington Bridge.

Her tires hit the bridge, and she could see the skyline

of Washington Heights in the rearview mirror. The outside world seemed to go quiet... no horns, no hum of the city, just her breathing. She gripped the steering wheel tighter, leaning forward.

Up ahead, a strange fog curled low across the bridge, thicker than she had ever seen. She glanced at the rearview mirror... behind her, New York was still sunny, untouched by the haze. She giggled to herself. "Of course, New Jersey has to be foggy."

But as the haze thickened, her laugh faded. She flicked on her high beams and entered the fog. The temperature seemed to drop. A chill crawled up her arms, and she turned on the heater.

After a few minutes, she exited the fog. Her chest loosened in relief—but then froze.

This wasn't New Jersey. She saw the sun setting now.

"What the heck?" She glanced in the rearview mirror—expecting to see Manhattan behind her. But it wasn't there.

She quickly turned her back to confirm what the mirror had shown her. The mirror was correct. This wasn't New York. It had hills and mountains and old homes. "Oh, my god, what did I do?"

A horn honked and grabbed her attention forward again. She almost rear-ended someone, but she was able to swerve on time to the side of the bridge, and she came to a total stop. She jumped out of the car. It was a city in front of her, but it most definitely wasn't New York.

"Young lady, what is wrong with you? You almost killed both of us." She turned her head and saw an older white man come out of a Ford pickup truck. He had on a cowboy hat and an old jean jacket. She stared at him with a blank stare. "Are you ok? You look like you seen a ghost." The wind was flapping her hair around. But she couldn't even notice that. She was having a complete meltdown right on the bridge. "Should I radio someone for help?" He passed his hand over his white mustache. He waved at a semi-truck coming through.

The truck halted, and the guy rolled down his window. "Is everything ok?"

"This young lady seems to be having trouble; she hasn't said a word. She seems to be frozen with fright." She glanced at her car... and froze. It wasn't hers anymore, but a 1965 Chevy. Chrome trim, old dashboard, manual windows. Nothing about it was right.

Her chest tightened—the last time she felt this sinking dread was the night Rodolfo died, when green fog spilled across the living room floor. She couldn't tell anyone then or now.

"I have a CB. I will call for an ambulance." The trucker reached for his radio.

"No!" She startled the two men. "I'm fine, I just... had a bit of a scare when I almost crashed into you. I'm sorry if I caused you any problems." She shook his hand and waved to the trucker. "Thank you. Really, I'm fine." She didn't let them get a word in and jumped into her car.

She did a U-turn and headed back the way she came, toward the hills and mountains, praying it would send her back to New York.

As she entered the fog at the end of the bridge, relief washed over her—she was sure this would fix everything. Once she got home, she'd figure it out. Her father would know what to do.

Then she looked around the car... and froze.

The dashboard, the knobs, the radio—everything looked decades older. The music player wasn't a CD player anymore; it was an eight-track. Willie Colón's old salsa, the kind her parents used to play at parties, blared through tinny speakers.

She took a sharp breath, forcing herself to focus. "You got this, girl. You got this," she whispered, gripping the steering wheel tighter.

But when she exited the fog, her relief shattered—she was still on the bridge, heading toward the same strange city she didn't recognize.

She passed the same car she'd almost hit earlier, but this time, it drove normally, and the driver didn't even notice her.

"Ah, freak!" She smacked the steering wheel.

She tried another U-turn. Then another. And another. But no matter how many times she turned back, she ended up on the same bridge.

There must be a reasonable explanation, she told herself—but the more she tried, the worse it got. Every time she came out of the fog, the same cars were in the same places. The same truck. The same old man. The clock on the dashboard didn't move.

8:28 p.m. Every. Single. Time.

Her chest rose and fell in quick bursts. Finally, she let out a shaky breath.

"Okay... fine," she whispered. "I'll go into this strange city."

She drove forward, heart pounding, until she reached the massive green sign overhead.

It read in bold, white letters:

WELCOME TO SAN FRANCISCO

"Wait! What?" Her breath caught in her throat. She'd never been farther than the Tri-State area or the Dominican Republic. "Ay, Dios mío..." Her whisper cracked. Was this God's doing? Punishment? A test?

She felt herself starting to freak out again. "Ok, let me find somewhere to park the car and figure it out."

She found a parking area at Golden Gate park. She shut the car off and took a deep breath. "Ok, now I can freak out a bit." She ran her hands through her hair—but stopped. Her curls were tighter, rounder, shaped into a perfect 1970s-style afro. Heart pounding, she leaned toward the mirror. Same face. Same eyes. But everything else… different.

"No way I'm time-traveling. I must be dreaming." She pinched herself "Coño." She covered her mouth. She wasn't the type to curse. "Sorry." She apologized even though she was by herself.

She opened her purse and counted the cash—$300. But the bills were wrong, the paper softer, the colors faded. She flipped one over and saw the print date: 1973.

Her hands trembled as she pulled out her ID. It wasn't the shiny new card she knew. It was an old, flimsy type, the kind anyone could fake.

Her eyes froze on the date of birth. April 11, 1957.

"No," she whispered, her throat tightening. "I was born 1977…"

She looked for her beeper, but she couldn't find it anywhere. She always kept it in the inside of her purse. She emptied everything out, but it was nowhere to be found. She noticed her purse and then looked at the clothes she was wearing. "This must be the 1970s. Look at me. When did I change clothes? I think the best thing to do is find a nice hotel and get some sleep."

She turned the key and pulled onto the street. She'd never been to San Francisco, but the city already felt alive in her bones—the wide hills rising ahead, the clatter of cable-car tracks, and the red glow of Chinatown lanterns lighting the blocks. She knew that the best place to go was up the hill. The same street the trolley drove on.

She looked out the windows, and her suspicions were confirmed. No doubt about it... this was the '70s. Everywhere she looked, people's clothes screamed the era—bell-bottoms, platform shoes, polyester prints.

She had no map, only her intuition to guide her. She drove a couple of blocks, then made a left. Somehow, she was able to navigate herself to a hotel. It was several stories high and not that big. But it looked decent, and didn't look like a place the ladies of the night would bring in their clients. She parked the car in the parking lot, grabbed her luggage, which again matched the era, and went inside.

The place had drawings of famous jazz artists on the wall. She walked up to the concierge desk. He gave her an odd look. He was an older white gentleman, well-dressed, with no facial hair. “Can I help you?” He said curtly, eyeing her up and down.

“Yes, I would like a room for the night.” She was as polite as her father had taught her, even though she could sense he was uncomfortable with her.

“The room’s $25 a night, plus a $25 deposit—total’s $50.” He was hoping that these high prices would scare her away.

“Oh, that’s it? Here you go, sir.” She reached into her purse and gave him a hundred-dollar bill. She was thinking in terms of the new century, when a hotel room could easily cost $150 a night.

He looked over the bill very carefully. He inspected the bill forever, holding it to the light. She sat there politely, only thinking of resting her head to see if she could make sense of this situation. He finally was convinced that the bill was real and gave her the change and the keys. “Room 235, and please leave everything in the room as you found it.”

She ignored his obvious ignorant remark. She was glad that she could safely find a hotel. She took the elevator up to the third floor and went into her room. She took a nice, much-needed shower and fell right asleep.

The next morning, the sunrays crept right into her room and woke her up. She stretched, half-dreaming she was back in the Heights... until her eyes opened. Until she opened her eyes and sat up in one shot. "Oh, crap, this is real. I have to find out what year it is."

She put on her robe, tucked her feet into some cozy slippers, and went to the door. As she suspected, the paper was right at the foot of the door. She unfolded the paper. **July 17, 1975**.

Her stomach dropped. She sat at the foot of the bed, her head turning. *How did I get into this mess? Best thing to do is get some breakfast and then figure out what to do. It seems I'm stuck in San Francisco. I could call my parents, but they only have Rodolfo. How will they react to their grown daughter who's not even born yet? My parents would be just a bit older than me.*

She pouted, and then she felt she would get familiar with this decade. The headline read: *Cosmonaut and astronaut shake hands in space.*

Her mind started to wonder. *I don't think I will find the answer here. Let me go out.* She opened her luggage, and head to toe, it was a time capsule in fabric form. She got dressed, looked at herself in the mirror and did a twostep to see her bellbottoms swing, and then went to the lobby.

In the lobby, there was a young Afro American lady maybe a few years older than her and displaying an afro. "Good morning, how is your stay so far?" The lady leaned in.

"It's quite lovely. Actually, I have a question. Do you know any good Mexican restaurants around here?"

"If you make a left and walk four blocks, there is a small place that usually sells to the local workers." The lady gave her a curious look.

"What's wrong? Do I have lipstick on my teeth?" She reached for her mouth.

"No, that's not it. I just don't see many people who look like us who are guests in this hotel. Did Bob give you a hard time?" She seemed to be genuinely interested in her.

"He was a little rude, but he let me stay here." Now that she said it, he was a bit of an unpleasant person.

"He deals with people like us, but he doesn't like us. I wish I could pop him one, but I need this job." She was surprised that she said that, but when Maria laughed, her shoulders relaxed.

“He was a little rude,” she admitted, “but I was too tired to care.”

“I’m Mindy,” she said, hand out.

“Maria,” she replied, squeezing her hand, grateful to find someone who felt familiar in this strange time. “Are you half-Mexican?”

“No, my family is from the Dominican Republic, but I was raised in New York.”

“Where is Domini—”

That’s right, Maria thought, *during this time, the people on the west coast wouldn’t be familiar.* “Are you familiar with Cuba?” She asked Mindy.

“Yes.”

“So, you have Cuba, and to the east, you have another island, which Haiti and Dominican Republic share.” She demonstrated with her hands.

“Ok, thank you for the geography class.”

"You're welcome. Oh, before I forget, I want to book another night. Is that possible?" She said, reaching in her purse to pay.

"Let me check." She scrolled down a list. Maria had to keep reminding herself that they didn't have the convenience of a computer. "Your room has not been booked, so it shouldn't be a problem. That will be $25 please." She reached out for the money.

"Here you are. $25 exactly." She said with a smile.

"Ok, you're all set." She paused for a moment. "I hope I'm not intruding, but if you wait fifteen minutes, I will go on lunch break, and I could take you myself."

"Would you? I don't know anyone in San Fran, and it would be nice to have the company." She was pleased to have someone to teach her. She had no idea what she was doing here, but if she was stuck here, then she'd better get comfortable.

"Great. Have a seat over there, and I'll be done soon."

Maria went and looked at all the brochures they had set out. *I might as well enjoy my vacation,* she thought quietly as she picked up a brochure about the Fisherman's Wharf. *Maybe*

I'll go here. Looks interesting.

Before she knew it, fifteen minutes had passed by, and they were on their way to eat. When they arrived, it was a hole in the wall. They were the only non-Mexicans in the restaurant. "*Terresa tienes una parde gringas.*"

Maria looked at him. He was a guy in his thirties. He guessed that she couldn't speak Spanish. "No soy gringa," She shot back without missing a beat—the whole room burst into laughter.

"Perdón, mi amor." He smiled, hoping to get back some cool points that he had lost.

"Don't bother the clients." The owner came around and sat them down.

"I'm sorry." He turned back to his food and ate quietly.

"What did he say?" Mindy asked, giving him a dirty look.

"He said a couple gringas are here, so I told him I wasn't one."

"Hello, ladies, what can I get you?" It seemed the owner was the only one working here.

"I think we should get whatever Tereza recommends. It's always good." Mindy's eyes popped a bit as she tasted the food in her mind.

"Ok, whatever you recommend, *por favor*." Maria showed her appreciation with her eyes to Tereza. She smiled back to Maria and patted her on the shoulder and left.

After a few minutes, she came back with an assortment of tacos. She put a small bowl of jalapeños on the table. Maria grabbed one, bit into her taco, then bit the jalapeño, and bit her taco again. Everyone, including Mindy, looked at her.

"Wow, where did you learn how to eat those?" Mindy looked scared for Maria.

"From my neighbor who would babysit me sometimes. The secret? Bite the food, bite the pepper, then back to the food. Never water. Ever." She was still chewing her food as she picked up a napkin and wiped her mouth.

"You're amazing," Mindy said, smiling.

"Nonsense." Maria waved her hand.

After lunch, they walked back to the hotel. Before they went in, Mindy stopped and turned to her. "Are you busy tonight?" She reached out and grabbed her arm.

"No, I'm not busy tonight," Maria said with curiosity.

"Great, then it's settled. I will pick you up at 10pm, and we are going to the disco."

Maria struck the *Saturday Night Fever* pose, finger pointed to the ceiling.

Mindy blinked at her. "That's... new," she said.

Maria froze—the movie wouldn't come out for another two years.

"I'll pick you up at ten. Tonight, we disco."

Afterwards, Maria went upstairs and freshened up, then walked over to where the trolley was and hopped on. She spend the day walking around, and for a brief moment, she forgot that she was lost in time.

Part of her felt like she was coming out of her shell. For the first time in years, she didn't feel trapped. San Francisco felt wide open, alive. It was something about this era that had more of a bounce. She remembered hearing some older guys saying that music from the seventies had this unique umph, no matter what genre.

She strutted down the boardwalk. For dinner, she sat at an expensive seafood restaurant and had a feast. Everything was so much cheaper. She was enjoying herself so much that part of her didn't want to go back. She headed back to her hotel and took a nap.

She woke up, took a shower, and threw on the best-looking outfit she could find. She went downstairs and met up with Mindy out front. When she stepped outside, she shivered a bit.

"San Francisco is chilly year around." Mindy rubbed her arm to warm her up.

"Let me go back upstairs and get a jacket." She took off and grabbed her jacket.

As she was walking out of the room, she felt an urgency to run downstairs.

When she reached the lobby door, she saw a black Impala stop in front of the hotel. Two men with big sideburns jumped out, grabbed Mindy, and pushed her into the car. She yelled, but the car was already gone.

Something snapped inside her; fear gave way to pure instinct. Maria wasn't the type to fight, and she was quite shy.

But not now.

She ran to her car, did a 180, and laid chase. She slammed the pedal down. Somehow, she handled the car like an Indy 500 racer. She saw the car do a sharp left and instinctually pressed the brake with her left foot while flooring the gas petal. She drifted. She now was right behind the car.

One of the guys reached out the window and started shooting. Maria had heard shots before, living uptown, and it always frightened her. She was 100% opposed to guns, especially after her brother's death, but now, she wished had one.

A bullet hit the hood of the car ricocheting off. Her car swerved, and her purse hit the floor—and a .38 revolver slid out.

She glanced down and, without thinking where it came from, reached for it. She picked it up in one stroke and tossed it to her left hand. She reached out the window, aimed at one tire and fired. *Bang.* The gun went off and hit the tire. The car swerved on the street.

Before aiming again, she froze for half a breath, shocked she hadn't dropped the gun. *Who am I?* she wondered as she aimed for the other tire. *Bang*, and the other tire popped. Now, the sparks from the rims made it look like sparklers, like the type you used on the 4th of July.

The car came to a halt, and the two men popped out of the car shooting. Maria jumped out of the car and rolled until she slammed into a building wall. People were running in all sorts of directions, hiding and ducking down. She turned quickly and fired, hitting one guy in the chest.

He fell back and landed in some garbage. Her eyes were scanning the area, looking for the other guy.

Her back slammed into the wall. He yanked her hair, ripping the gun from her hand.

She didn't think… just reacted.

Her hand shot back, grabbed his jewels, and squeezed hard. He screamed, folding over. She snatched the gun back and fired twice.

Bang. Bang.

He dropped where he stood.

She ran towards the car, where Mindy was shaking. She took Mindy in her arms. "We must go." She put Mindy into her car and sped off. Mindy kept looking back, and with the same fear she'd had towards the men, she looked at Maria. "Who are you?" Little pearls of sweat were forming on her forehead.

Maria couldn't honestly answer her. This wasn't her. Had someone or something taken over her head?

"Are you going to kill me?"

Maria was disrupted from her own self-doubts. "Of course not." She patted Mindy on the leg to give her some assurance. "I'm going to take you home. You had a rough night. What do you say?"

Mindy looked at her and smiled. "Please."

They drove the rest of the way quietly. Mindy only spoke to give her directions. As soon as they got to her house, Mindy bolted out of the car without saying goodbye.

Maria couldn't blame her. She would've done the same thing herself.

All of sudden, her own insecurities came rushing back, and she still had the gun in her lap. She suddenly felt nauseous; she opened the car door, fell to her knees, and hurled up all the contents of her stomach, then sat back and cried. "I just killed two people." She stared at her trembling hands as if they belonged to someone else.

She'd never even killed a spider without guilt—now this.

After five minutes of sobbing, she was able to get herself together. She stood up, grabbed the gun, wiped the prints off of it, and tossed it into the storm drain, then got in the car and drove off. Where she was heading, she had no idea.

She decided to head back to the Golden Gate bridge. Since that was where she began, she would try again to leave. She took the much longer route, trying to avoid the area where the incident took place. She played some music to relax herself.

She just remembered she had left her luggage in the hotel. No matter. She would figure it all out when she got to where she was going. When or wherever it was.

She reached the bridge, but there was a lot of traffic. It was moving, but really slow. She needed to get out of San Francisco. She kept tapping the steering wheel and looking around, making sure the cops weren't coming.

She couldn't take it. The opposite side of the road was empty. She drove to the other side as fast as she could.

When she got towards the end of the bridge, a fog started to form. “I hope this works ,or at least it sends me back to yesterday.”

The weather inside the fog began to warm up. She took this as a good sign, and for a brief moment, she felt relief.

CHAPTER 4

Chapter 4

As the fog cleared up, rays of the sun started to break through. She paid attention to her car. Everything changed right in front of her, morphing into a much older car. It looked like something out of an Al Capone movie. Her hair fit the era, but she wasn't sure when she was.

She stopped the car and looked around. Cobblestone streets. Stone bridges. Roofs pitched like storybooks. This wasn't America anymore—this was Europe, and everything screamed 1940s France.

The disappointment settled in. She quickly shook it off and got out of her car to look around. She was on a stone bridge and decided to get back in the car and drive a bit.

She saw so many villas, it had to be very early in the morning. This had to be France, judging by the beautiful architecture.

She decided to stop in front of a house. She didn't know why, but it felt right. She turned off the car. It had seen better days of care. The road was made of gravel.

Somebody opened the door to the house, and a young blonde lady came out. She was startled when she saw Maria, who had a dark complexion. Her features showed a black, Taino and Indian background; like most Dominicans, you could see her African roots, but also other mixes. She stood out in what appeared to be the 1940s, judging by the car and the lady's hair.

"Can I help you?" She walked towards Maria cautiously.

"I'm sorry to bother you. I'm a little lost." She smiled, hoping to relax the lady.

"Your French is really good, where did you learn?"

Maria was about to answer, but then she thought about it. "In school. I'm from America." She didn't realize that she could speak French.

"Are you a jazz singer? I heard your people sing beautifully." The lady looked a lot more relaxed.

Maria could dance, but she couldn't sing to save her life. "No, no, I'm here visiting France." She felt she'd better play the dumb tourist role.

"Oh, my name is **Alice**. You picked a terrible time to visit. The Germans just invaded a while ago." She waited for Maria to answer.

"Do you know a place I can stay?" She looked around the area, but there wasn't much around.

"Please come in. France is quite dangerous now. Especially for your people." She grabbed Maria by the hand and dragged her in. As soon as they were inside, she bolted the door. There wasn't much in the house. She sat Maria at the table and went to the kitchen. "I was going to prepare breakfast; I don't have much, but what I have, we can share." She grabbed a pan from the cupboard.

"I'm sorry to intrude, but I'm quite famished."

"No need to worry. It's been a while since I've had company." Alice smiled and began cooking. After she served breakfast and coffee, Maria was pleased to fill up her tummy.

"I can't believe this is happening. The Germans have just crossed the French border." Alice put her hand on her forehead. At least now, Maria knew it was during WW2.

"I know. I was so surprised." She was careful not to mention too much.

"If you want, you can stay here until we can get you to the American embassy." She patted Maria's hand.

"Thank you so much. I can pay you for the trouble." She dug in her purse, hoping she had some francs.

Alice waved her hand. "I can't accept your money, but to pay me back, you can help me with the chores."

"It would be my pleasure." Maria looked around to see if there was any sign of anyone else. "Do you live alone?"

"My husband was killed during the invasion." She began to weep.

"I'm sorry. I didn't mean to pry." She stood up and put her arms around Alice.

"It's ok." She tapped Maria on the arm to let her know she was ok.

They began the chores in and out of the house. By lunchtime, Alice walked to the market, which was a few miles away. Alice told Maria to stay behind, since she would draw too much attention.

She brought Maria the newspaper. It was May 29th, 1940. It was still hard for Maria to comprehend that she had travelled through time, but she had enjoyed the people she met so far. She thought to herself that she might be here to help this lady, like she had helped Mindy. She was also very scared, as she knew how dangerous it could get. She had so many questions, but no one she could ask. She sat at the table reading the newspaper.

Alice cooked dinner, and they drank wine. Maria wondered if she had a gun since she had tossed the other one. She excused herself and went to go get her luggage. When she opened the trunk, there was a Tommy gun in the back, and next to it, a German Luger. She grabbed the Luger and put it in her purse. She passed her hand over the Tommy gun, shook her head, and closed the trunk. She left it in the trunk. The last thing she wanted to do was scare the life out of Alice.

Where are all these coming from and how? Nothing makes sense. She thought about it while she dragged her luggage. She walked in the house and left her luggage by the door.

Dinner was ready, and they sat down to eat. Her house had no electricity, so they had to light some candles. Maria wondered how she was going to take a shower. After dinner, they drank more wine, and Alice told her how she'd met her husband.

Maria didn't know what time it was, but she was feeling sleepy. Alice told her that they could share the bed. She found this a little awkward, but she noticed there was only one place to sleep unless she was going to sleep on the floor.

Alice heated some water and told Maria she could take a bath. Maria was glad to take a bath. When she got in the bath, Alice walked in with her glass of wine. Maria covered herself up with her arms. Alice didn't even notice; she started to take her clothes off. *Is she making a move on me?* Maria pondered it, but said nothing. Alice got in the bath as if this were normal.

"It takes so long to heat up the water, I hope you don't mind." She took a sip of her wine, placed it on the table, and grabbed a cigarette tin that was sitting on a stool.

"Not at all." She tried to act cool and just dipped her head under water. Alice started chatting away. Maria was actually enjoying herself. They got out of the bath and got ready for bed. Alice and Maria jumped into bed, and they both turned opposite each other. Maria closed her eyes and fell asleep.

When she woke up, she had her arm over Alice. She quickly moved it and turned to the other side, hoping she didn't notice.

"Good morning." Alice sat up, stretching her arms.

Maria wondered. "Good morning." She sat up and put her feet on the floor, then quickly picked them up.

"You should put the slippers on. I will put some firewood in the wood stove." Alice put her robe on and walked into the living room area. Maria shook off her worries and followed her into the other room.

There was a large blast that shook the whole house. It felt as if it would all come crashing down on her. "The Germans are here. We must leave the area. If they catch us, it won't be pleasant."

Maria understood that if they caught her, she be in a world of pain, but why Alice? "Are you Jewish?"

Alice lowered her head and rushed over to the wood stove, where she picked up a couple of old boards. She pulled out a rifle and a handgun, then passed the handgun to Maria.

Maria reached for her purse and pulled hers out. "We should get dressed."

Alice smiled at her. Another blast went off, but this

time, it was closer. They could hear a firefight off in the distance.

They got dressed and ran to her car. Maria opened the trunk and pulled out her Tommy gun.

"You're not a tourist, are you?"

Maria just smiled and pointed for Alice to get into the car.

"Let me drive. I know where the resistance hideout is." Maria tossed the keys, and the two ladies with their uncombed hair jumped into the car. Maria put the handgun on her hip and the Tommy gun between her legs. That confidence came back. Alice floored the car so hard that Maria's head hit the celling. She then remembered that the cars from this era had no seatbelts.

"It's the Nazis! They are blocking the stone bridge." It was the same bridge she had come from. They had blocked it off with a truck.

Maria put her head outside the window and opened up on them, spraying several of them.

They turned on to a muddy road that headed up into

the woods. She still had her head out the window, scanning the area.

When she spotted them, she wished she had some grenades. "What the hell?"

Alice looked at her, not sure what she was talking about.

Maria reached into her purse, and without fail, there it was: a beautiful grenade.

"Slow down a little, then speed up when I tell you." Alice did as she said and slowed down just a tad. Maia yanked the grenade from her bag, pulled the pin, and rolled it low. "Ok, now." Her head banged the edge of the window.

She counted it down, and *boom,* the truck went up in flames. They could still hear the gunfire in the distance.

Maria was keeping her eyes peeled. For the next twenty minutes, they drove in silence. The whole time, Maria was missing her family. Would she ever see them again?

"Are you an American spy?" Alice paused and looked at Maria, who just kept looking around making sure they weren't driving into an ambush. "It's ok, I belong to the resistance."

Maria looked at her. "You could say that." Honestly, she

didn't know what she was, nor did she care at the moment. The road was getting more treacherous by the minute.

They drove another half hour, then Alice pulled into a smaller road that was full of mud. When they pulled next to a house similar to hers. She sensed something was wrong.

They both grabbed their weapons and approached the house. The door had been broken open. There were some men and women dead on the floor.

"Noooo!" Alice cried out and fell on the floor. Maria threw her arms around her.

Then, they heard someone coughing. They went over to an older man. He was laying on his side. "Claude, what happened?"

He coughed some more. "A man... And a woman came and shot everyone." He fought to speak. "They took your daughter."

"No, no, no! Where did they go?" Droplets of Alice's tears fell. Claude took a last breath and died in her arms. She closed his eyes. The look on her face scared Maria. "We have to find her; can you help me?" She stood up and braced both of Maria's arms.

"We will find her."

They grabbed their weapons and ran outside. Maria looked around and saw tracks heading into the woods. There was no way they could take the car.

"This way," She told Alice, and they ran into the woods. They walked up a treacherous hill. There air was brisk, and Maria could see her breath. She shivered and felt her clothes becoming damp.

After twenty minutes or so, they heard a little girl scream. Alice became frightened, but then she looked determined. They ran towards the sound as stealthily as they could by keeping their heads low and stepping like cats.

They came up on a road. When Maria's head came into a clearing from the corner of her eye, she saw them. She pulled out her handgun, aimed, and hit the man in the ankle.

There was a bridge up ahead. Maria somehow knew she couldn't let them pass. She aimed carefully, making sure she didn't hit the little girl, and hit the lady in the arm. Alice shot the man with the rifle before he could take a shot.

The lady veered back into the woods. She shot her gun at them. Maria and Alice took cover before continuing to chase her. Maria pointed for Alice to go left while she went right. Maria was running so fast, for a quick second, she remembered that she wasn't athletic at all. In high school, she'd never joined any sports team.

A bullet flew by her and hit the tree next to her. The sun was coming through the trees. The little girl was slowing the woman down. Alice caught up to them. The lady pushed the little girl to the side and shot at Alice, hitting her in the leg. She was about to take another shot when Maria hit her with perfect aim right between the eyes.

Maria froze for a moment, chest heaving, watching Alice collapse around her daughter. Relief and guilt tangled together. She'd just killed again... but she'd saved a child.

"Mommy, who is that?" Maria smiled at her.

"This is mommy's friend, Maria. She helped me save you from those bad people."

"Hi, what's your name?"

She hugged Maria and looked up at her. "I'm Mari." Maria kissed her on the head.

"We need to leave." She helped Alice up, and they walk

slowly towards the cabin. It took them a long time, and Alice's leg was bleeding a lot. She tore a piece off her clothes and tied it around her wound. "I should have something for that in the car." She hoped that the same way she got the guns, she could get medical supplies.

They got back, and Maria sat Alice in back of the car. She opened the trunk ,and there was a medical bag. "Thank you," She said to herself.

"Mari, I need you to be my nurse. Can you do that?"

"Yes!" She was jumping up and down.

Maria put on some gloves and helped Mari put her gloves on. They both cleaned the wound. She then got the morphine. "This will numb the pain." Mari looked the other way as Maria injected Alice. "Ok, now I will take out the bullet. Mari, I need you to be brave and hold the wound open so I can help mommy. Can you do that?" She nodded and held it open. Maria went in and, as carefully as a surgeon, took out the bullet and threw it on the ground. "You're doing great. Now, wipe the wound again." Mari wiped it as carefully as possible. "You're a natural." Mari smiled at her.

She got the stitch ready and began sewing it close. Once

she was done, Mari cleaned it again, and Maria injected Alice with antibiotics. "Ok, all done."

She quietly hoped for a map. The bombing in the distance began again. "I'm going to take you to Switzerland. The Germans won't find you there." Alice's eyes were half-closed as she was getting comfortable in the back, so she just nodded. "Ok, Mari, hop in the front." Maria went to the back of the car and looked in the trunk.

She put the medical bag back in and found the map. She stopped for a moment. "How is this possible?" She shook it off and was just glad. The map was already marked, and even had places to avoid and where to stay.

Maria handed over to Mari and explained to her what to avoid, then jumped in the driver's seat, and they took off. They took the longer route to avoid the Nazis. When they arrive at the border, it was busy with French refugees. The line was so long.

By then, the blood in Alice's face had returned. "How will we get through? They won't let us cross," She said.

"Don't worry." Maria got out of the car, went to the trunk, and before she opened it, said, "Please have three Swiss passports." She opened the trunk, and there they were: three perfect passports with all the stamps and their pictures. She ran to the front and handed Alice both their passports.

Alice gasped. "Where did you get this from?"

"Do you want me to tell you, or do you want to cross the border?"

Alice pointed towards the crossing.

Maria looked around and saw a guard. "*Officer, officer,* we are Swiss citizens." She waved the passport around.

He looked at her and walked over. She handed over her passport to him, and he inspected it. He looked at her with suspicion. She didn't really quite fit a typical Swiss. "Let me see their passports." Alice handed over the passports.

"She was shot by a Nazi soldier." Mari pointed at her leg, and Alice showed him. His face became urgent.

"Get in the car, and I will get you through." Maria hopped in the car, and Alice gripped her hand and followed him as he walked in front. "Everyone move! Out of the way." He cleared a path for them. When they got to the booth, he ran inside and explained the situation to the guard. The guard fumbled through the pages to stamp their passports and lifted the bar. The guy ran back and gave them the passports. "Two kilometers from here, there is a hospital."

"Thank you." Maria kissed him on both cheeks. His face became red, and he grabbed his cap and fumbled with it.

"Bye." His smile was so huge. Alice just giggled. Maria gave her a look. She was loving this side of herself. Her new personality made her feel important, not like a shadow.

Don't get me wrong, Maria was beautiful, but she hid herself most of the time.

They drove off to Zurich. When they finally got there, Maria stopped at a hotel. She helped Alice out of the car. She went into her purse and asked for some Swiss Francs quietly. She handed everything over to Alice.

"I can't take this." She said, handing it back.

"You and your daughter are safe now. You will be starting a new life, and you need this to get an apartment until you find a job. Or do you prefer to sleep on the street with your daughter?"

Alice put the money away and hugged her. "Without

you, we would have never made it out of France, and they would've taken my daughter."

Maria hugged her again and jumped into the car. She drove off and looked for a bridge to cross. "I hope this takes me home."

When she found one, she sped up a bit, and at the end of the bridge, there was a fog forming. "Yes!"

She had enjoyed France and Switzerland, but it was time to go.

CHAPTER 5

Chapter 5

The car twisted beneath her, changing faster than the last two times. The steering wheel dissolved under her hands. Her body felt like it was rippling through time itself. There were all these panels and holographic dials.

She looked up... and froze. The moon wasn't in the sky. It was right there, massive, close, alive with hundreds of lights. Cities. On the damn moon.

She looked around, and she was in a spaceship that could hold up to four people.

"Wow, I'm in space, with my own ship. My mother would have a heart attack." She look back at the controllers. "I hope I know how to drive this. If not I will be a splat on the side of the moon." When she said that, on the side of her window appeared a diagram on how to drive. "Oh, this must be voice control. Can you find me a three-star hotel?" A list popped up. "Please navigate me to the closest one."

A small map popped up. "Would you like me to drive you there?"

Maria jumped in her seat. "Who said that?"

"Your ship's AI, of course."

"Oh, sorry. Please take me there, and what is today's date and year?"

"Today is February 7, 2274."

"2274?" She almost jumped out of her skin.

"Yes, that is correct."

Maria was glued to the window as they came closer to the surface. Below her, massive crystal domes stretched for miles, glowing like glass cities under starlight. Outside of it, there was a long line of vehicles; the ship got online, and Maria's credentials popped up with a QR code on the window. A drone flew over and scanned the QR code, and a green light turned on.

She went inside and followed the rest of the traffic. As she passed through the barrier, her jaw dropped. Towers spiraled upward like twisted glass, glowing from within. Times Square and Shibuya would look like candlelight compared to this. No steel, no concrete, the buildings shimmered like living plastic.

"Welcome to the future..." she whispered to herself.

The buildings glimmered from within, with no light fixtures anywhere. Everything felt alive, even the walls. But she didn't like the constant swarm of drones.

The streets were crowded with every kind of person... and then she noticed one—not human. Then another. Then dozens. "There's life... outside of Earth?" she breathed.

She finally reached the hotel, and the ship parked itself. She got out of the vehicle; some drones came and picked up her luggage and whisked it away. The floor moved by itself and brought her to the concierge desk.

A beautiful android waited for her. "Good afternoon. How can I help you today?"

The android was stunning... same complexion as Maria, but her eyes were sharp and Asiatic. The small sign on the desk read: **Angie ~ Concierge Android**.

"I'd like to stay for two nights," Maria said carefully, unsure how to speak to a machine.

Angie stood still, expression soft but unreadable. Maria blinked, frozen, until Angie finally said, "Your wrist, ma'am."

"Oh, sorry." She gave Angie her wrist, and Angie scanned it with her palm.

"Your total is **0.00000021 Bitcoins**. Please place your wrist next to mine."

Maria obeyed, watching as a glowing screen popped up across her own wrist.

"All done." Maria looked at her wrist, and it said she had .08723487 Bitcoins.

She glanced at her balance. "What's... a Bitcoin?" she muttered, shaking her head.

A drone chair floated up, sleek and silent. "Enjoy," Angie said, waving as Maria was whisked away.

The chair glided up a vertical shaft and stopped at one of the upper floors. The door slid open smoothly, releasing her into the room. Inside, the drones had already unpacked her clothes.

Her wrist pulsed once. A thin line of text scrolled across the glass. **If you don't understand something, just ask your**

wrist.

"Who is this? What am I doing here?" she whispered, pulse quickening. Finally... someone had contacted her.

The wrist display glitched... letters stacked wrong before settling clean: **Stay on mission.** Green fog seeped out and dissipated.

"What mission? I never agreed to any of this!"

Silence. The wrist went blank. The lights dimmed for a breath, like the building was listening... then pretended it wasn't. "Coño!" She slapped the wristband. No response.

She decided to take a nap. Maybe she'd wake up back in Washington Heights. The bed contoured perfectly to her body, soft as clouds.

"Wow... that's so cool," she whispered.

She must have slept for hours. When she woke, the room glowed with soft morning light, and the Earth was rising beyond the horizon. "That's the most beautiful thing I've ever seen," She breathed.

Maria stepped into the bathroom and frowned. No knobs, no handles.

"Everything must be voice-activated. Warm water, please."

Two robotic hands slid out of the wall.

She screamed, clutching her chest. "What the hell is that?!" She smacked the hands.

"Apologies. I am the shower assistant. Would you like me to disengage?"

"Yes, please. From now on, I handle all bathroom things myself. Understood?"

"Understood. Please forgive me."

She finished up without further drama.

She opened her luggage and froze. "What the hell is this? It looks like a stripper's suitcase."

She picked up a garter belt. "I'm not wearing this shit."

Then she covered her mouth. "Ah, fuck... I cursed again." She frowned, confused by her own sailor's mouth.

"Computer, show me the latest outfits of this decade."

A 3D model popped up—women in garter belts.

"Que mierda... I don't want to look like a dinosaur."

She slipped on the garter belt anyway, revealing more skin than she wanted. “This century doesn’t leave much to the imagination.”

She grabbed her purse and searched for a weapon. Only a pair of gloves. She slid them on. “I guess I don’t need a weapon.” As soon as she opened the door, the chair was there. It took her down to the lobby and she walked outside.

Everyone seemed to be wearing the same thing—even the men strutted around in assless underwear. Maria shook her head and kept walking. She was still admiring the towers when she bumped into a man with curly hair and light skin.

“Oh... I’m sorry.”

“Not a problem. are you new in town?”

“How do you know?” She gave him a questioning look.

“No one stares at the buildings unless they’re not from the Moon.”

“Well, they’re quite beautiful.” She glanced at the buildings

“I can show you around if you like? By the way, my name is Sherik.” He smiled and he shook her hand.

"I'd love that. My name's Maria."

For the first time, she wondered if she was catching feelings. She'd never wanted a boyfriend before... yet butterflies stirred in her stomach.

He took her to the Armstrong memorial, which was the most visited site in all of the moon.

"This was built in 2037. Ever wonder what it was like to live back then?"

Maria giggled.

"What—did I say something wrong?" Sherik asked, frowning.

"No, no, no... I was just thinking they were a lot more dressed."

They both laughed. She didn't dare ask, but she wondered when fashion became so loose.

There was a statue of a guy pointing to the stars, the name plate said Elon Musk. She wasn't sure who he was. What caught her attention was the gravity—it didn't feel different.

"I thought we were supposed to be lighter," She muttered. *They must have figured out gravity,* she thought to herself. “Can we grab something to eat?” She said, grabbing her stomach.

“What are you in the mood for?” He asked with a smile.

“What is the moon famous for?” She said looking around.

“How about Chinese? I know a place that grows all their own stuff.” He pointed with his hand.

“Sounds good to me.” She just remembered she hadn’t eaten since two nights ago, when she was in France. For a brief moment, she forgotten that she was wearing a garter belt and a bustier. All the shame came back; she worried about getting food between her breasts. Her mother would have a patatun if she saw her like this. She had always taught her the importance of dressing like a lady. Her bare skin felt uncomfortable.

“Is there something wrong with Chinese?” He said.

She shook it off. “No, I was just worried about getting food all over myself.”

He gave her a strange look. “You do know that they have foodtecters?”

What’s a foodtecter? she thought to herself. She didn’t

want to give him the impression that she was out of place. "That's right. I must be tired from my trip."

He accepted that answer, and they made their way to the restaurant. They waited for about fifteen minutes, and a drone sat them down.

Come to think of it, she haven't seen anyone working. All the jobs were being done by robots. *How are people making money in this century?*

She was taken out of her thoughts when a drone came and put a clear poncho over her. He gave her a strange look when she seemed to be surprised again.

"Sorry, my mind keeps wandering. Are we allowed to go outside the bubbles to walk on the surface of the moon?" She was getting better at deflecting attention.

"Yes, we can go right after lunch." Her taste buds were lit, and her skin as well, with his company. Her skin called for his touch.

After their walk on the surface of the moon, she was going to invite him back to her hotel, she thought. She was eighteen, and it was about time.

She treated him to lunch. After lunch, he called one of those portable chairs on his wrist. She still didn't understand how to use her wrist as a device. Did they implant something in her, whomever they might be?

The chairs zoomed across town. They were sitting in a double chair. She let her bare leg brush his... a tiny contact that sent a thrill through her. If she'd known it felt like this, maybe she would've gotten busy back in high school... like so many girls in her class.

He was too busy pointing out all the things of the city to even notice. *Does he not find me attractive?* She wondered.

They arrived, and there was a drone renting out space-suits. She was glad to cover herself up, but at the same time, she was tempted to pull her undies aside and let nature take its course. But she could never be that raw.

She felt herself getting moist. She wondered if he could see the wet spot. But she couldn't look down without drawing attention to it.

When she was younger, she would hear her classmates talk about it, and she found it outright disgusting, but not now. She would have to wait until she took him home. She didn't know how long she would be in this time, so she threw caution to the wind. *I probably will never see him again, but he must be the person I have to save.*

She glanced down at his junk and felt a tingle. She took a deep breath and clung to his every word. The drone dressed them, and she barely listened to it.

They walked into the depressurizing room. She felt lighter. "Wow, this is so cool."

"Right! But be careful when you walk not to use too much strength. If not, you will lose your balance." She held onto his arm when they walked outside. She hung on to his muscular arm so that she could feel it through the suit. Here she was, walking on the moon, a once-in-a-lifetime experience, and all she could think about was putting his sausage in her mouth.

"What is wrong with you?" She muttered, scolding herself.

They had rented a replica of the Lunar Roving Vehicle that was used during the Apollo missions. They drove in the direction of the Earth, passing by some craters. There were at least four other cities that she could see in the distance.

Something in her loosened, and without thinking, she drifted toward him.

She felt a push, and she fell out of the vehicle. Because of the low gravity, she didn't roll; instead, she hit the ground, then bounced in the air. She could feel herself rolling in the air, and then she hit the ground again. She had done this five or six times before she came to a stop. Her face was in the ground.

Suddenly, someone yanked the hose from her helmet—she gasped, lungs burning, twisting to see who it was.

To her shock, it was him.

"Why?" she cried.

"You think I don't know who you are? It was obvious the moment I met you. Out of place... wrong. And no one is going to stop my mission—not like you stopped the other two."

She was starting to lose consciousness when it dawned on her that she was still wearing the gloves under her space suit.

She wasn't even sure how the gloves worked, she thrust her palm forward... energy gathered around the outer space suit gloves, bright blue, then erupted in a blast that killed him instantly.

Her wrist was lighting; it said, **Vehicle is on its way.** Everything was so foggy, and her head hit the ground.

When she woke up, she was on the floor of her vehicle. Her mask was off, and she was able to breathe. “How did I get here?”

“I detected your oxygen level was very low, so my robotic arms brought you in.” The computer said. It startled her a bit, but she still wasn’t used to talking to computers.

“Thank you for saving my life.”

“You are very welcome.”

She received a message on her wrist. “Stay on mission. Objective complete. Police drones inbound.” A voice came from her band.

“Who the hell are you?” She yelled at her wrist. She was tired of this. She had been about to give her booty to a guy who tried to kill her in the twenty-second century.

“Go now or spend your time in prison.”

“Since you put it that way, I’ll take option one.” With that being said, she had no choice but to skedaddle.

She got in the seat and, without knowing how, she got the ship in high gear. When she was leaving orbit, the space drones were hot on her tail. She armed the ship's weapons and blasted the drones one by one.

As soon as the last one was shot, a fog started to form, and she raced in.

CHAPTER 6

Chapter 6

While she was in the fog, she prayed she'd land in a more familiar time.

Shapes began to harden around her—the interior twisting until it became a military jeep, but not American. As the fog cleared, distant bombs rumbled through the air. "Perfect... I landed in the middle of a war." Maria slammed her hand on the wheel, breath quickening.

Rain pelted her face, cold enough to make her shiver. Bullets streaked through the air like burning needles. She glanced down; her uniform carried a Canadian flag. The jeep was armed to the teeth, weapons systems humming beneath the dash. She dug through her bag, searching for any kind of comm device, but found nothing.

Definitely the future... but what year?

A translucent map lit up across the windshield, shifting

symbols until the date appeared.

“2076,” she whispered. “I’d be ancient by now...”

A small red dot pulsed on the display, three miles away, almost like a heartbeat.

“This is 38 tango passcode Charlie, 798 Beta 87delta.” She heard it coming from the jeep’s computer.

“Passcode confirm, come in.” She heard from the stereo. She scrambled to get her bag, and then she heard something chiming. She looked in the bag.

“Do you read? Please confirm.” She finally found what was chiming. It looked like a rolled-up piece of plastic. She unrolled it, and it was a smart phone. A text came up: **Give this password.** “Alpha 9123foxtrot.” She read out loud onto the phone.

“Confirmed, we are under heavy fire. Can you come pick us up?” She really wanted to turn around and run, but she had no choice. She could see the target on her windshield. She targeted it with some knobs on the steering wheel; when it locked, she let out a small missile from the back of the vehicle, then stepped on the gas, and was now racing through an open field. Wherever she looked at, her vehicle targeted that area like it automatically knew the enemies.

Some missiles were coming her way. She fired upon them and destroyed them. She kept targeting enemies automatically, but a thought cut through the chaos: *Who am I even fighting?*

She finally arrived, and three guys approached the vehicle, but when she looked at them, it wouldn't target. "I hope this is not the same mierda from the moon."

They jumped in the vehicle. "Go, go, go!"

She stepped on the gas. The guy in the front opened the glove compartment, which had a control panel. "I will handle the bogies." He tapped onto the dashboard and put in the coordinates, and the jeep started firing like crazy. Drones were coming in from all directions.

Behind the tree line, enemies were waiting. She saw them just in time to veer the vehicle. The machine gun pointed in their direction started firing. The vehicle was being bombarded by bullets. She looked to her right and saw a guy holding a grenade launcher. The jeep started to slide on some mud. "Take cover," she screamed. The blast turned the jeep on its side, and for the second time in her life, she was unconscious.

She awoke to some cold water being splashed on her face. "Nice of you to join us, sleeping beauty. Go get the captain." Her eyes were still foggy, and her head was throbbing. She looked to the side and saw her companions. The guy in front of her was an American. *Is America at war with Canada? Impossible,* she thought to herself.

He grabbed her face and forced her to look at him. She yanked her face from his hand and got a couple of scratches in the process. "Don't fucking touch me, *mama guebo.*" She glared at him after cursing him in Spanish.

He laughed at her comment. "Hey, guys, we got a feisty one here. I like Latinas. What are you, some kind of Mexican? "

"I'm Dominican, you ignorant motherfucker." She knew if she had the chance, she would kill him. Never had she wanted to do someone harm the way she wished upon him.

"Oh, excu-se me, I meant a Dummy in a can." The rest of his men all laughed. He put his hand close to her breast.

"Don't do that, unless you want to be tried for war crimes."

The room went silent when a tall Black female officer walked in. The other soldiers stiffened instantly. She must have been his superior, because he had straightened up real quick.

"Thank you." As soon as Maria finished, she received a backhand that rocked her chair almost to the point of falling.

"You speak when I say so. Is that understood?" She got close to her face.

"Yes. ma'am."

"Take this one to a separate room." Two men grabbed her chair and carried her to the back, separating her from the rest. Her face was hurting, but her eyes scanned the room, looking for an escape.

The same guy nonchalantly brushed his hand up against her breast. "Pardon me, young lady." He bowed his head and grinned at her. She nodded, knowing he was a dead man. He laughed at her evil eye.

The lady walked in with a no-nonsense attitude, almost strutting. She closed the door behind her and pulled up a chair that was up against the door. She stared at Maria's eyes for a few seconds. Maria's heart started to pound. It felt like it went up into her throat.

The woman leaned close to her ear. "I'm here to free

you. Sorry about this."

She got up suddenly, knocking Maria over. Maria fell to the side, and the lady jumped on top of her. She pulled her knife out and cut all her ties. "Don't move until they come in, then let your body naturally do its thing."

The lady got up quickly and ran behind the door. "Help!" She yelled out. Maria stayed perfectly still as she was told.

The men ran in; Maria turned onto her back, popped her body up, and immediately went into a roundhouse kick, landing it on the first guy. The lady went behind the other one and snapped his neck. The last one came in with his gun, and Maria grabbed the dead guy's gun and shot him.

An alarm went off, and they headed to the other room. They both cut the three men loose and they grabbed some weapons that were on the wall. The lady signaled the men to cover the windows. They looked at Maria, and she nodded. They fired up the field in front of them, unloading everything they had.

"Maria, check your bag for disk grenades." Maria tilted her head, unsure what she meant. "Just check your bag, they put it in that corner."

Maria ran to her bag and searched feverishly. She found small disks that had pins on the top. She brought them over, being careful not to drop them.

"What are you waiting for? Pull the pin and toss them! They have a ten-second delay."

Maria followed her orders and flung them like a frisbee. They glided through the air and right over some sandbags. "Fire in the hole." Maria called out. One by one, she threw them and cleared the area.

"Everyone, follow me! Maria, make sure to bring your bag."

She grabbed it and slipped on the floor. She balanced herself with one hand and kept running. The floor was muddy, and they were getting soaked. She was able to see her breath as they headed towards a hummer.

The lady pulled out her rolled-up phone. "Bring vehicle to my coordinates." A drone vehicle came out of the woods and headed towards them. "Lay down cover fire. A platoon is coming."

Maria pulled more disk grenades and was tossing them like they were candy. That help keep them at bay while they piled into the drone. “Someone take the guns.” Two of the guys grabbed one on each side and began firing.

Maria paused for a second at the thought of killing Americans. She had so many questions about this time, but kept them to herself.

“Maria, take the wheel.”

Without hesitation, she jumped on and took them up into the air. She knew their best bet was to go into the clouds. Bullets were flying past their aircraft. Somehow, Maria didn’t pee her pants. Right before they hit the clouds, one of the propellers was hit. They started spinning out of control, but luckily, they were able to hit the cloud.

She relaxed a bit, knowing she was safe for now.

CHAPTER 7

Chapter 7

The aircraft landed on what looked like **solid fog**. A soft green haze stretched forever... no landmarks, no horizon.

"Welcome to the **In-Between**," Lakisha said. "This is the fog's home—safe inside the bubble. I'll be in charge of training you."

"What do you mean training—and where the hell are we?" Thomas asked, scanning the endless mist.

Lakisha glanced back at the group. "The fog pulled us straight here after 2075."

"All I can tell you is that in 1995, I was on my way to college when a fog hit me, and then I was in 1975, 1940 France, 2274, and that's when I ended up with you guys. Since then, I've been shot at, suffocated, and had bombs going off around me." Maria said.

"What?" He said with skepticism. "Time travel is impossible." Said the white guy with a beard.

"I wish it was, but I also have a lot of questions as well, so let her start." Maria gave her a stern look.

"I promise I will explain, but I could surely use some sleep." Lakisha walked over to the fog, and two rooms appeared—one for the guys and the other for them, both equipped with bathrooms and kitchenettes.

"Wow!" They all said.

"By the way, what's your names?" She turned and gave Lakisha a look.

"I'm **Kyle**." The white guy with the beard said. "And this is **Thomas**." He was the Native Canadian. "Last but not least is **Kevin**." He was the heavyset white guy.

"It's pleasure to formally meet you all. I need sleep. Good night." Even though she had not eaten, she wasn't hungry. She went straight into the shower and then fell asleep.

When she awoke, only Lakisha was awake. "Good morning, I made us some breakfast."

Maria didn't even answer her.

“Stop right there. For your information, I didn’t pull you from your time and get you involved in this mess.”

Maria turned to her. “Really.” She said resentfully.

“Yes, I’m just the one who saved your ass. The vehicle got destroyed, so even if you had escaped, you would have been stuck in that godforsaken place.”

Maria took a breath. “I’m sorry. Can you imagine being pulled out of your time and being thrown into crazy-ass situations without a simple explanation?” Her eyes softened.

“Yes, I can. How do you think I got involved? I’m from 2019. I was driving in Atlanta, went to cross a bridge, and was pulled to 1989 New York, where I saved a young boy.” She softened her tone. “So, trust me when I say I do understand.”

“Then can you explain why we are here and why are we doing this?” Maria sat down at a table that wasn’t there last night. Or was it night? She couldn’t tell the time of day.

“Well, the first thing you should know is that this fog is alive. This is its home.” She continued scrambling some eggs.

“What? Really! How? Huh?” Maria put a hand on her head. “Oh, shit.” She placed both her elbows on the table.

"Oh, shit is right. This being doesn't have a form, and it can only exist within linear space briefly. That's why the fog appears and then disappears. We are in a time bubble; if they don't make this for us, we will go insane, but we can survive for short periods of time in the fog."

"So why are we doing this?" Maria pleaded.

"Ah, the million-dollar question. Ready to have your brain fucked?" Maria just waited. "There is this gene called the Chronos gene. It gets discovered way in the future, about 12,000 years to be exact, give or take a century. Every person alive has it. But it's usually dormant. Every once in a while, it turns on and helps maintain time. But people like me and you, it's on all the time. It's very rare; it's what allows us to go into the fog. From my understanding, that gene is from the fog itself. How that happened, they don't even know themselves." She served Maria some breakfast.

"So, the people who discovered this in the future learned to tap into it and manipulate it. Basically, giving them the power to do the same thing as the fog. They have basically weaponized time. But when they use it like that, it literally pulls apart the people who have this gene awoken atom by atom. So, the more they use it, the more people they have to kidnap throughout time."

"So, the guy I killed was from the future?" Maria asked.

Lakisha shook her head. "No, they hire mercenaries from each time period to kidnap. He was warned about you, so he never had a chance to find her. For some reason, we are unable to get things from other times and bring them to another. I also think the fog does not want to pollute the timeline." She sat down to eat her food.

"So, why not go back again and grab those people after we leave?" Maria asked, rubbing her head.

"Like I said, it only turns on for a couple hours. After that, they are unable to harness it." Lakisha looked towards the guys' room. "These three guys will be part of your team." They looked at Maria.

"I don't know the first thing about commanding a team." She scrunched up her face.

"Well, you didn't know how to shoot a gun or fight, and yet you shoot like a trained expert." Lakisha put a hand up. "Before you even ask, I suggest you walk into the fog."

"Walk into the fog? You said it can make someone go

insane." Maria looked at her suspiciously.

"For a normal person, but for you, you can handle a few minutes. I will tell you this: nothing in there is linear, and you will experience weird time shifts. I will let it explain. "

"Are you sure it's safe?" She got up slowly.

Lakisha got up with her, and they walked over to it. "I know you don't trust me, but you can handle it." She stared into Maria's eyes.

"Alrighty, then." She took a deep breath and walked in.

"Breathe normally." Lakisha yelled, but her voice became distorted.

Her body felt as if it were expanding and contracting. She had become the motion of the water. Rippling, crashing, spreading, evaporating, and falling all at the same time. The night the fog first visited her, the news of her brother, the day she beat up the boy. She felt like she was jumping through time to different parts of her life. "It, you, stop, must."

"What?"

"Them, you, stop, must. Malleable, time, is." Every second in there made her lose touch with herself. She felt a hand grab her.

"Are you ok?" She was out, but her mind was still bouncing around. "Focus on you now."

She listened to her, and her eyes tried to focus on Lakisha's face. Her mind started to slow down, and she felt herself being whole again. "Wow."

"What did they say?" Lakisha gripped both her hands and gave them a squeeze.

"'Malleable, time, is,' and 'Them, you, stop, must.'" She sat down in a chair.

"I got it. Yeah, that's how they talk. Their time is not linear."

Maria put her head on her lap. "Nothing made sense in there."

"No, it doesn't. I'm going to wake up the others."

"How long was I in there?"

"A few seconds." She turned around to answer Maria.

"What? It felt a lot longer."

Lakisha walked into the room and woke the guys up.

They came out and sat at the table to eat. Lakisha explained to them what was going on and that Maria would lead them through time. Everyone's face looked stumped. After the guys ate and groomed themselves, Lakisha started showing them the backpacks and the vehicle and explaining how they could get equipment when they needed it, but only equipment of that time.

While she was explaining, the fog started flashing different colors. "Shit, we are under attack."

Before Lakisha could explain, soldiers came through the fog wearing these suits that covered their face, which gave them an aura of being menacing.

Maria grabbed her bag and reached inside. The moment she needed weapons, five gauntlet-gloves were waiting. "Put them on, they're weapons."

Thomas turned the table on its side. Maria finished putting on her gloves and stood up. With one hand, she created a forward shield, and with the other, she fired energy balls. She hit a few of them so hard it blasted them back into the fog. "Those are **chrono-suits**!" Lakisha shouted. "They shield them from the fog—**rip the masks off**!"

Even three of them attacking at once couldn't break through her barrage of punches and kicks. *If only my brother could see me now...* She grabbed the mask off one woman, and the fog shot into her and she disappeared. There must have been two dozen. One of them threw a ball into the fog, and when it exploded, the fog receded back. Lakisha was able to rip the mask off another one; he was pulled out of existence as the fog engulfed him. Every time Maria would hit someone, energy would come out and blast them back.

"We have to retreat—too many!" Maria and Lakisha raised shields while the others dove into the drone. It morphed into a ball of light and launched into the fog.

Behind them, the In-Between bubble **snapped shut** — erasing the unmasked intruders instantly.

Inside the sphere, the walls began to shift...

CHAPTER 8

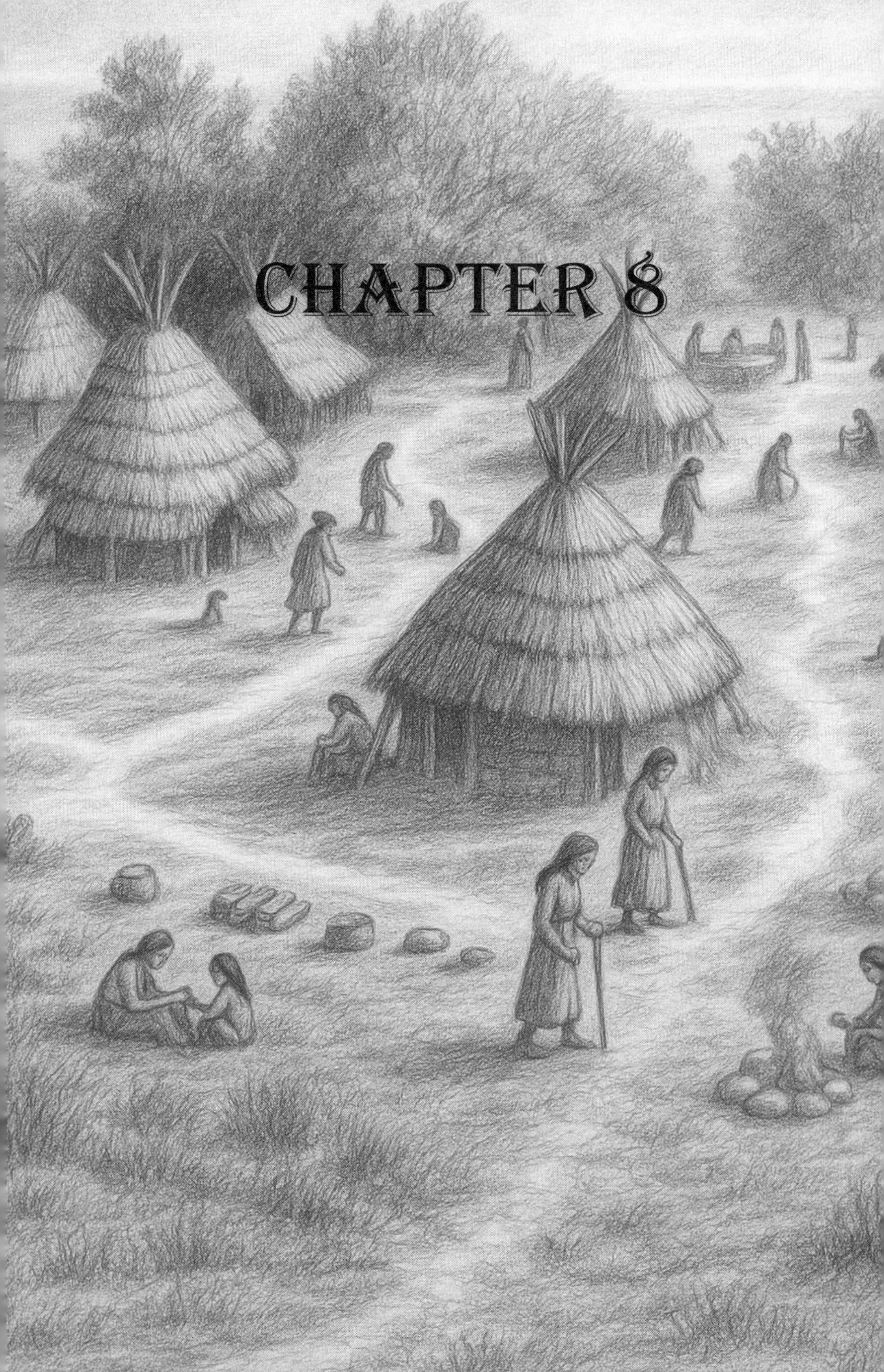

Chapter 8

Maria felt that she was on some kind of animal. As they cleared the fog, she saw that they were in a wooded area. Her hair was braided back. Their clothes were native American, and they were riding bison.

Lakisha scanned the dense forest, watching bison shift beneath them.

"This has to be **precolonial America**, before European contact." She said quietly.

Everybody's hair was longer. Maria looked at her waist and saw a traditional stone tomahawk. They all looked at Thomas. "Why are you looking at me?"

"Well, your heritage is Native, right?" Kyle said.

"It's native Canadian, you dickhead?" Thomas said, glaring at him.

"My bad." Kyle apologized, laughing.

"How do you know this is precolonial?" Maria asked.

"Judging that we are riding bison." Lakisha answered.

"These beasts are temperamental." Thomas said, looking really nervous.

"No worries. The animal is completely controlled by the fog, and if we get into some shit, they can bulldoze over several people." Lakisha petted her bison.

"Here's a good question: How do we know that they are not controlling us?" Kevin said.

"I've been wondering that myself. There's too much cloak and dagger to understand what's going down," Maria said, staring at Lakisha.

"Well, we really don't, but what else can we do? You three are from one era, I'm from another, and Maria is as well. We all have been thrown together. What do you suggest we do? I believe we are here hiding, but it won't be long before they come hunting us down. If we go back to our regular lives, they will just kidnap us and do horrendous things to us. Which do y'all prefer?" Her southern twang was finally coming out. No one said a word. "That's what I thought. Now, keep your eyes peeled, because any moment, we are going to be scrapping for our lives." They nodded and looked down.

Maria also nodded, but something was gnawing at her in the back of her head.

Off in the distance, she saw a group of native men. "We have company."

"Let me try to communicate with them." Thomas got off his bison. "Do we have anything to trade?"

Maria opened her bag. "What do you need?"

"Whatever you've got," Thomas said, forgetting, for a moment, that the bag always provided tools native to the current era.

"You know I can get you anything from this period." She got off her bison.

"Oh, that's right, give me some furs and dry bison meat? Everyone, put your weapons on the ground."

Maria pulled out some furs and dried meat. "Remember, you can speak their language." He looked at her, wanting to ask, but with no time, as they were approaching.

"We are from Lenape tribe. Why are you here?" They looked at their weapons on the ground and did the same.

“We are from the **Gitxsan** tribe, about one moon’s ride from here. We are looking for shelter. We brought you these gifts.” He handed over the furs and dried meat.

The man inspected the trade goods carefully, then froze, his gaze flicking between them... Maria, Lakisha, Kevin, Kyle.

He’s never seen Black or white outsiders before. Maria wondered how far back in time they were.

“You are welcome to come to our village.” He pointed north. “You are able to tame the bison; you must teach us how you did that.” He stared at the beast with awe.

“For friends, we are willing to help. This is Sunshadow.” He was giving everyone native names so they wouldn’t stand out as much. Lakisha was Sunshadow; Maria was Fightingdeer. Kevin was Snowcougar, Kyle was Raincloud, and Thomas was Tamingbull. They introduced themselves to the Lenape men, who walked ahead of them.

Maria remembered her history lesson. “Ask them the name of this island?”

“Excuse me, what is the name of this area?”

“This here is **mah-NAH-tah**.” He said slowly.

Maria's eyes widened. "Manhattan... that must be the original **Lenape** name."

She glanced at the hills. "Back home, this'd all be paved over. Thank you." She said.

"I was correct." She looked around to see if she recognized the landscape, but it would be so different in her time. "This is Manhattan. That must be the original pronunciation." Everyone looked around to see such a beautiful place, and it would all be paved over. They were going up a hill that snaked a little; then she knew where they were, able to see both sides of the island. "This must be the Dyckman area. I recognize this hill. Mah-NAH-Tah means 'island of many hills." She said.

"Beautiful and nerdy." Thomas smiled at her.

"Damm proud of it." Maria blushed.

They were able to see tipis and little kids came running towards them. The younger kids were very scared of them.

"I've never seen such strange people." One kid said.

"What tribe are you from?" A little girl asked Maria.

Maria dismounted her bison and knelt down next to the little girl. "We are from Gitxsan tribe, which is Thomas's tribe, which is in western Canada." The little girl giggled and ran away.

The chief and his wife were standing by his tipi, staring at them. He opened the tipi and invited them in to sit. His wife started stoking the fire. After introductions, the chief seemed very suspicious of these newcomers. He was surely worried they might be scouts for an invasion.

"We want nothing from you but a place to stay. But we can also leave if you feel uncomfortable." Thomas said, pointing at the door.

"I think it might be best if you do, but please take food if you need it. We are not used too strangers." He stared at Kyle.

"Thank you, but we are fine." Thomas said, gesturing to the others to get up. They got up and headed towards their bison.

They road towards what would become downtown, which was south. Crossing a few streams as they headed downhill, Maria realized that this would be around 135th Street.

She tensed suddenly, eyes narrowing on movement in the tree line. "Get your bows and tomahawks ready." She whispered. "Something's coming from the east."

Everyone else was trying to figure out what she was talking about. They came from behind a ravine, and Kyle shot the first one with his bow. Maria kicked her bison forward, leapt off mid-stride, and swung her stone tomahawk in one clean arc. She hit a white male right in the head, rolled to one side, came up, and hit a woman in the face.

Kyle was shooting his arrows so fast that it must have been one every three seconds. Lakisha ran her bison over one guy, but she was knocked off her beast with an arrow. Kevin grabbed her and dragged her to safety. Thomas yelled out in his traditional language with a tomahawk in each hand. He threw one at a guy, then spun around and hit the last one in the back of the head. They threw Lakisha onto the bison and rode west towards the river.

When they got close to the river, Maria went to work on her wound. She pressed down on the bleeding wound. "We need to get Lakisha out of this era." She said, voice sharp. "The fog can get us proper medical care if we can reach it." She had some leaves in her satchel. "Kyle, chew these." She handed them over to him. "Ok, Kevin, hold her down. Here, bite on this stick." Lakisha opened her mouth and bit down like a great white biting down on its prey. "Ok, ready? One, two, and... three." She pulled out the arrow. Lakisha screamed at the top of her lungs.

Maria packed the wound with the leaves, which stopped the bleeding. She then gave her another leaf to chew on and wrapped the wound in a rag. They picked her up and helped her walk.

"We must get on the bison and... get close to the water." Lakisha could barely speak. The color from her skin was draining fast. Her eyes were squinting, trying to cope with the pain. They picked her up and put her on the bison.

They rode down a ravine, Maria's memory clicking. "One day, this'll be **Riverside Park**," she muttered. "Hard to imagine right now." When they reached the riverbank, Maria led her bison halfway into the cold water.

The fog rolled in fast, curling around them, humming faintly. Maria exhaled with relief.

Her eye fixed on Lakisha.

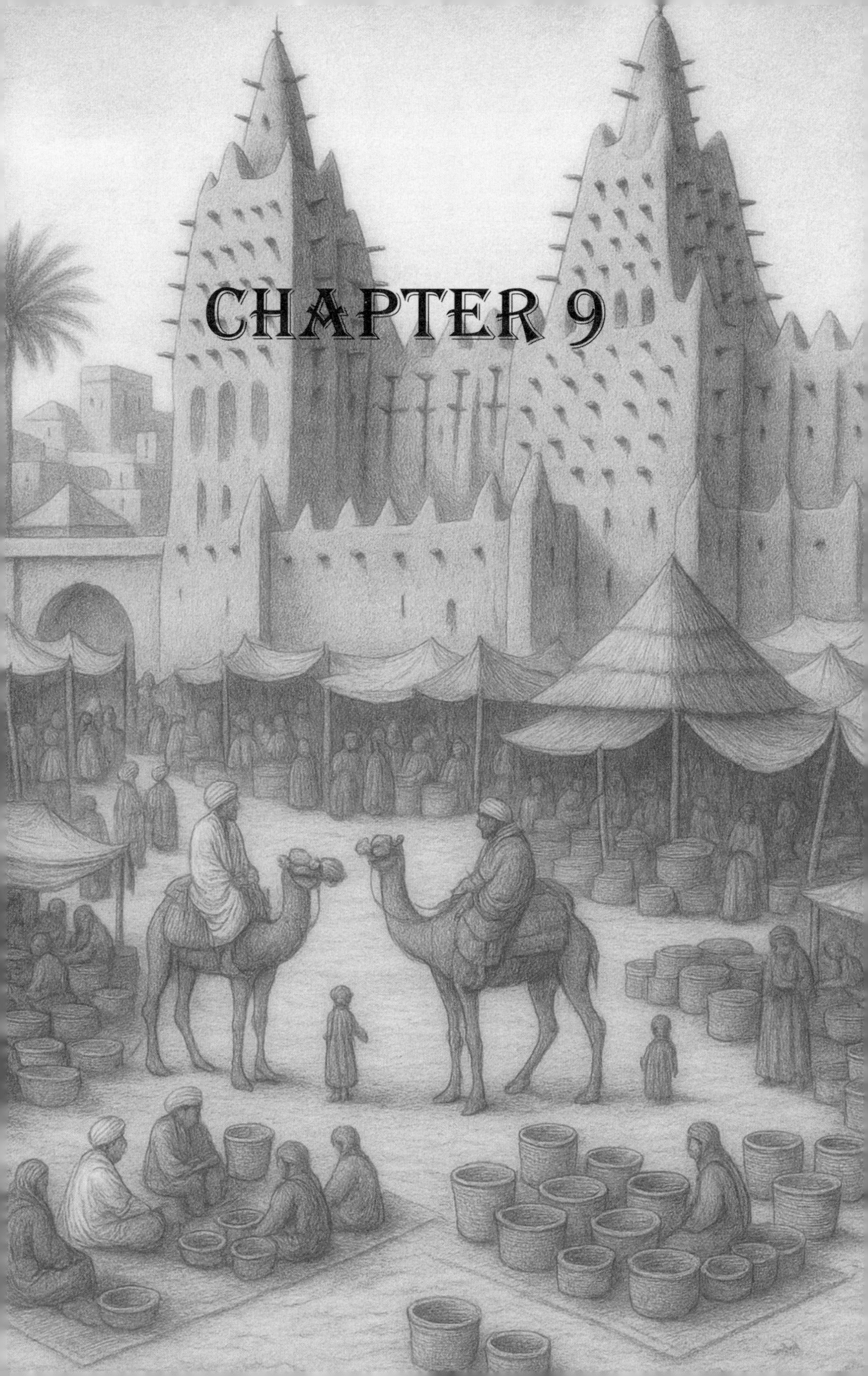

CHAPTER 9

Chapter 9

Lakisha's wound was starting to heal, and the color in her face was coming back. As the fog dissipated, they found that they were wearing African clothes. This time, they were on camels. Lakisha was back to her old self. She looked at her wound, and it was completely healed. Not even a trace of the scar. "I can never get used to this." Kyle said, leaning in from his camel to look at her.

She shoved him a bit. "Can I have some privacy, or do you want to see my breast too?"

"That wasn't my intention, but if you're offering..." He leaned to look some more.

She gave him a sideways look and covered herself up.

Maria checked her satchel and found a bag of gold coins, each stamped with intricate Arabic calligraphy. "**Empire of Mali**." She said softly.

"Empire of Mali... yes, I have heard of it. Wasn't it one of the richest empires of all time?" Kevin said.

"How do you know that?" Maria wondered, because when she was growing up, they'd never taught her that.

"We learned that in school, didn't you?" Kevin looked at her in a questioning look.

"They didn't teach us that in my time. I'm glad to see things got better." Lakisha said.

"What's our mission here?" Maria asked.

Lakisha sighed. "The fog sends us to a time and place—we don't get instructions. We wait for the target to surface."

They wandered through the desert on their camels for an hour before they reached an oasis. "Let's head into town." Thomas suggested.

Kevin leaned over. "We should act like traders. Maria, anything fancy in your satchel?"

She unzipped it and found **silk, incense, and polished beads**, all matching the era. "It's not much, but should keep our cover." It was a busy square with plenty of markets and guards all over the place watching them as they strolled in.

They dismounted from their camels and walked around. They saw traders from almost all over the world. "It's too bad we can't take any souvenirs back with us." Kevin said, looking at a weapons trader. He had all kinds of swords.

"What now?" Kyle asked.

"Let's check into an inn and get some rest. It should be dark soon." Maria pointed to a place that was made of mud, but was huge. They checked into a room they all shared. Maria lay her head down and fidgeted a bit, pressing her hand up against the hard floor.

Suddenly, guards stormed their room, weapons drawn. Maria reached for her sword but stopped when Lakisha gave a sharp shake of her head. There were too many guards in the small space.

They were dragged to a jail cell beneath the main market, stripped of weapons and Maria's satchel. It smelled of feces and unwashed butthole. No one would answer their question. Her satchel was taken away. The room had no windows, just a candle to light the room that was near the guard. Kyle kept telling them that they were merchants.

"What we going to do now?" Maria asked. She felt

something very ominous.

"Let's just wait and keep our eyes open for an opportunity." Lakisha got comfortable on the floor.

They were there for hours, not knowing what time it was. A few guards came, and they chained them up and brought them outside. It was early morning, and they saw one guy handing over a huge bag of gold to them.

Maria froze as she watched the man hand over a bag of gold. "They're selling us." She hissed under her breath, scanning for an opening, but the guards' swords were so close that she couldn't even swallow without cutting herself.

The man had fourteen other people with him, and they kept their swords at their throat. As much as Maria wanted to fight, she couldn't risk it. They were crowded into a cage that was on top of a wagon. Maria was looking for weakness, but nothing stood out. The guards surrounded them and kept their swords inches from their bodies.

"They aren't taking any chances," Maria whispered. "They know who we are."

The lead guard turned, smirking. "We've been tracking you for days."

"What do you want with us?" Kyle was trying to back away from the tip of the sword.

"You kidding? You're worth a fortune in the future." The guard said with a grin. "You're very special to the organization that hired us. Now, be quiet before my friends slip and poke you." He looked at the other guard.

They rode for hours without stopping. Their camels got tired, and they stopped. Half of Maria's body was cramping up. Her foot and shoulder fell asleep.

As the caravan stopped at an abandoned oasis, Maria noticed the temperature drop sharply. A ripple of **black fog** swirled near the water, crawling toward them like it was alive. Their clothes didn't change.

Maria couldn't wrap her mind around it.

CHAPTER 10

Chapter 10

She wondered how they found them. How were they able to track her?

They arrived at a room that was made of stainless steel, with no decorations, just pure blandness. They chained them all up against the wall using magnetic chains. These people had taken all the precautions from the fog by making the air dry as a desert.

Maria wondered at time, who was the real enemy—the fog or these people or both. Was she caught up between a war that had no good guys?

As they strapped her down, they ran a laser light over her, and she felt her old insecurities come back. She knew she no longer had the fighting skills she once had. She felt comfort that she was with three trained warriors, but she already missed that part of her that could kick ass. "Let's see how well you fight now, little girl." A man said to her.

Her stomach was in knots, and she wanted her big brother. She knew too well what they were going to do to her. She had to muster the courage to find a way to escape. Her heart was pounding, and she had to bite her lip so she wouldn't go into a full panic attack.

Everybody but Lakisha was strapped down. They were uncuffing her, and with one arm loose, her hand turned into fog, and she reached out for a man's face and aged him to the point that he was so old, he dropped dead.

For the first time, Maria saw Lakisha fully; she *was* the fog.

She got the rest of herself loose and turned the whole room into the fog, killing everybody but her group. Her face came out of the fog, which scared Maria so much that she thought she peed a little in her undies. Her arms extended out and released all of them. "Walk into the fog." She commanded.

Maria froze. Kyle grabbed her and ran into the fog. Once in the fog, they noticed a car started forming around them. When they finally came out of the fog, they were in Atlantic avenue in Downtown Brooklyn. Maria was in the driver's seat, and she looked over to Lakisha and screamed. The car swerved a bit, and she regained control.

As soon as she found a spot, she park the car. "What the fuck are you?" She wasn't the only one who was freaked out. The guys jumped out of the car.

Lakisha got out of the car as well. "Everyone, relax. I will explain everything. Let's get a hotel room and do this in private." She gestured with her hand.

"No, I'm not going anywhere with you until you explain." Kevin said. People started looking at the commotion. Lakisha pointed to the people who were stopping to look at them. Maria noticed they were all wearing masks.

They got in the car, and Maria set the GPS. She looked at the year, and it was May 7, 2021. She found a hotel on the GPS and drove the rest of the way quietly. They got to the front of the hotel and saw a giant poster that said, *Everyone must wear a mask or you will not be allowed inside.*

Maria reached into her bag and took out a mask.

After they checked in, they all piled into the elevator, and Lakisha lost her strength. Kyle caught her. "What's wrong with you?" Maria just gave her a sideway glance. "I knew there was something off about you."

"You have the right to be angry. But right now, in order for me to maintain this form in this reality, I need water. It took a lot out of me being in fog form in that room." She held herself up by holding the wall. "Let me take a shower, and then we can talk."

Maria just stubbornly turned around, ignoring her the rest of the way up. Kyle and Kevin helped her into her room and actually helped her get undressed. They put her in the shower, and she told them they could leave now. They didn't seem thrilled to see her naked, now knowing what she was.

Maria went into her room and took a nice long hot shower. Maria came out of the shower, and one by one, they went to her room. Thomas was the first one to arrive. "Ok, Maria, what the fuck?"

"Who are you telling? What is her true purpose?" Maria answered

A minute later, Kyle walked in. He didn't seem to care and just raided her mini bar.

"You don't care what's going on?" Maria was annoyed that he was raiding her stuff.

"Of course, I do but I was fifty-five years in the future,

fighting a very stupid war with your country, then I was in limbo, then I spent a night in a medieval jail and was brought way into the future, where they were going to de-atomize me. And now, I'm with a woman who is not even human. So forgive me if I want to drink first before hearing her side." He pounded one of those airplane-size whiskies.

"In that case, give me one of those as well." She said, snatching the bottle out of his hand.

"Dammm, miss, where's your manners." He said.

"Time travel is a motherfucker, as you said." Maria drank the whole thing, and it didn't even seem to faze her.

Kevin walked in with Lakisha, and Maria just sat down quietly. The rest of the guys sat next to her on her bed.

Lakisha held her hands together, looking for a way to start. "As you know, I'm not human. But I can exist in this reality as long as I have a human form. When you guys were in trouble, I had to do something." She took a deep breath. "I took this form and came to help you," she said, looking at all four of them.

"Nah, you need to go further back with this story." Maria said, waving her hands.

Lakisha put her hand up so Maria could relax. "Ok, so, as you know, I help maintain time as you know it from my realm. But from time to time, I seep into this reality, and it causes problems. Rare weather patterns that I myself don't fully understand." She sat on the floor and crossed her legs. "Have you ever heard of people who had timeslips?"

"Yes, the story of the man from the 1800s that found himself in 1950s and was killed by a cab." Kyle said.

"Like that." She pointed at him. "For my entire existence, I was unconscious of my existence; I just existed. Until I seeped into your living room that night when you were a child." She said to Maria.

"I saw space and green fog. You were there?" She asked with her mouth open.

"Yes, I carried you into my fog. For the first time, I felt compassion. When I surrounded you to keep you company, it gave me consciousness, but I was quickly pulled back into my reality. I couldn't take this form yet, not until later. I found that I could jump around different years like walking into another room, but I could only stay there for a few minutes and would be pulled back. Well, one time, I was way into the future in that place we just came from. I came into their lab. They quickly scanned me, since their tech is so far advanced, and they figured out what I was. They tried to hold me there but couldn't. But they were able to take a sample, and they invented time travel. That's when they started abducting people across time. I then recruited you to stop them because it was causing problems with the timeline."

Maria stood up. "You didn't recruit me you abducted me and threw me into 1975 without knowing what the hell was going on." She raised her voice.

"I'm sorry, Maria, but I knew you were a target, and I downloaded into your mind & body every self-defense method humans had invented. I should have asked you first, and I know that now. Please understand my intentions." Maria stood quietly. "I realized you needed help, and that's when I recruited these three gentlemen, who have vast experience."

Maria seemed to be partially convinced.

"Again, you didn't ask me neither whether I want to join this craziness." Kyle said, standing up and going to look for more booze.

"Listen..." Lakisha took a deep breath and put her hands

on her lip. “I thought I was doing you guys a favor, but you know what? Fuck it. Any you mo’fuckers want to go back, let me know. I’m tired of explaining myself.” She stared at everyone. No one said a word. “That’s what I thought.”

“Ok, then what is our mission?” Maria asked with less attitude this time. She didn’t like it, but she knew with them, she had a better chance than on her own.

“Now, we rest. As much as you guys bitch, you earned the rest.”

“Woo hoo.” Kyle jumped up with excitement.

“But! Not too much. You don’t want to call attention to yourself.” Lakisha warned them.

“Well, with that being said, I’m crashing. Everybody scoot.” Maria waved them off with her hands. She must have slept fourteen hours or so. Her body still ached from the cage they were in.

After she got ready, she went to see the others. She knocked on Lakisha’s door first. Lakisha let her in. “So, what’s the plan?” Maria asked. She was wondering where they would go next.

"Have a seat." Lakisha was wearing her worries on her face. "Here is the problem: we need to destroy the machines, but the area they have the equipment in is shielded. So, I cannot travel there, and if we travel to an outside place in that time, they will notice immediately, and we will be overrun. Believe it or not, I do care what happens to you guys. Especially you."

Maria was taken back. "Why me?"

"Weren't you listening? You gave me sentience, and that's a big deal for me." Lakisha said with soft eyes.

Maria sat there quietly and didn't know how to respond.

"Anyway, do you have any ideas?" Lakisha broke the awkwardness in the room.

"We need to learn more about them." Maria was poking in the dark because she felt she was out of her league.

"That could work, but we need to bait a trap. How can we?" Lakisha now looked at her for answers.

"That part is easy. Who is their next target?" Maria had a plan.

"I have to get in the shower to find out, but I need your

help." She started walking towards the bathroom without even waiting for Maria to answer, taking off her clothes and leaving them wherever they landed. She jumped into the shower and turned on the warm water.

Maria wasn't feeling comfortable seeing her naked. Nevertheless, she stood by the shower, waiting for her impatiently.

Lakisha finally stuck her hand out of the shower. "Grab my hand. I need you to anchor me here while most of me goes back to the no-time zone."

Maria rolled up her sleeves and embraced her forearm. Lakisha's feet started turning into fog. It engulfed the rest of her except for her arm. The fog was absorbing all the water and started surrounding Maria. It overtook the bathroom. She looked around and made sure not to touch the fog. The majority of it was disappearing into the no-time zone.

Maria's mind had gone into a trance. She could see the no-time zone; Lakisha essence was reconnecting with the fog. Maria's perception was that Lakisha was the whole fog, but no, it was only a small portion of her that was forming the body of Lakisha.

Her mind moved from the no-time zone and saw flashes of the different points in time, scanning thousands of places, seeing the rise and fall of societies. Her mind was fixed in one point in time. She got it; they both knew where they had to go to find a little boy, who was the next target.

Slowly, the fog came back and started transforming back into Lakisha. After she came back, Lakisha got out of the shower, and Maria gave her privacy. When she came out of the bathroom, she quickly got dressed. “Did you see it?”

“Yes, I did. We have to go to 1893 Colombia. It’s a little Spaniard boy.” Maria was sitting on the bed.

“Let’s get the others and head for the car.” Lakisha said, getting her bags.

“But we have to be careful. Colombia is very racist during this time, but not as bad as America.” Maria cautioned as she got up.

“So was the rest of the world.” Lakisha said with a grim face.

Maria headed to her room to collect her things. She got her bag and knocked on the guys’ doors. “Pack your stuff, we are heading out.”

They were all hungover from the night before. "We need half an hour to get ready. We will meet you downstairs."

"Take your time." She remembered that they'd had time to get ready, but not the guys. She took the elevator down and met up with Lakisha, who was checking them out of the hotel. "Where's the rest?"

"They must have gone out last night, so they need time to get ready." She put her bag down. It felt different never to have to worry about money.

"In that case, why don't you go and get the car and meet us in front of the hotel?" Lakisha suggested.

"Sounds like a plan." She left her bag with Lakisha and walked out. She first headed for a Korean deli to get coffee, but when she came out of the deli, she saw so many police cars racing past her. "Oh, shit." She knew at that moment that they were coming for them. She dropped her coffee and raced to the car. She jumped into the car, fumbled with the key, and couldn't seem to get it into the ignition. She dropped the keys right when the police car passed by hers.

Maria got it into the ignition and the engine revved up. She drove past the hotel, and Lakisha, Kevin, Kyle, and Thomas were all in handcuffs and being thrown into the wagon. She was able to make eye contact with Lakisha. What her mouth couldn't say, her eyes said, so she kept driving.

"But where can I go?" She couldn't go to her family for obvious reasons. She didn't know what to do or where to hide until she could come up with a plan to break them out.

She drove out of Brooklyn and headed for Queens. She found a two-star hotel in Sunnyside, Queens and stayed in her room, where she ordered Dominican food from a nearby space. This would give her comfort and help her think. She wanted a drink, but knew that would impede her judgement. "Think. If you were the enemy, what would you do?" She paced around her room and, in frustration, threw her luggage to the floor. A smart phone slid across the floor. She picked it up and looked at it for few seconds as, in her time, the cell phones were still big and clunky.

"Before, I was able to get knowledge that I didn't have before. So, I should be able to hack the system and find out where they are being held." She checked her bag for a laptop, and yes, it was right in there. "Of course, the fog will help me. It wants me to free Lakisha." She opened it up and got to work. At this point, she wasn't even surprised anymore that she was able to hack the system without prior knowledge.

"They will be transferred to the CIA, according to the 84th Precinct. But I bet you they're not even the real CIA." She snapped her fingers together. "They have to find a secluded spot to jump into the future. I need special weapons. Glock with a silencer and a fifty-round drum clip." She meant business.

She checked the bag, and there it was. She paused for a second and wondered how the bag worked.

She put her hand inside, and she could feel the fog, though it was very little. "Somehow, the fog must be pulling in moisture whenever it sends me something."

She grabbed her stuff and drove back to Brooklyn. She didn't even bother to check out. They were moving them in the evening, and she needed a better vehicle. As she was driving over the Brooklyn bridge, she asked the fog for a Hummer. A deep fog set into the bridge; she could barely see a few feet. The car morphed into a white Hummer.

She parked herself across from the precinct in an area that gave her the best view of the back, where they were bringing perps in and out. An SUV pulled up moments after she got there. She waited for them to go inside, then went into her bag and got a tracking device.

Maria walked in the back. When she got close to the SUV, a police officer noticed her.

"Excuse me, ma'am, can I help you?"

She had to think quickly. She acted like she lost her balance and fell to the floor, stretching her arm under the car and placing the device before the officer ran to her. He helped her up.

"Are you ok?" He was looking her over, trying to make her out.

"I'm so damn clumsy. Thank you for your help. You're a true hero." She placed her hand on his chest with a smile.

He smiled at the compliment. "How can I help you?"

"Sorry, I just need directions to the two train."

"Not a problem. Just follow this avenue, and it will take you there."

"Thank you so much." She walked away, turned her head, and smiled at him, waving goodbye. He smiled and looked down.

She waited until he headed back into the precinct, and she jumped into her car and drove a few blocks away. She didn't want to draw any more attention.

Ten minutes later, the SUV was on the move. She knew they were going to a secluded spot, so she would wait until then to ambush them. They drove towards Williamsburg Bridge and headed under it, near the Dumbo area.

Night started to set in. She turned off her car lights and sped up to the car. She crashed right into it, sending it onto the sidewalk. A commotion soon ensued inside the car.

She jumped out of her car. But as soon as she came out, more SUVs turned the corner, and six extra men jumped out shooting at her. She hid behind her car, timing her shots. Maria closed her eyes and calculated in her head where they would be standing. Her head popped up, and she hit two of them.

Kyle and Thomas had one guy on the floor, and Lakisha was struggling with the other. Kevin ran towards her, and she opened the car door and tossed him her bag. He dug into it, pulled out a few guns, and tossed one to Kyle and Thomas. Lakisha made her way towards Maria.

It was a barrage of bullets, but Kyle and Thomas bided their time and popped them one by one like ducks at a county fair.

"Hurry, the cops should be here at any moment." They jumped into the car. Maria backed the car up and did a 180-degree turn. She drifted the car at the corner. Several more SUVs came, almost out of nowhere, and gave chase. They got on the bridge, and Maria was honking the horn so the other cars can get out of their way. She was swerving through traffic.

The fog started to come, and they were home free.

But right before they entered the fog, one of the guys took out some homemade gadget that had wire protruding from it and fired a laser beam at the car. As it entered the fog, Maria could feel the car breaking apart, as if it had split into individual pieces. She was thrown clear from the car and flew through the fog.

Her mind started jumping around to different parts of her memories. She finally hit reality, and she remembered hitting water.

Then everything went dark.

CHAPTER 11

Chapter 11

When she awoke, pain shot throughout her body. She slowly opened her eyes.

"I think she is awake." a strange male voice said.

When she looked at him, she saw that he was not human. He was a crystalline humanoid. She sat up and screamed. Even though she had been time-traveling, she couldn't hide the expression on her face.

"You are safe. We won't hurt you." A female-looking being came to his side. "Can you understand us? Are you able to speak?" He asked with care in her eyes.

Maria gasped at their sight, but shook it off. "Yes, I understand what you are saying, but I feel groggy." Their skin looked like a soft crystal; he was an off green, and she was an off blue. Their eyes looked like little emeralds.

When Maria moved, she felt broken glass in her leg.

"Don't move; your leg was broken." She glanced at the splint, and her breath caught... her leg wasn't human flesh.

It was silvery-blue. Crystalline. Like theirs. Her fingers trembled as she touched it, half-expecting to change back.

She passed her hand over her leg. It felt like silk with a bit of oil. She then looked at her hand, and she really didn't have a hand; it was more like her fingers were all fused together, and her thumb was long and flat.

"Do you know who you are?" The lady asked her.

"My name is Maria." She placed a palm on her chest.

"That is a strange name. I've never heard a name like that."

"My parents wanted something unique." She looked around and quickly realized they were preindustrial. Where the hell had she been flung to? Their way of reading the calendar wouldn't help her, so she could be anywhere in the galaxy and time. She could be a billion years in the future or a billion years in the past. But somehow, the fog changed her face and body to fit these people, so Lakisha must know where she is at.

"Our name is **Lkankt,** and my husband is **Ucyftre**."

That's why they thought my name is strange, she thought to herself.

"Are you hungry? We don't have much, but you're welcome to stay with us until you get better."

"Thank you. Did you find anything else around me?"

"Oh, just this satchel. It's very pretty." She tried to get up, but the man gestured for her to sit back down.

"When we found you were floating in the water, we were afraid you had drowned." The man said.

The lady handed over her bag, and Maria rummaged through it. "Thank you for saving me."

"How where you injured?" She said it slowly, not wanting to intrude.

"I…" She had to think quick. "I slipped and fell into the water. I must have banged myself into something."

"You poor thing. Your family must be worried." The lady said, sitting next to her.

She then thought about her family. She had lost count of the days since she had gone to college. But would they even notice? She shook the thought away. "Yes, but I live really far away, about three months' walk from here." Maria said, half-believing her own lie.

"Oh, dear, we've never met anyone from so far away. Why would you travel so far?" She leaned closer to look at her skin.

"I had never left my area, but I wanted to see the world, all of its wonders, and get to meet nice people like yourselves."

The lady looked bashful. Her skin glimmered a bit, and Maria stared for a moment. She had to change her face quickly. "Thank you, you're a brave girl. Are people from your area explorers?"

"No, ma'am, they are not. I'm just very different." Maria smiled.

"I think the furthest we've travelled must have been a day's walk." She got up. "Let me get you something to eat." She went to a wooden stove and got her some soup. Maria told herself not to look at the food, as she knew it would be strange. She immediately started eating. "This is good. You're lucky to have married such a good cook."

They both glimmered, and it threw Maria off again. She dug into her food, hoping they didn't notice. She finished it all up; it actually tasted like salty honey, so for her, it was easy to consume.

"I'm sorry, but we don't have any more." She said with concern.

"Ooh, I'm sorry to eat all your food." Then she saw them glimmer again.

"That's not what I meant; I just wish we had more in case you were still hungry."

"Oh, no worries. I'm very satisfied." Maria rubbed her belly.

"I will start a fire. The nights get cold around here." Ucy-ftre got up and went outside.

"I wish I could help." She saw her skin glimmer again. *Wow, this is not cool."* Maria thought to herself.

"The only thing you have to worry about is healing your leg." She helped Maria up, and they went next to where the fire would be in the middle of the room. She placed something that look like petals and squeezed a leaf; when the drop hit the petals, a blue fire ignited.

Maria flinched at the sight of fire.

"Don't you have grthsa where you from?"

"Yes, but it still fascinates me when I see it."

The lady looked at her eyes, then looked away.

The husband came back in and added wood to the fire. "So, tell us about your family." He sat next to her to listen.

I guess before the tv, this is what families did. She told them about her brother, but changed it to fit her circumstances.

After she told her story, the lady stared into her eyes. "Where are you from, really?" she said softly but stern.

Maria squirmed a bit. "Why would you ask me that question?" Her face became very serious, the same way your grandmother's face would look if you had lied to her.

"Because if you were truly Pklyan... you'd know we *cannot* lie. Our eyes betray us when we try." Maria nodded slowly, filing that away for later.

"Let me show you: You are my daughter." Her eyes glimmered.

Then, Maria's body glimmered. She took a couple of breaths and stared at them for a second. She had no choice.

"I'm sorry. I'm a time traveler, and I'm lost in time." She was waiting for a reaction, but it never came.

"That is the first truthful thing you told us, but we understand why you lied. The truth is, we had no idea if we were the only ones in the galaxy. But you have now answered our question. Please continue." She didn't seem as surprised as Maria would think. She was starting to like these people more than humans.

"I'm human, and I come from a planet called Earth." She continued telling them about Earth and how she got there. They were on the edge of their seats and wanted Maria to tell them everything. They were shocked by the violence. According to her, they had never ever harmed one another in her species. Maria found this incredible. She now wished she could change her form, but she wondered how the fog missed that. It must be aware of only some things. They traded stories into the wee hours of the night.

The next day, LKankt went out into the forest and made them breakfast. For the first time ever, Maria felt at peace. She had never felt this kind of honesty from any human. *Are we even capable of it?* She thought.

After breakfast, LKankt helped Maria to go outside. The air was warm. Now, Maria could be openly fascinated with the smallest things. Everything seemed to be made of crystalline structure. She no longer cared about leaving; she was home.

After a month, her leg became strong enough. She still had a limp, but she could walk on her own. She was worried that her leg wouldn't heal correctly, but it did. Two weeks after, she barely limped. It only bothered her when it rained. She helped LKankt around the house.

They finally took her to town to meet other people. This time, she was honest; some people couldn't believe their ears, but they knew she was telling the truth. Maria thought this would be her permanent home. Judging by looking around, these people were in the iron age.

One day, she was walking around the forest. A gleam through the trees stopped her cold. A ship... Earth insignia sharp against its hull.

Her chest tightened... images she'd grown up hearing about slammed into her: the stories of the Taíno, the natives of Dominican Republic, wiped out by *explorers*.

And now, another ship. Another discovery.

Her pulse pounded—history was repeating itself … this time on a different world. She was frightened by what might happen to these people. *Will history repeat itself?* She was 100% sure they were here for resources. No way would they contact a preindustrial civilization if humans had advanced in the ways that mattered.

She ran back to the house, crying and panicking.

"What's wrong?" Ucyftre had never seen her like this.

"We need to warn the others!" They helped Maria to sit down.

"Slow down, tell us." LKankt stroke her hair to calm her down.

Maria was hysterical. "My people are here, and on my own planet, when they would arrive to an area such as this, they would conquer it and take all the resources."

LKankt's skin glimmered wildly. Maria got up and looked for her satchel. She hadn't paid attention to it in a while. When she found it, she tested her theory. She looked in the bag and found an energy rifle that fitted to her arm. The insignia was a human company. Before she could only get what was available to these people, and now, with the human threat, things had changed.

"See this?"

They were scared of it. "Is that a weapon? Get it out of my house now." LKankt had never demanded anything from Maria.

"I can only get what is available in this time, and with the humans showing up, this is what they carry." She went into her bag and got another one. "We must arm the people and fight them off the planet."

"Your people may be killers, but we are not. Have you even seen one argument amongst us? And the answer is no. Because we are peaceful. Why don't you put these away, and we will go and talk to them?"

Maria realized what she was asking them to do: to throw centuries of values out the door.

"Ok, but I will hide this under my sleeve." They didn't like the idea, but they agreed with her.

By the time they got there, it was full of local people.

Men in military suits were looking around. They had men posted guarding equipment and their ship.

LKankt became frightened. "Don't worry, Maria is a fighter." Her husband said.

"That's what I'm afraid of." Maria didn't hear LKankt; she was marching to the front. She thought for a minute to see if her English would come out. "Testing, testing." She was able to switch back and forth, just like English and Spanish.

Some scientists were taking readings. She looked for the man in charged. He was a short, stocky man who looked like he was of Hispanic descent, possibly Columbian or Venezuela. "Why are you here? We are a peaceful people. Don't come to exploit us like you did to the indigenous people on your own planet."

Every human stopped to look at Maria. The Pklyan didn't know what she was saying. "How do you speak English, and how do you know about our planet?" He was trying to make sense of how this alien knew so much about them.

"Don't worry about that. Answer my questions." She got really close to his face, and the other soldiers pulled up their weapons and aimed at them. All the Pklyan cringed in fear.

Maria realized that she could turn this into a massacre if she didn't calm down. She knew all too well that when humans were scared, that was when they were the most dangerous.

She stepped back. All the Pklyans backed away. These people were not fighters whatsoever. How was she supposed to help them fight these pricks off?

"Relax, papi." She put her arms out. She didn't want them to know that she was armed. "This is what I'm talking about, you people are quick to pull the trigger. Why can't yah chill?"

The head guy in charge just couldn't wrap his head around the idea that not only was she speaking English, but it was classical English. "Seriously, where did you learn English? You speak an archaic English."

Maria had to come up with a quick answer. "What year is it on your planet?" She was trying to devise a plan.

"Jan 15, 2732." He was trying to find her angle.

She was about to come up with an answer, but she remembered she couldn't lie. "Anyway, why have you come to our planet?" As she waited for his answer, she looked around and saw their instruments. If she could get her hand on one of those devices, she could do research and find out more.

"We just want to get to know you." He said with a smile.

"Bullshit, not buying that. Your company wouldn't spend so much money just to get to know us." She sat down and waved her hand for him to sit. He sat down. "So, you're telling me that those eggheads over there are not scanning for minerals?" He waved at them, and they went back into the ship. She knew better now not to lie; she just avoided his questions.

"Why are you so mistrusting of us? We've done nothing to your people." He was trying to find her soft spot, not knowing that she was human.

"Your history. I'll tell you what: let's take a short recess, and we will offer you some drinks and food." She needed to buy time.

He agreed, and she told some of the Pklyan in their language to get them food and drink. They were so afraid; her heart broke at the sight of seeing these defenseless people.

She met up with the couple she was staying with. "I now understand your people are not fighters. But I have an idea."

She reached into her bag and took out a device from Earth. "There has to be a planet that protects civilizations like yours." She gestured for them to walk away from the crowd. Her hunch was correct; she found an intergalactic internet. She pored through the information, looking for a species that she could call as an arbiter. After half an hour, she finally found one. "I got it," she said to them.

She called them up. The device had a translator, so she spoke in English.

"This is the **Barbenkus** intergalactic affairs office. How can I help you?" Their chins were pushed back and long. He had white hair and spots all over his face.

"Hi, there, I'm representing the Pklyan people. We are having a dispute with the humans. These people are preindustrial, and I'm afraid that they will colonize them."

His face went from friendly to serious. "When you say humans, are you talking about the Earth humans or the New Lemurian humans?"

The question threw her off. "Earth humans, of course."

Then his face went from serious to disgusted. "Of course it's Earth humans. "Don't get me wrong; individually, they are quite friendly, but their companies will do anything to make a profit. We will dispatch a few ships, and we will alert the **Cradark** as well. Please send me the coordinates." Maria sent him their location. "I have a question: how are you able to use technology?"

"I'm not really Pklyan. It's a long story, but we really need you here."

"Ok, they will be there shortly. Stall them for now."

"Thank you." Maria answered and disconnected the call.

She explained the situation to LKankt and her husband, and they went back to the group.

Maria sat down with him again. The whole time, she was able to avoid giving names. They went back and forth; he was trying to convince them to let them set up a colony, but Maria was stubborn and would not. After three days of this, they finally got tired and started setting up their colony. He believed they weren't a threat, so there was nothing the natives could do.

Maria moved the village very far from them. "Is there somewhere you could hide?"

An old man in the village stood up. “I believe there is an old cave system about half a day’s walk from here. We should be safe there.”

“Good. I need you all to go there until the Barbenkus arrive. I will stall them until then.” They took as many provisions as possible and headed for the cave. When they were walking towards the cave, Maria spotted a small scout ship that saw them. “Everyone hide.” They jumped into the bushes, hoping the ship didn’t spot them. It didn’t seem like they were looking for them. All they cared about was mining their minerals.

Maria went with them to the caves they settled in. If she fought them, that could be disastrous for the Pklyan.

The humans would get too far ahead with the mining by the time the other aliens came. She saw the ship again, and this time it got closer. It landed half mile away.

Maria went to check it out. She had to make sure they didn’t find out where they were hiding. She slowly got closer to the craft. If she shot them, that would call attention towards them. There were three of them with their helmets on. One of them decided to take his helmet off.

“Kyle!” Maria called to him. She was so happy to see

them. Like seeing old relatives. Obviously, he didn't recognize her. She had started running towards him when he let out a shot. She quickly threw herself to one side. It barely missed her. "Put your weapon down, stupid. That's Maria." Lakisha pulled down his hand.

"Oh, shit, I'm so sorry. You were running towards me, and I got scared! You look so different." Kyle said, apologizing.

Kevin and Thomas ran to her to help her up. "I'm ok. You racist bastard. Just because I'm silver." She dusted herself off and walked towards him and Lakisha. "You're lucky I like you. If not, I would kill you."

"You know, she could." Lakisha said, laughing to herself.

"You look hot as an alien." Thomas said.

Maria glimmered. "Why, thank you." She did a turn to show off. "Feel." She said to him. He passed his hand on her arm.

"Wow! That is soft. You want to go over there for a minute?" He pointed to some bushes.

"Only a minute? No, thank you." She teased.

"That's not what I meant." He said, blushing.

"Why do you look like that, and we look human?" Kevin asked, helping Thomas out.

"That's because I arrived here before the humans."

Everybody laughed. "So, should we get going?" Lakisha pointed at the ship.

"Not yet These people need our help, and they took care of me for over a month when I broke my leg." Maria pointed to where they were hiding.

"What's the problem?" Thomas asked.

"They are indigenous to this planet, and here come the humans, wanting to colonize. I called another alien race to intervene, but we must wait until they get here." She was trying to appeal to his indigenous heritage.

"We have to help them." Thomas spoke proudly.

"Alright, let's do it, but keep our eyes open for the futurist." Lakisha said.

"What should we do?" Kyle asked, loading his weapon.

"Well, that's just it: I want to avoid armed conflict. These beings are extremely friendly, and don't believe in violence. They won't defend themselves, so we have to."

"What if we fool the humans' sensors? Trick them by showing them that ships are coming." Kevin was throwing ideas into the air.

"That could work, but I don't want to alert them to the Barbenkus coming." Maria said, and he put down his head.

"What if we let out explosives away from here?" Kyle leaned up against the ship.

"They're to trigger-happy, and wouldn't want to take the chance." Maria was being a little hard.

"What if...well... we want to time it right? We'll give them what they want." Thomas wasn't sure of his plan.

"What do you mean?" Maria asked.

"Well, they need resources. So, show them where, but don't sign any treaties. They will be busy looking for it, and it will make them relax, so when the other ships come, they will be caught off-guard."

"That just might work." Lakisha said, slapping him on the back.

"She's right. I think that's excellent deception. I like it." Maria said.

"You will have to do this almost on your own. We will find it for you." Lakisha said, going into her satchel. She pulled a device out, then pulled out a small disk, and it took off flying. "This planet has never been mined, so it should be fairly easy to find something close to the surface." She searched until she finally hit something close to the camp. "Got it." She went into her bag and pulled out some mineral samples. "Here. Take this to them, show them this spot, and help them in any possible way."

Maria grabbed the samples and took off. They were going to monitor her to make sure she was safe.

She arrived at the camp, and the head guy was talking to some people. "I was wondering when you would show up. Where did you guys go?" He said, sitting on the floor. He must have thought this was their tradition, but it was really Maria's.

"Honestly, we are hiding from you." She had to be careful with her words so her eyes didn't glimmer. "Here. I brought you this." She put it on the floor in between them.

He picked them up and looked at them carefully, then called over a guy and passed it off to him. "Do an analysis on this, and let me know the findings." He turned back to her.

"Where did you find it?"

She turned her head to hide her eyes. "I found it over there, about two kilometers away." She closed her eyes as well in case anybody was looking at her. She took a few seconds to turn back, hoping the glimmer was over. "I will take you to the deposit, and you will leave us alone. "

"Yes, of course." He had a great big smile on his face. He quickly got up and extended his hand to help her out. When he pulled her up, she stared at his face. She'd just noticed that she was attracted to him. She shook off that feeling as quickly as it came.

"What is your name?" It seemed that he had noticed.

"The important thing is that you leave us alone." There was a lot more she wanted to say, but she didn't want to tip him off. She began walking and was not waiting for them. He called some other guards, and they caught up to her. She kept her head down and didn't bother to make small talk.

"Tell me about your planet?" He tried to walk side by side with her.

"It's nice and comfortable." She was keeping the conversation minimal.

He fell back a little and told his men with gestures to keep an eye out. He wasn't buying her story.

They finally made it to the spot, and they began looking around. They could clearly see the minerals. "This is a great find. What do you want in return?"

"For you to leave us alone."

"Ok, I got it."

Another guy came to him. "This is an amazing find. They are going to be happy back home."

He turned back to Maria. "Thank you. We will leave you alone."

"Thank you. I will leave you now." She got up and walked away. She started heading back to where Lakisha and the others were.

She was halfway there when she was suddenly ambushed by two men. They came out of nowhere and threw her on the ground. "I never had crystalline pussy before," One said to the other.

She hit her face up against the floor. She had gotten dirt in her mouth. She turned around to see her attackers. They were big brutes, and one of them had scars along his face. "It's ok, little one. We just want to teach you some Earth customs." He was getting closer to her.

Maria had never ever been in a predicament like this before. She'd been shot at and beaten up, but never raped. Times like this, she was glad she wasn't the same Maria from before.

"You can scream if you want. No one can hear you scream." The other one was getting closer from her left.

She had to buy herself time.

"I like screamers. Let's see what alien vagina looks like." He reached out to grab her arm. She quickly grabbed his arm and lay back so her body weight could pull him down. She twisted his arm. He fell on his face, and she rolled over his body and got up. She kicked him in the head.

The other guy was taking out his weapon, so she jumped and kicked him in the chest. She twisted her body in the air and did a round house kick to his face. He fell back.

The other guy went to get up. She was tempted to shoot the guy, but that would give her unwanted attention. Instead, she did a flying knee and knocked him out cold.

The other guy bounced up and squared up with her. He was so much bigger than her in weight and height. The only advantage she had was her kicks. She aimed at his face with a hook kick. He weaved back and clocked her right in the face. Maria fell right on her ass. Blood was dripping right from her lip. The color of her blood was light blue.

“Alright, sweetie, ready to get busy?”

Something clicked in her. If she didn’t subdue this guy, he was going to rape her, and she couldn’t let that happen.

She spun up. Right when she did, he took out his knife, and she’d had enough. She jumped, aimed with her arm, and shot him. The other guy was gaining consciousness, so she went over to him and clocked him with a downward fist, putting her weight into it, knocking him out again.

She ran off, knowing they’d heard that shot. Her team came on the ship, and she jumped on as they took off. She was still fuming. Lakisha went into her bag and took out her medical kit to patch up her busted lip. “You guys could’ve gotten there sooner.” She was venting her anger.

“We got here as soon as we could, but you handled yourself, as I expected.” Lakisha was wiping her lip.

"Can you tell how far out those ships are?" She asked.

"They should be here in six hours or so." Kevin was in the co-pilot's seat, looking at the computer.

They hid the ship close to the cave. If they come looking for them, they would use the ship in defense. They lay in the ship waiting. Maria knew they would want revenge.

"We got movement. There's about thirty of them, armed."

When they got close enough, they formed a perimeter around the area. "We want the girl for killing one of our men. We will leave the rest alone."

Maria and her team heard a sound from behind. They jumped around and aimed their weapons. "Put your weapons down." It was LKankt; she became frightened, but once they put their weapons down, she ran over and hugged Maria.

"We were so worried for you." She looked at her face and touched her busted lip.

"I'm fine. Why are you here? It's quite dangerous. You should run back and hide. This will be over soon."

LKankt looked at the others and was curious. "Are these

your friends you were talking about?"

"Yes, this is my team." She introduced her to everyone.

The voice interrupted them. "We will give you one minute to come out, or we will come in for you."

Maria shoved her to leave. "You must go now. Things might get a little dangerous." To her surprise, she listened to Maria and ran back.

"Any ideas?" She asked her team.

"I say load them up and aim." Thomas said, aiming his weapon out to the field.

"I hate to say it, but we ran out of options." Lakisha also aimed into the crowd.

At that very moment, a shot was fired across the horizon. Two ships were coming into the atmosphere. The crowd of humans aimed their weapons up. The two ships landed, and two battalions came out.

"Kevin, go get LKankt." He ran off without asking a question. Maria stepped out from her hiding place with her hands up. The humans aimed their weapons at her. "I suggest you put your weapons down. We wouldn't want a slaughter here, would we?"

As the two battalions got closer, it became clear that there were too many for the humans to fight off.

The human ordered his men to put their weapons down, and he walked over to the aliens that had arrived. "How dare you? This land has been claimed by the Earth."

"I am Ambassador Garek of the Barbenkus. You have seized this planet illegally. There are indigenous people here, so this land now falls under our protection until they become a spacefaring civilization.

"I am General Mario Gomez. Under whose authority?" He demanded.

Another person walked up to them. "Under the agreement your planet made with 200 other planets. I am Council Pizau of the Cradark. I suggest you honor that agreement. You can only mine non-inhabited planets."

LKankt finally came, and her people followed behind. Maria gave her the device. "Speak for your people." Maria pushed her forward.

So many different types of people. This was more

excitement than she'd had in a lifetime. "I'm LKankt. I will be speaking for my people." The device was translating for her.

"Did you give these people permission to mine on your planet?"

"No. We told them to leave, but they started mining anyway."

He turned to General Gomez. "You have to hours to leave this planet, or we will make you. Is that clear?" He said, stretching his chin back.

Gomez was going to say something, but then he turned around and order his men to retreat. Maria was able to breathe a little easier, knowing they would be safer now. She went back into the crowd and met up with her team.

"We should go before anyone asks us questions." She said. They scurried back into the ship and took off at low altitude.

She was sure they were seen, but they went over a river before anyone could do anything. The fog engulfed them, and they were gone.

CHAPTER 12

Chapter 12

The fog cleared, and they were on a creaky wooden bridge. Maria was in a carriage. She looked at the others, but Kyle was missing. They were all wearing classical clothes. Both she and Lakisha had big dresses, and she had to take extra breaths just to breathe in it. It was so tight around her chest, and her boobs were popping out. “Is my face back to normal?”

“Oh, no. You’re green now.” Kevin teased.

“Fuck you, but seriously.” She insisted.

“You’re good.” Lakisha said.

“Where’s Kyle?” Thomas looked around the carriage, but it wasn’t that big. Kevin stuck out his head “Eh? Is that you, Kyle?”

“It’s me, but I have no idea where we are going.” The rest of them could hear his voice.

Maria got a good whiff of horse’s ass. “Damm, what the

fuck is that?" She said, grabbing her nose.

"I think that's the horse's ass." Thomas started laughing.

"I think that's your ball sack." Kevin said.

"Close that curtain, but tell Kyle to pull over." Lakisha demanded. Kevin yelled it out to Kyle, and he pulled on the straps.

Maria almost fell on top of Thomas. "This is not as glamorous as the movies make it seem."

"This must be Colombia." Lakisha said.

"Why are we here?" Kevin played with his beard.

They got out of the carriage and looked around. With nobody in sight, Maria felt it was safe enough to tell them. "First thing, protect the boy. He's the target... which means whoever wants him knows *we're here*. We will use that to our advantage and capture one of them and find out more."

"Who is the boy, and how come we didn't know ahead of time?" Thomas asked.

"I am the fog, or at least part of it, but I don't have all the answers. Hence, we are going after one of the futurists."

"I think the best thing to do is go into town. That's where I usually bump into the person?" Maria said, trying to adjust her dress.

They jumped back into the carriage and rode into town. "You have to remember that during this time, not everybody had horse-drawn carriages, and especially not people of color. So, all eyes will be on us," Lakisha said.

"Oh, it's so nice that I can lie again." Maria remembered how hard it was. "We need a cover story."

"That's easy. Just say we are from Dominican Republic, looking to invest in Colombia." Kevin said. That reminded Maria to look into her bag, and she pulled out a few pistols and some silver. "I think we have the necessities." She smiled, handing silver pouches and the pistols to everyone.

There was a young light brown-complexion boy walking on the side of the road. "Excuse me, do you know where there is a hotel?" She said in her Dominican dialect.

"Yes, it's over there." He pointed, but Maria wasn't sure. The sun was bothering her eyes, and she squinted to get a better view.

"Can you show us?" Lakisha asked.

"Yes, I can." He was about to start walking ahead of the carriage.

"Jump up and ride with me." Kyle tapped on the chair next to him.

The boy smiled and got up on the chair, and they took off. He looked around, smiling at people like a movie star.

They came to a house that was as big as a mansion, with so many helpers cleaning everywhere. The carriage rode right through the gates, and the servants bowed. They rode on the stone path right to the front of the house, which had a rounded path for the carriages. Some men rushed to get the stoop for them to get off. They put their hands up to help them down. Their mouths fell open when they saw the little boy, but they all started murmuring when they saw Lakisha, Thomas, and Maria riding in such glamour. Well, to Maria, it smelled like horse's ass, but that was this era's version of balling.

"Kevin, you should talk to the concierge. I don't know how welcoming he will be to us." Thomas said to him.

"Why is that?" He said with a blank face.

"Really?" Thomas pointed to the back of his hand. "Civil rights movement is not for another hundred years."

"Sorry, I don't see color, just my peeps." He put Thomas in a headlock, and Thomas pushed him off.

The servants grabbed their bags, and they walked inside. Kyle and the little boy walked side by side. They seem to have bonded on the ride to the hotel.

"I'm sorry, sir, he can't be in here." A servant said. He pointed at the boy.

"Why not? He's with me." Kyle raised his voice a bit.

"Oh, I'm sorry." The servant bowed his head and walked away.

A well-groomed man came. "Good afternoon. How can I help you?"

"I would like a big room for me and my family." Kevin put his pinky up to his mouth, and Maria slapped it when the man turned around to get a key.

They went upstairs to the room, which was huge, with four different rooms. The whole mansion had old Spaniard decor. The little boy gasped. "It's great, isn't?" Kyle said to him.

Maria turned to Lakisha and said in a whisper. "Do you think that's him?"

Lakisha took a good look at him. “I think so he should stay with us.”

Maria walked over to him. “What’s your name?”

“My name is Carlos Bermudez Sanches.”

Maria extended her hand and shook his hand. “Where’s your family?” She crouched down next to him.

“I don’t have any family.”

“Where do you sleep?” Kyle asked.

“I sleep in the horses’ stables.”

“Oh, no. Tonight, you stay with us. Would you like that?” She asked.

“Yes, ma’am.” He gave Maria a big hug. He smelled a bit. *Sleeping with the horses rubs off on you,* she thought to herself.

“I’m going to set up a bath for you, and then Kyle will take you to buy clothes.” He almost cried; Maria’s eyes got watery as well. She warmed up some water and set the bath for him. After that, Kyle took him to a tailor and had few outfits made for him. In the meantime, the rest of them walked around the town to see if they could get a whiff of the futurists.

“We have to be careful not to piss off the Catholic church.” Maria warned.

“Yeah, we wouldn’t want them to burn us at the stake.” Kevin made a gesture, but Lakisha and Maria found it in poor taste. Thomas was quiet, just observing the landscape.

They got back to the mansion and waited for Kyle and Carlos to come back. They didn’t have much time, and they had to brainstorm about how to capture the assailant and what to do with him.

Kyle ran in. His face was injured. He was breathing deep. “They took the boy!”

“Coño!” Maria said, ripping off her dress. “I can’t fight in this shit.” Lakisha did the same, and they opened the trunk in a hurry, pulled out clothes, and threw them in the air. She found a peasant outfit that was comfortable to fight in. “Let’s go.” She grabbed a dagger and pistol.

They took the horses to town and wondered which way they would have gone. “The river is south of here, towards the jungle.” Lakisha pointed the way.

According to Kyle, they were on foot, which gave them a chance to catch up with them. They were right at the edge of the jungle. This time, it was two ladies with Carlos. The boy was slowing them down; he was feisty and was trying to fight them off. They got close enough, and Maria threw her dagger, planting it right in the back of the neck of one of the ladies. The lady saw she was outmanned, and she took off running, leaving the boy behind. Thomas and Kevin took after her and were able to tackle her down. Kevin being a little heavyset he put his weight on her to hold her still while Thomas bound her by the arms.

They were walking back to the carriage and Thomas and Kevin were holding her each by one arm when a group of farmers were walking by. They seemed startled.

"Help, they are trying to sacrifice me to pagan gods!"

The farmers took off running.

Thomas elbowed her in the face, knocking her out. "We need to leave this time now. If we are caught, there is no way to explain this." He said.

"I agree." Kyle said.

Thomas picked up the woman and ran for the carriage, but just as they got to it, five men on horses came and surrounded them. They had their pistols all aimed at them, and there was no way they could fight their way out.

"Put your weapons down. You are all under arrest for kidnapping and witchcraft." A man said, aiming his pistol at Thomas's head.

"*Coño*, this lady tried to kidnap this young boy. Just ask him. That's why we captured her and were going to take her to you." Maria said.

"Save your excuses, you can explain it to the judge."

"Yes, her and her friends have been nothing but nice to me." Carlos said, pleading with them.

The man looked at the boy. "Aren't you the bastard who sleeps in the horse's stall?"

"Yes, and I'm telling you, if it wasn't for them, this lady and her friend would have taken me into the jungle."

He scanned everyone's face. "He may be a dirty little boy, but I've never known him to be a troublemaker. But just in case, arrest that lady as well."

They were all arrested except for the boy. Maria hugged him and slipped him her satchel. "Keep it safe for me." She whispered to him.

"Let me see that." One of the guards grabbed the satchel, and it was full of boy's clothes. He gave it back to the boy.

They dragged them all to a cell and threw the woman in a different cell. Again, the cell was filthy and smelled like excrement. "Fuck, another jail cell. Is this going to be our common theme?" Kyle sat in the corner.

"Well, at least there's some hay to sleep on." Lakisha said, getting comfy.

Thomas and Maria looked around for a way to escape. The windows were high up with bars. Even if she climbed up on someone, she wouldn't be able to reach it.

The next morning, they were dragged in front of a cardinal and a judge. Carlos was sitting there.

"Please explain." The judge pointed at the farmers.

"Well... your honor, we heard a commotion, and when we went to go see, we saw this woman." He pointed to Maria, and she just cursed under her breath. "Throw a dagger and kill one woman. Then, we saw those two men tackle that woman, and that's when we ran away to get help."

"We are fucked." Kevin whispered.

"Do you all agree with him?" He asked the rest of the farmers. They all nodded in agreement. "What about this child? What did you see?"

"As you know, your honor, I don't have anyone to take care of me. When they came into town, they asked for me to show them where they could stay. Once they learned I don't have anyone, they took pity on me, gave me a bath, and bought me clothes." His eyes were welling up. He grinded his teeth and looked at the lady. "This gentleman told me to wait outside while he went into the tailor's shop. That's when they grabbed me against my will."

"I was saving him from those demons." The lady blurted out.

"No, you weren't, hija de *puta*." María responded.

"Quiet." The judge demanded. "Please tell me your side of the story?" He asked Carlos.

"They were preparing him for the devil! Don't be fooled." The woman yelled out again.

"Would you shut the fuck up?" Maria retorted.

"Quiet! Let this be the last time I have to tell you two

to be silent." He said to both of them. "Now, what evidence do you have that they are practicing witchcraft?"

"I saw them appear from a fog like the devil, and that's when they picked up the child." She greatly exaggerated, playing into the fears of this time. The court room gasped. Maria put her head down.

"Ok, I ask you where you come from?"

"We come from Dominican Republic." Maria answered the judge.

"We haven't had a boat come from there in a long time, so you didn't come on a boat."

She scanned the room with her eyes. "We took a boat to Mexico and rode our carriage down. We did cross from some fog on our way into town, but we did not come from fog. I believe in Christ." She did the sign of the cross. "See? I did not light into fire." She looked at the others. "You see? None of us turn to ash." She felt she'd made a good point, and the people were buying it.

"The truth is, this young man helped us, and we wanted to do something nice for him, so when he was kidnapped, we went into action. Instead of kidnapping him, if she felt he was in danger, why didn't she call the authorities?" The lady was about to say something, but Maria cut her off. This wasn't about the truth; it was about who could bullshit the courts best. "I will tell you why we... didn't go to the authorities." She pointed to herself with pride. "He was just kidnapped and we had to act fast, but she had time to get you. Didn't you?" She had to put her in the spotlight before the woman did the same to her.

"But..."

The tailor walked into the courtroom. "It's true! I saw that woman take him, and this man." Pointed his finger at Kyle—"Was buying this poor boy clothes. This boy has no one, and that is the kindest thing I've seen, and doesn't our Holy Bible tell us to give to those in need?"

"Amen!" Kevin and Maria said at the same time.

The judge looked at the cardinal, who was quiet. "Cardinal what do you think?"

He stared at us and the woman. "Well, I think to prove that you are children of god, you should donate to the house of god." Maria nodded. He then turned his attention to the lady. "Why did you try to take this child, and where are you from?"

"I'm from—"

At that very moment, four men burst into the court, shooting the guards and firing at Maria and her teammates. Lucky, for them they all hit the floor, but they took the boy and the lady. Maria still had handcuffs on.

"Can you release us, and we will capture her and bring back the boy safely?" She pleaded with the judge, who was standing up and adjusting himself.

"Release them and give them back their weapons. There are some horses you can borrow." He said.

"Thank you. We won't fail you." They grabbed their stuff and ran out of there. "It took a minute to bring the horses to them. They jumped on the horses and galloped away.

After a few minutes, they were able to catch up to them. But the pistols they had only allowed one shot, and the accuracy wasn't great. They had to get closer. At a time like this, she wished she had a bow and arrow.

Kyle fired his gun and missed. *Why would he fire his gun?* Maria thought to herself.

Thomas's horse was gaining on them, and a man slowed

down to confront him. Thomas aimed, but also missed. He threw the gun at the guy, hitting him on the head. That was when Thomas jumped from his horse, knocking the other guy off and falling with him.

Maria and the team continued. If she was going to fire her gun, she had to make it count. Kyle again wasn't as fast as the others, but Maria ignored it. Lakisha aimed and hit one guy, and he fell off. "We will take care of the others! You get the boy." She yelled to Kevin. He sped up.

Maria was aiming at one of the guys when the lady slowed down and jumped on her. They hit the floor and rolled. It knocked the wind out of her, but her body kept moving. They both lay there for a minute or so.

Maria knew she had to fight or this bitch would kill her. She stumbled to her feet and looked for her knife. Her knife and satchel were nowhere to be found. Maria decided to rush her as the lady was getting up, and she was able to tackle her back to the floor. She got right on top of her and started letting loose a fury of punches. She busted her nose, but she kept arching her back.

Maria had her thigh close to her face, and she bit into

it. Maria wailed with excruciating pain. She reached for her armpit and pinched it, which had the same reaction. She rolled forward, and they both got up, but it hurt when she stood up. Maria swung a cross hook, and the lady ducked and came up with an uppercut. Maria lost her balance and went back a few steps, then came in with an elbow and hit her in the face.

Maria fell on her ass. The woman went to kick her in the face, and Maria weaved her head to the left and gripped her leg with her right hand, then extended her leg and put it right on her knee, leaning back at the same time. Her knee collapsed and she fell forward. Maria grabbed her crotch and yanked on some meat. She wailed. Maria then punched her in the stomach, and she fell back, then turned on to her stomach to get up.

Maria took the chance and jumped on her back and started choking the living daylights out of her. She was fighting back, whaling her arms and legs, but Maria was able to snap her neck. She tossed the body to the ground and rubbed her leg. She got up and looked for her bag. She saw it a little way back and was walking towards it when she saw some man walking towards her. He was too far to tell if he was friend or foe.

She grabbed her bag, reached inside, and pulled out a

pistol. The man put his hands up. "Don't shoot! It's me, Thomas." She squinted. She was relieved when she noticed it was him. As he got closer, she noticed that his shoulder was drooping down. His eye was shut closed, and he had blood trickling down from the side of his head.

"What the fuck happen to you?" She said, laughing.

"You don't look so hot yourself." They leaned on each other for support and walked in the direction the others went. After twenty minutes or so, they saw them coming back. Kevin had had some guy lying across his horse, and Carlos was riding with Kyle.

"Are you guys ok?" Lakisha asked.

"We both need medical attention." Maria gasped for air.

"Once we are through the fog, we will be fine." Lakisha reached down her hand to help Maria and Thomas up.

They rode back close to town and dropped Carlos off. "Say we rode off. You should be safe. Here, take this money, and build something with it." Maria said. Everyone gave him their money.

His eyes welled up. "Thank you."

"Be careful no one steals your money." Kyle said.

"Thank you, thank you." They waved goodbye and rode the horses back to the bridge.

CHAPTER 13

Chapter 13

They arrived back in the no-time zone, and neatly, there was jail cell waiting for their new guest. They put the man inside, and everyone crashed without saying a word. Since they all knew her secret, Lakisha entered the fog to rest.

After much-needed sleep, they all got up, and the man was looking at them. Lakisha came out of the fog. "I feel better, don't you?" She said to the guy.

"I'm not telling you shit." He spat on the floor.

"Let's start with your name?"

He made a gesture of zipping up his lips.

"Ok, then, I'll go first. I'm Lakisha, that's Maria, Kevin, Thomas, and Kyle. Can we know your name now?" He gave her the middle finger. "How about breakfast, then?" She calmly said. She began cooking for everybody, and after she was done, she put a plate in the cell for him. At first, he didn't want to touch it, but after seeing them dig in, he tried a little bit and devoured his plate. "Do you need juice?" She asked him. Maria wonder why Lakisha was being so polite.

"Yes, please." Even he became polite.

"Ok, would you like to talk to us?" She asked calmly.

"Fuck, no. You can beat me, and I still won't talk." He waved his hands around.

"Let me beat his ass." Thomas said, punching his hand. The man glared at him.

"No one is beating anybody's ass. Well, since he's not talking, let's relax for a bit." Everyone looked at her like she was crazy. But they were still tired.

Maria went to go take a hot bath. After her bath, she felt nice and relaxed.

Lakisha went up to the man's cage. "Would you like to talk now?"

He gave her a sideways look. "I will not."

She opened the cage.

"What the fuck are you doing?" Kevin said, standing up, ready to tackle the man.

"Relax. He can't go anywhere." He came out his cage and put his hands up. Lakisha put her hands up to gesture for the others to keep their distance. "How about now?"

"Lady, you must have lost your marbles. That's not how you interrogate someone." He pointed at her.

"Oh! How do you interrogate a person?" She put both her hands on her hips.

He waved his finger at her. "Oh, you're not tricking me."

"What trick? Why are you nervous? We haven't mistreated you. We even fed you." She grabbed a chair and sat down. Everyone else was scratching their heads.

"Ok, enough. I'm going back in my cage. You're fucking weird." He walked back to his cell and closed the door.

"Ok, have it your way, but let me know when you're ready." She smiled at him as if they were old friends.

Maria grabbed her by the arm and dragged her to her room so they could talk in private. "What the fuck are you doing?"

"Trust me. I got this." Lakisha had such confidence. "Let's watch tv or a movie." A tv and a couch appeared from the fog, and they all started watching tv. After a few hours, they all trained together and did a few things to entertain themselves, then ate dinner that she cooked and drank beers. Even the guy drank some beers. He kept trying to figure her out, but even the others couldn't. They went to bed. He had a nice comfortable cot in the cell, and even had a private bathroom.

The next day, she made breakfast and trained them. He started doing exercises. After three days of this, she let him out of the cell again. "Ok, would you like to talk now?"

This time, he was more confident, and he sat down at the table. "No, not about the future, but we can talk about other things. I'm really starting to like you guys."

The bottom part of her body turn to fog, and she came up behind him and dragged him into the fog. He kicked and screamed all the way in. After three minutes, his eyes were out of focus and he was jabbering. She put him back in the cell and closed it. "I'm going to rest. Keep an eye on him." She walked back into the fog. Everyone was surprised by her action but Kyle stared at her.

After twenty minutes or so, he regained consciousness. “Are you ok?” Kyle asked him.

“Man, it was fucking crazy in there. Time is all broken-up.” He said , standing up.

“Tell me about it. I was in there longer than you.” Maria said, softening her eyes.

“What? Why? What for?” He seemed confused.

Lakisha came back out. He jumped at the sight of her.

She walked over to the cell and opened it up again. “So, how about now?”

“Uhm, well, I mean, if I talk, what will you do with me?” He looked at the floor.

Kyle excused himself and went to the bathroom. Maria gave him a look.

“What would you like us to do with you? Why are you frightened? I didn’t hurt you, did I?”

“No, ma’am.” He waved his arms.

“Ok, then what would you like?”

“I have to think about it, but I can’t go back to my time.”

He said, rubbing his head.

"Whatever you like, but whenever you go, you lay low, or I have to come get you." She pointed at him.

"Yes, ma'am." He sat down.

Suddenly, some men came through the fog and shot at him. He fell face-forward. They all scrambled for the fog to grab weapons and lay down cover fire until they could get into the car. Maria pulled the gloves out of the satchel and shot her energy weapon, hitting one guy. The fog started seeping out, and they had to get out of there. Thomas had an assault energy weapon, and he started spraying them from behind the car. The space was closing in. "Get in." Maria said. He got in, and she drove into the fog.

"Wait for me." Kyle cried out, running towards the car. Thomas held the door open for him. Maria stepped on it and blasted into the fog. The fog seeped out, and the men were crushed by reality.

The fog dissipated, and they were in an old Ford. It looked like a 1920s model. Maria looked at her clothes. It resembled something Josephine Baker would wear. The guys all looked like they were working for Al Capone. She remembered what just happened. "How the fuck did they know? One of you motha'fuckers is a chota. Which one of you is a stool pigeon?" She looked at everybody.

"That doesn't make sense. If, and that's a big if, how the fuck would they convey the info?" Kevin said defensively.

"Think about it, Kevin! When we travel somewhere, they show up right away, except when I went to that planet. I was there for over a month, and you guys weren't there long enough." Maria was losing her cool, making everybody else irritable.

"Didn't you say that they tracked you down when you went to the 1970s?" Thomas leaned forward so she could see him while she drove.

"Then it must be you?" She looked at Lakisha's face.

"Bitch, I'm tired of your shit, always accusing me of something or another." Lakisha's anger let loose.

"Bitch, you got us in this mess! We wouldn't be here if it wasn't for you!" Maria was ready for it.

"You know what? *Fuck you!* We can step out the car and settle this shit!" Lakisha wasn't as calm as she usually was.

Maria took out a switchblade and was waving it around as she drove. “Bitch, I will cut that pretty face of yours.” Kevin put his arm on Maria’s chest and grabbed the knife. The car swerved a bit. He tossed it out the window. “What the fuck is wrong with you?” They were about to rebut. “I don’t want to hear shit. Somehow, they are finding out. So, we”—he pointed to all of them, including himself—“have to plug that leak, but you two fighting won’t help. Shake hands, and let’s find a place to rest.”

They shook hands, and everyone was quiet for the rest of the ride.

Thomas broke the silence. “This must be China. Let’s stop there, that looks like a nice hotel.”

They drove up to the hotel and a man wearing traditional Chinese suit open the door for them. Inside, it had old Victorian décor. They checked in. “Excuse me, do you have an English newspaper?” The concierge passed one to Thomas. “May 3, 1921, *Shanghai Times*.” He read out loud.

“There were many gangsters in this era, and they were no joke. I mean, are.” Kevin said.

Maria was still pissed, but she looked over at Kyle, who

was unusually quiet. They had their bags taken up to their room. “Let’s get some tea at the hotel café?” Kevin said.

“Sounds like a plan.” Thomas agreed. No one else said anything, so Thomas and Kevin walked ahead, and the rest followed. They sat down and ordered some tea. The tea came in expensive-looking China. “With all the drama, I forget to appreciate all these relics we come across.” Thomas was focused on his cup.

“Look at you, aren’t you sophisticated?” Kevin was making failed attempts to lighten the mood.

Thomas put his pinky up, following his lead. Maria cracked a smile. She’d noticed how she really did like being around Thomas. He was tall, strong, and smart. She could see herself dating him, but it wouldn’t last, because she thought they were from different centuries.

Kevin broke her thoughts. “I wonder who this guy is. Must be one of those gangsters.” A Chinese man walked in; he had on traditional Chinese clothes with a western-style gangster hat of the type you would see in the movies. He had four guys with him. They walked by the table, and his goons stared at them, being that they were the only westerners in the room.

They sat at a table not too far from them. The air felt thick with drama; these guys looked reckless, but the boss was calm and was very polite to his waitress.

"I think he's the next target." Lakisha drank her tea.

"How the fuck are we going to protect that guy? 'Hi, we're time travelers, we've come to stop some futurist from kidnapping you and turning you into spaghetti sauce." Kevin said.

"Not exactly like that, but one of us can get close to him." Maria said.

"Which one of you can sing? Because if this is the 1920s, a lot of black jazz singers traveled around the world singing." Thomas added.

"He does have a point. I've never tried. How about you, Maria?" Lakisha asked.

"Wouldn't the fog have fixed that? Because I've found myself talking different languages, so we should be able to sing." Maria replied.

"I bet he owns the biggest club in town." Thomas added.

"Ok, then who will go and talk to him?" Kevin looked around.

“Thomas, I think you should. You have a somewhat Asian look, but not really, so he might be more open to you, maybe. But we should offer him something.”

“I know.” Thomas lifted his finger, then gestured to Maria to pass him her bag. He pulled out a bottle of Canadian whiskey. This was during the American prohibition, so Canadian whiskey was a big deal. He took off his newsboy hat and jacket, fixed up his suspenders, and walked up to them with his hands up.

The man’s goons got up and blocked Thomas off from the guy. “I just want to introduce him to my two jazz singers from America.” One of the guys pushed him back.

At this point he was speaking Shanghainese, which was a Mandarin dialect. “I have this gift for him.” One of the thugs was holding Thomas by the shirt.

Maria and everyone else stood up, making loud noises as the chair dragged across the floor. The men looked at them like they were ready to brawl.

“Stop your foolishness, and let me hear what he has to say.” The last thing a real gangster wants is negative attention. “You give him your seat.” He ordered one of his men. “I’m sorry.

You can never be too careful. Please sit. What can I do for you?"

The rest of his team sat back down, and the thugs surrounded Thomas, still trying to show their might. Thomas sat down. "My name is Thomas. I brought you some Canadian whiskey." He handed the bottle over.

"Thank you. My name is Chao Hung." He took the bottle in his hand and looked it over. "Now, why do I deserve such a nice gift? This is not easy to come by in China." He looked at Thomas, trying to analyze him.

"To be quite honest, I'm managing these two jazz singers from America, and I heard you have a beautiful club. I would like for them to perform at your club, if it's possible."

He looked at Maria and Lakisha. "Very beautiful. Tell them to come here. Move your dirty old asses." He pushed two of his henchmen off the chairs and waved for the ladies to come join him. They got up and strutted across the floor, full of smiles and sex appeal.

"Why, hello, sir. My name is Marcela."

"And my name is Laritza." They both spoke in English and put their hands forward.

"Ah, yes, I learned this." He kissed each of them on the hand. He looked like he was going to cum in his pants from the excitement. He was all smiles. "So, you are singers?"

"Yes, we are." Maria leaned back and put her hands on her cheeks.

Lakisha put a hand on his chest. "Would you like us to sing for you?"

"That would make me so happy." He raised his head and leaned towards Lakisha, showing her his puppy eyes. She smiled and started singing "Cry Me A River" by Ella Fitzgerald. Maria tuned in, and they sang together. After they were done, he clapped so hard. "Yes, yes, yes, can you sing tonight? I will have a car come pick you up at 6:30 from this hotel."

Thomas reached over to shake his hand. "Thank you, Mr. Hung. We will see you then." All three of them got up, and Mr. Hung waved bye at Lakisha. She took advantage and blew a kiss at him.

They went up to their rooms to get much-needed rest. Maria picked out her outfit and jumped into the shower. She slipped on a dress that had slits coming up to her knees. She grabbed to gun holsters and placed them on each thigh, then placed a dagger in each long glove. She looked at herself in the mirror, spun around, and left her room.

She went downstairs, and a car came to pick them up. The chauffeur opened the door for them, and they piled into their seats. A bottle of champagne and flowers awaited them. "Now, this is riding with style." Kyle poured himself some champagne.

"Hey, what about the rest of us?" Kevin claimed.

"Sorry, guys, was caught in the moment." Kyle poured the rest of them some, and they toasted.

When they arrived at the club, Mr. Hung was waiting for them at the front of the club. As soon as Lakisha got out the car, he wrapped his arm around hers, and they strolled into the club. "What are we, chopped liver?" Kevin complained.

They were sitting at his table up high above the other people. Where they can overlook his miniature empire. His area must have at least twenty goons around them. *How would they be able to take him with all this protection?* Maria thought. She kept her satchel close to her leg just in case something popped off. She scanned the room, and she breathed in some relief when she saw everyone's smiles.

He brought them down to the stage and introduced them to the audience. He was clapping the hardest. Maria didn't know what hit her; all of sudden, she was singing and performing like a veteran. She and Lakisha had the crowd in the palm of their hands. She'd never felt so alive.

That was when the Shanghai police turned on the lights and came marching in. They were accompanied by the British police. "What should we do? It's obvious that's not the British police." Maria said to Lakisha.

"Follow me." She gestured to the guys, who were still sitting high up in the chairs. Everyone was running all over the place. Maria took out her gun and fired at the British police. They jumped offstage, and Lakisha grabbed Mr. Hung, who was watching the performance from the side of the stage.

"We should go to the kitchen." Mr. Hung pointed the way.

The guys lay down cover fire from above. Maria pointed to the kitchen to let Thomas know. His men attacked the police to give him time to escape. Lakisha shoved Mr. Hung behind her, and Maria stuck her head out the kitchen door, looking for the guys. Thomas saw her, and all three of them dashed towards the kitchen. In the kitchen, he had one of those speakeasy doors; when he pulled a pan, it opened up, and they all ran in.

The staircases went down into a brick tunnel that was damp and humid. They raced through, and it didn't look like anyone was following them. They came upon some stairs and headed up into an old factory that was closed. They went to the back, and there was a car sitting there. "Who's driving?" Mr. Hung inquired. He wasn't expecting to drive.

"I got it." Thomas said. Mr. Hung tossed him the keys, and they all piled in. Thomas turned the car on, and they sped out of there. He glanced back at Mr. Hung. "Which way?"

"Head towards the mountains. I will show you. I have a house there, and we can hide out." They passed some police cars, and they all ducked. Maria realized there wasn't much traffic because not everyone had a car.

After a two-hour drive out of the city, they arrived at a small town up in the mountains, nothing but trees and bamboo. They stopped at a cottage that had a rice field. An old lady came out to greet them. She paused for a second when she saw all the foreigners. Mr. Hung came out and greeted the old lady.

"This is my mother."

"He really must like you if he brought us to his mother's house." Maria whispered to Lakisha. They all greeted her, and they wondered quietly where they were going to sleep. She went inside and got them some tea. They sat outside and planned the next move.

Mr. Hung went inside to help his mother bring out some food. Even his mother was surprised that he would do that, but he must have really wanted to impress Lakisha or was grateful that they saved him from going to prison. What he didn't know was that they didn't want to put him in prison. If he only knew.

"Is he safe now?" Kevin asked.

"I believe he is, but we should stay a couple of hours just in case." Lakisha said.

"Where would we go to next?" Thomas asked.

"I'm not sure, but I believe we should put an end to this. If not, we are just going to be jumping around time for the rest of our lives." Maria was getting tired of this, and she desperately wanted to get back to her life.

"There must be a way to hit them on their own turf?" Kevin asked.

"That' so far into the future that we would be like Neanderthals in our time." Kyle said.

"He does have a point," Lakisha agreed with him.

"We just can't do nothing. I'd rather hit them with everything we've got and be captured than to spend the rest of my life jumping through time." Maria wasn't sure where this frustration was coming from.

"I understand your frustration, but if we go in half-cocked, we might as well give ourselves to them now." Thomas played with a stick.

"Thomas is correct. We need the best plan ever created in history, or close to it." Kevin was shooting in the dark.

"What if..." Maria felt like she had nothing, but was trying to reach that place where great ideas came from. She tapped her lips and closed her eyes. She was trying to picture herself being at that place. Everyone waited for her idea. She slowly let her thoughts sink into that unknown abyss. Things would be so different in that world. "How do you walk in a world that you have never been to?" She said out loud, but she was really talking to herself.

"Huh?" Kyle said, interrupting her.

She waved him off and concentrated. "What information is missing?"

"Everything," Kevin said.

"Maria, it's ok. We will come up with a plan together." Lakisha said, putting a hand on her lap.

"Can we travel that far into their future?" Thomas asked.

"No, that's the problem. They disrupted time so much that they collapsed it."

The food came, and Maria's stomach grumbled at the sight of it. She had two plates of the food before she felt full. She leaned back in her chair and inhaled nature's essence. Mr. Hung's mother picked up the dishes and went inside.

"Thank you for helping me." Mr. Hung said, sitting up in his chair and taking out a pipe.

"You're welcome." Kevin said.

His mother came back out with tea and picked up the rest of the dishes. "What are you planning to do now? Because…" He lit his pipe. "I could use help like yours. I saw how well all of you fight."

"I'm sorry to interrupt you, Mr. Hung." Lakisha said, bowing her head. "But we must get going soon. But we are very grateful for your hospitality."

"If you stay, I will make sure you are well off. Not only you, but all of you." He pointed to the group.

"She is right. We have other affairs to take care of." Thomas said, getting up. They said their goodbyes to him and his mother.

"We don't have a car." Maria said to Lakisha.

"Take my car. It's the least I can do for saving my life." He said, standing up.

"Are you sure?" Thomas asked.

"Of course. I mean it—if you are ever back in town, let me know."

They all hopped into his car and left his house.

CHAPTER 14

Chapter 14

As they were going through the fog, it started to pulse erratically. The vehicle shook, and Lakisha screamed in pain. Her body was between fog and physical. A black fog was coming into the greenish fog.

"Something is wrong!" Lakisha's body was convulsing as she cried out.

"Kyle, what are you doing?" Kevin grabbed Kyle's arm. He was now half black fog, half physical. Kyle's other hand started to fog up and paralyzed Kevin and Thomas.

Maria looked outside the car, and the black fog had pushed out the green fog and started swirling around. She reached into her satchel to pull out a weapon, but by then, the fog from his chest had reached out, strangling her by the neck, squeezing the life out of her. She tried to reach into her bag, but it was to no avail. She felt the blackness coming around her eyes and lost consciousness.

They woke up in a similar room as before. Same old sterile environment. She looked at the straps, and they weren't your typical straps. Her wrist and ankles were infused into the metal. *How the hell will I get out of here?* She thought to herself.

Kyle walked into the room with a grin on his face. "Bet you didn't see that coming, did you?" He got very close to her

She snapped her teeth at him like a pit bull. He pulled back his head. "You're a wild beast, aren't you?" He winked at her.

"You treacherous bastard, how could you?" She paused for second. "What the hell are you?"

"Oh, you mean this?" His hand turned into the fog and then became solid again. "I'm just like Lakisha." He looked up, filling himself with pride. "I'm better. Unlike Lakisha, who became human, I was human and became black fog. So, you could say I'm the next evolution—a masterpiece created by grief, not that different from you. But unlike you, I was able to take it to the next level." His eyes came close to her in a cautious manner.

"I'm nothing like you." She wiggled in her constraints. "I

knew there was something off about you, but I never realized what you are. You must be off your rocker."

"That maybe the case, but all great men are a little off." He pointed to his head.

"What about your friends? You just gonna do them dirty like that?" Her lip twisted and her head tilted to one side.

"Friends? Those two scumbags? Please... I infiltrated their unit so long ago, while I was still running things on this side, even your stupid ass didn't realize it." He waved his hand at her.

"Wow, you really do buy your own bullshit, don't you?" Maria was keeping him busy by talking, but really, she was looking for a way out.

"Look all you want, but there is no way you can break out of that unless you saw off your wrists and ankles, and I would pay money to see that." He taunted her.

She tried not to show her surprise. "Where are the others? Where is Lakisha?"

"Oh, now you're Lakisha's friend. Didn't you try to cut her pretty face?" He waved his index finger at her. "Ok, enough talking. Now, you sleep." A bubble came over her, and she was out.

The first thing she remembered was some shaking. Everything was fuzzy. Boom, another shake. "Is there a battle going on?" She said. She noticed the bubble was down, but her wrist were still infused to the metal plate she was on. She could hear fighting going on outside, but her eyes were barely open, and it was hard for her to stay conscious.

"You was drifting in and out."

For a moment, she saw some men in suits similar to the ones the futurists had worn when they attacked the no-time zone. "Who... are... you?"

And she lost consciousness again.

When she woke up again, she was on a more comfortable bed, and some lasers were pointing at her head. "She's awake." A voice said. She tried to see who was there. She moved to sit up, but she was still too weak. "Save your strength."

She finally got to see who it was. It was a Barbenkus woman.

"Your Barbenkus, aren't you?" Maria asked, laying her

head back down. Her long chin gave it away.

"So, it was you all those millennia ago." She seemed so happy to see Maria.

"Do you know me?" Maria seemed confused.

"My people have talked about your stories for a very long time. Especially the Pklyan. Is your name Maria?" She asked.

"Yes, it is. How?" She said she was still feeling groggy.

"After you left, my people were wondering how these primitive people were able to call them to protect them. The Pklyan said that you were a time traveler fighting people from the future. Of course, at the time, they didn't believe them, and it became one of the most famous folklores. I mean, we have a whole play on this subject. Once we confirmed the fog existed thousands of years later, we knew you were real, so we devised a way to track your signature in case you came to our time. We know what the humans are up to, and we have to stop them. What they are doing not only affects your world, but all existence. So, we are here to help you. But you should rest now. The rest of your team is safe, including Lakisha. Please rest. You have people who want to meet you."

Maria was looking for words, but nothing came out. But she was burnt-out. Her exhaustion took over, and she fell asleep.

She woke up, and there was a suit with a glass of water. She gulped down the whole glass of water in one shot. When she started to put on the suit, it adjusted by itself. It fitted right to every curve on her body. She stepped out of the room, and the nurse came right to her. "All rested?"

"Yes, I feel much better, thank you. By the way, what is your name?" Maria asked.

"Oh, I'm sorry. I was so excited to meet you that I forgot to tell you. My name is Ekasta."

Maria stuck her hand out to shake it. Ekasta shook her hand. "It's a pleasure to officially meet you." Maria liked her, and she seemed really cool. "Can I see my team?" She said looking around.

"Yes, right away." Maria followed her through a corridor and went through a door. Kevin and Thomas were there, eating some food. When they saw her, they got up and hugged her. "Where's Lakisha?" Maria looked around for her.

"She's recovering. Kyle did some serious damage to her."

Thomas' face saddened just by saying his name.

"Yes, what the fuck? I thought you guys knew him for long time? Are you guys working for him or are you just like him?" Maria questioned them.

"Come on Maria, seriously? Do you really think we would do that?" Thomas stood up, saying it defensively.

"Yeah Maria, think about it, have me or Thomas ever done anything to show you that?" Kevin stood up as well. He took a breath and calmed himself down. "That's what I don't understand. We all served together for the last five years."

"I'm just as upset as you, he was an asshole most of the time but..." He turned around took a breath and held his head. He turn back around and look at her in her eyes. "He even saved my life once when the war started between the United States and Canada."

She looked at them both. "You guys are right." She put her hand over her mouth. "I knew there was something that was always off with him."

"What do you mean?" Kevin asked.

"Think about it? When we were attack in the in-between place, he was in the bathroom."

"And he almost shot you when we first saw you at the Pklyan planet." Thomas added.

"Exactly and for someone who is military trained he would take shots that didn't make sense. Like he did in Columbia.

"Your right, the clues were right under our nose. How stupid of us." Kevin said showing disappointment in his face.

"Because we weren't looking for it that's why. So, when did he become fog?" Maria wondered.

"Well, with time travel, it wouldn't matter, would it?" Kevin said.

There was a knock on the door. "Come in." They all said.

A Pklyan woman came in. She had a silver blue crystalline color to her complexion. She was smiling at the sight of Maria as if she were an old relative. She thrusted herself on to Maria and hugged her. Then she kissed her on the cheek. Maria stepped back. "I'm sorry, Maria, I'm a descendent of LKankt, so your stories have been told in my family for many centuries now. My name is Maria as well. Your name is quite popular in my family. You're a heroine on my planet."

"Me, why?" She pointed to herself.

Kevin did the cross on himself. "Mother Mary." He put his hands together in prayer form.

Human Maria pushed him. "Be quiet."

"You saved my people long before we reached the stars, and because of you, we were protected until we reached the stars. You told my ancestor that you were a time traveler. Here you are." She was so excited that she hugged Maria again and gave her two kisses on each cheek. Maria didn't want to be rude, but then she remembered that she'd taught her people that tradition. "Anyway, we are here to help you in whatever you need."

"But I didn't do anything special. All I did was to make sure that what happened to indigenous people on my world didn't happen to your people." Maria was trying to make sense of all this admiration.

"You mean like the Tainos? They lived on the same island where your family is from. My people know that story very well, and that's why we admire you. Because you didn't have to help us, but you did." Maria Alien—let's call her that—was going to explode from excitement.

"Of course, I had broken my leg and was stuck on a distance planet. I had no idea where I was or if I would ever leave. Your ancestors took care of me in my time of need. It's only right I did the same for them." She said with pride.

"And that, Maria, is why you became a heroine on my planet. Every school child knows your story." Her face was full of admiration.

"Sorry to change the subject. Can we see Lakisha?"

"Yes, of course. Follow me." She felt Maria was a little uncomfortable, so they walked out back into the hall. They took the stairs up one flight and walked into a room that had glass all around it. Inside was the fog. The fog transformed back, and it was Lakisha. She opened a glass door and came out, then hugged all of them like it had been years since the last time she'd seen them. "You don't know how happy I am to see that you are all ok." Lakisha smiled.

"Are you ok?" Thomas asked.

"It was touch and go for a bit. Kyle caught me by surprise, but he won't next time." She balled up her fist and gritted her teeth.

"Why are you in here?" Maria said with care.

Lakisha took a deep breath. "He was literally feeding on me, making himself stronger. Our new friends" She pointed to Maria Alien—"created this chamber that mimics the no-time zone so I can recharge myself." She lost her balance, and Kevin caught her. He helped her get her balance back. "Thank you, Kevin. I need to go back in. I'm not at a hundred percent yet." Thomas opened the door while Kevin put her in. When they closed the door, she reverted back into fog.

Maria turned to Maria Alien. "I'm going to teach you a new word. It's a Spanish word. It's *tocaya*—it's what you call someone who has the same name as you."

"To-ca-ya," Maria Alien said slowly.

"Yes, that's it, but I think we will call you Mari from now on. Just so we won't get confused. Is that ok with you?" Maria said.

"Yes, that's great." Mari said with a little too much enthusiasm.

"Ok. How long does she have to be in here?" She placed her hand on the bubble.

“About...” She thought about it. “A week, but in the meantime, I can get you up to speed on this whole new era and come up with a plan to stop him. Follow me. There are a lot of people who want to meet you.”

They went back into the corridor and walked for about a minute. Maria and her crew all gasped at the scene. “Wow, this is fancy.” Kevin said.

They were way above the clouds, and they could see other buildings, which didn’t look as solid as the buildings she remembered. When they looked up, they realized that they were very close to the upper atmosphere. “Holy crap, how high are we?” Thomas sounded like a young child during their first time at the zoo.

Mari giggled. “We are about twenty-eight miles up.” She said.

“How are the buildings not crumbling below us?” Maria asked her *tocaya*.

“Remember, it’s been more than 10,000 years, so our technology has advanced significantly.” She gave them a second to take it all in. “Let’s go meet some people.”

They got into a force field bubble and shot straight

down. Maria looked around but didn't see any controls. They hit the floor they were going to, and they came right into the middle of a room where all these people were. They all looked at each other. "Don't feel overwhelmed. They just want to talk to you to figure out an attack plan to stop Kyle and his group. Believe it or not, it's a small group who is doing this. If we don't stop them, by this time next year, there will be no more time. He will turn this reality into his no-time zone."

"No pressure." Kevin said to them.

"Let's see what we can do." Maria said to her.

There were many Barbenkus, Pklyan, and humans. They sat down at a big round table.

This Barbenkus man stood up. Maria could never get use to their long chins. "My name is **Krudus.** Me and Pklyan Maria will be in charge of helping you with your mission." He bowed and sat down.

A human female got up; she was of Asian descent, but you could tell someone was black in her linage. "My name is Sue, and we have been fighting Kyle's group for a while now. But until you came to our time, we didn't even know who was behind this, so thank you." She sat down. The rest of the people introduced themselves, but there were far too many to remember their names.

"One of the problems we have been having is that he is very mobile. By the time we locate him, he has moved on or jumped through time. We found evidence of your group fighting them throughout time, but could not locate you until now. Do you have any idea how to locate him?" Mari asked them.

"We can't, but I believe Lakisha could. What we do know is that they need a special type of people with a chrono gene that is activated so Kyle can feed on it. They have this device that turns that into black fog, and it wasn't until recently that we knew that." Maria said.

"I know we all have it, but we need an activated sample." Sue said.

"If it's not evasive, you can take a sample from me." Maria volunteered.

"Thank you. That would help us figure out a way to track them."

"But Lakisha is probably your best bet to track him." Kevin interjected.

"We believe so as well." Krudus said.

"Where to start, then?" Maria waited for their reply.

"Take them." Krudus ordered, and about twenty guards came from another room.

"What?" They all said. Maria looked at Mari with disgust.

"No, no, no, I have nothing to do with this." She then turned to Krudus. "How could you betray us?" Both Marias, to more Pklyans, Kevin, and Thomas got up.

Maria threw her chair at the guards coming. "Don't kill them! We need them alive." Krudus ordered.

That made Maria feel good, because now, she could let loose. She did a spinning roundhouse kick and knocked the first one out, then punched another guard. Mari was right by her side fighting. A guard came towards Kevin. He ducked and picked him up, throwing him onto the table. Thomas elbowed one in the face, but there were too many of them. They piled up on top of him. Sue just sat there, looking at the commotion. Mari kicked one in the balls.

The two Pklyans were subdued. Now, it was just the

three of them fighting. One grabbed Kevin by the neck, and two more pulled him down to the ground. Maria was fending off three of them who were coming at her. They shocked her with some device, and she fell flat on her stomach. Mari was the last one standing. They were able to grab her. "You've just declared war." She yelled as they knocked her out.

When Maria woke up again, she was bound down the same way. "Not again! How many fucking times?" She was in a room all by herself. A laser pointed at her stomach. The table she was on suddenly flipped, and she could feel something coming out of her spine. "What the fuck are you doing to me? Is this how you treat your friends?" She struggled in her confines. A machine flipped her over.

She was awoken by the nurse Ekasta. "We have to go quickly." Maria didn't even know what was going on. The nurse injected her with something. "This should make you feel better." It felt like a fresh cup of coffee after a hangover. Not that she really knew what that was like.

"Thank you." Maia said, pumping her arms.

"Let's go find the rest. I need to get you out of here before they notice." They ran into a few rooms and got Kevin,

Thomas, the other Maria, and her two friends.

Then, they went to go find Lakisha. Kevin opened the door, and she became solid again. "I still need more time." She collapsed right into Kevin's arms.

"I can carry her." Kevin hoisted her up on his shoulders. They took the bubble up to the roof. "Here, just attach these to your chest. The air is really thin up here, and you will suffocate." Maria felt like she could jump and be right in orbit. They attached the disks, and they turned into suits that covered their whole bodies.

"Aren't you coming with us?" Thomas asked.

"No, but I need to help you. They have good intentions, but are going about it the wrong way." She handed the other Maria another disk.

"What's that?" Kevin pointed to the object in her hand.

"This is like the bubble we took to get here, but this one will take us to my ship." Alien Maria said, going into the decompression chamber. They walked onto the open roof. "Stay low, or a gust of wind can carry you right off." They all crouched down and slowly walked to open space. "This is a good spot. Everyone stand in a circle." She laid it in the middle, and the bubble came around them. It took off at a freakish speed. Maria felt her stomach go into her throat—not because of the G force, but because everything was moving past them so fast that it made her dizzy.

"Don't you dare hurl in this confined space." Kevin reached for her. She grabbed on to him and closed her eyes. He was feeling the weight of both women on him. The bubble was shooting straight down and zigzagging through buildings. They finally got to a spaceship parking lot.

"That's my ship on the left. Open door." The ship opened up, and they ran in. It was pretty sleek. Maria wondered what a ship like this would cost. She wasn't even sure if they still used money.

Mari told them it would take three days to get to her planet, so the first thing Maria did was take a nap.

CHAPTER 15

Chapter 15

On the way to the Pklyan homeworld, Lakisha took a turn for the worse. She had a high fever and was unconscious. None of the modern medicine they had had any effect. She had to go back into the no-time zone, but how would they get there? They tried the shower thing Maria did at the hotel, but that didn't work. She was unconscious and it seemed she needed to be conscious to do it.

Maria checked her bag; maybe the fog had sent something. When she opened the bag, there was a disk, just like the one they used on the ship, but it was a little different. She just knew how to attach it to the hull of the ship. It became part of the ship, and a fog started to appear, soon enveloping the entire ship.

"You did it." Kevin said, picking Lakisha up. They all came out the ship.

"Her pulse is fading... we have to move now." Maria

snapped, her voice sharp with panic.

Kevin ran towards the fog and threw her in. "What do we do now?" Mari said.

"We wait." Maria walked towards the table. "I suggest we get some rest."

The Pklyans were mesmerize by the no-time zone. They were asking so many questions, and honestly, Maria just wanted to sleep. She excused herself without being rude and went to bed.

When she woke up, Thomas was cooking. "I didn't know you could cook." Maria said with a smile.

"There's many things you don't know about me." He winked at her.

"Like what?" She got a little closer to him, and that was when she noticed that she was flirting with him, and he was flirting back with her. She shook it off and backed away, trying not to be obvious.

"How's Lakisha?" She changed the subject.

"No change yet." Relief came over his face when she changed the subject.

The two male Pklyans came in from the bedroom. “Something smells good.” One of them said, looking around.

“Just in time. I’m making Earth-style breakfast. I hope you’re hungry?” Thomas was putting some food on plates.

“I have never eaten Earth food before. I’m looking forward to it.” The other one said as they sat down. They’d been quiet since Maria met them.

“Maria, can you get them some coffee? By the way, what’s your names?” Thomas handed them the plates.

“My name is Klav, and this Taran.” Klav was the taller one; his skin was a lighter green crystalline, and Taran’s was blueish green crystalline.

“Here, try this. We usually drink this in the morning to help wake us up. If I remember correctly, your people like sweet things, so add some sugar—about two to three spoons.” Maria handed them the coffee.

They took a sip. “Wow. Oh, we should get some on our planet. The taste is not so great, but it wakes us up.” Taran said, gulping it down.

***

They were in the no-time zone for about a week before Lakisha finally came out. “Hello, everyone.” She was looking very chipper. Her skin was very shiny, and she seemed to be glowing. Everyone gathered around her.

“You’re back from the dead.” Kevin remarked.

“I was very close to it. Kyle pulled so much energy from me. He had me so close to death, and he could have killed me if he wanted to. But for some reason, he didn’t.” She grabbed a chair and sat down. “Oh, hello.” She said to the Pklyans. She introduced herself, and they did the same. She turned to Maria. “We need a new plan to stop Kyle.”

“Yes, we do,” Thomas said.

“I feel like we are stuck at square one.” Maria leaned back in her chair and looked up at the ceiling. “How the hell is he so strong?”

“That’s easy. He keeps feeding on people who have the gene turned on.” Lakisha answered.

“There must be a way to use that against him.” Kevin had some food in his mouth.

“That’s not a sexy look, Kevin.” Lakisha teased.

He wiped his mouth. “Sorry.”

“Somehow, he is able to block me from reading him.”

“What if we go to the source, when he was infused with your fog?” Maria was throwing ideas into the air.

“That might work.” Lakisha agreed with her.

“Do you have any idea when that happened?” Kevin asked.

“For that, I have to go back into the fog.” She got up without saying a word and walked right into the fog.

Mari just looked at Maria. “She could’ve said something, or is that weird?”

“You’re right, she should’ve. Sometimes, she is a bit rough around the edges, but she means well.” Maria said, patting her on the back. “By the way, how come you guys don’t glimmer anymore?”

“Oh, that’s right, you would’ve seen that. Around eight thousand years ago, we were advanced enough to turn the gene off. We still can on command.” She glimmered for Maria, and she found it so elegant and beautiful.

“Wow, you look absolutely gorgeous.” Maria gave her

such a big smile.

"Thank you." Mari said, putting her head down.

Maria caught Thomas giving them a strange look. She gave him a look, and he acted like he was looking somewhere else.

With perfect timing, Lakisha came out of the fog. Everybody got up and walked towards her, not even giving her time to reach them.

"Did you find anything?" Thomas said.

"When are we going to?" Kevin jumped in.

"How can we kill Kyle?" Maria said, which surprised everyone, and they glanced at her.

Lakisha put her hands up. "Can you guys back up a bit? Damn, let me sit down first." They moved back, and Lakisha went to the table and sat down. They all crowded around her, waiting for the plan. "I'm sorry, but he is completely blocking us. I can't find him."

"What do you mean, you can't find him?" Maria stood up, and tears started running down her face. Her fists balled up, and she turned her back to everyone.

"Has he gotten that strong?" Mari asked.

"I'm afraid so. I can't even find anything about his life before he became fog."

"Don't you remember when you where there?" Kevin said.

"I remember what the room looks like, but that's it. At that time, I really wasn't self-aware."

Maria turn around. "We can't just sit here and do nothing."

"Did I say that? Of course we have to do something, but we have to be extremely strategic in what we do. Here is the problem: his fog is shielding his whereabouts in any time, future, past, and present. The only good thing is that he can't find us anymore the way he was finding us before."

"I still can't believe that you weren't able to sense him when he was here with us." Thomas said.

"Could you?" Lakisha retorted.

"Don't get defensive; I'm not accusing you of anything." He said.

"He seems to have no weakness." Mari said.

"Everything has a weakness. We just have to find it." Maria said.

Kevin put his hands on his head. "The question is, how do we find it?"

"We won't find it here." Thomas pointed at the table. "Let's go somewhere and look for something."

"I agree. I'd rather go around and find nothing than stay here twiddling our thumbs."

"Wherever you guys want to go, we can go."

"Can you check whose gene is ready for harvesting? Then let's go there."

Maria got up. "Let's go into the fog, Lakisha. Maybe... just maybe we can locate something together."

"Are you sure that's a good idea?" Thomas asked, putting his hand on her shoulder and squeezing it. For a brief moment, she almost kissed his hand, but brushed it off instead.

She stood up. "Like you said, we have to do something." She looked at Lakisha.

"Alright, let's see what happens. But no longer than five minutes."

Maria extended a hand towards Lakisha. “This time, you will be anchoring me.”

Lakisha grabbed her hand. “Anchoring you? Shouldn’t I be...”

Maria pulled her into the fog before she could say anything else. She could feel Lakisha’s smooth fingers, but couldn’t see her.

A car sped off.

“Time, what, it, is?” She heard in her own voice. She saw plancha falling down some wooden stairs next to her building. Green fog entering her fingertips. “Professional, I, hit, think, it, a, was.” Two detectives talking in front of her building. Car peeling off again the window of the car coming into view. She felt a tug.

The room spun, and she sat on the floor. “Maria, Maria, are you ok?” Voices in the distance getting closer.

She blinked a few times. Then her eyes focused on Thomas’s face. “I’m ok.” She held her forehead.

She felt a hand on her shoulder. She turned her face to see. “What did you see?” Lakisha asked.

"I, I..." She ran it through her mind a few times before answering. "I need to sleep, and maybe... I can make sense of it."

She held a hand out, and Thomas helped her up.

CHAPTER 16

Chapter 16

Maria got up and walked across the room. She lay in her bed and went to sleep.

"Wake up."

Maria heard a voice. She sat up in bed, and everyone was still asleep. She took the covers off and walked into the bathroom. She brushed her teeth and walked into the living room then grabbed her satchel, glanced around, and got into the ship. She set the ship to stealth; it hovered without making a peep.

She headed into the fog. The ship started to transform into a car. As the fog cleared, she saw a bridge and recognized it. "George Washington Bridge." The orange lights from the bridge shined over her. Not many cars coming from New Jersey. She glanced at her wrist. The time was 11:55pm. She headed for the exit towards Fort Washington Ave and drove towards downtown. Once she got to 164th Street, she parked the car next to a hydrant on the corner. "It's ok if I get a ticket."

She grabbed her satchel and got out of the car, closing the door. She walked up the hill heading towards Broadway, on the Northern side of 164th Street. An older lady was walking towards her. "Excuse me."

"Yes, my dear?" She answered with a smile.

"What date is it today?" Maria smiled.

"Well, it's past midnight, so it's October 15."

"Gracias, what year is it?"

The lady gave her an odd look. "It's 1988. If you are forgetting the year at your age, what happens when you get to my age?"

"I know. Sometimes, I forget it's not 1987." Maria replied.

The lady studied her face. "Are you related to Altagracia? You look just like her daughter Maria. But she only has two children, and she's the good one. The other one is selling that crap up the block." She pointed with her lips.

Maria looked up the block, but couldn't see them yet. "Yes, I'm his cousin. I'm trying to get him to stop selling that crap." Maria focused her attention towards Broadway.

The lady grabbed her hand. "May God bless your words so you can make him stop. He comes from such a hardworking family."

Maria's eyes got watery. She took a deep breath. "Thank you. Let me go now. Don't tell my aunt you saw me; she will just get worried."

"Ok, mija, adios." She waved and continued walking.

Maria went into her satchel, grabbed a Glock, cocked it back, and put it in her waist. She got in view of her brother. She felt something welling up inside her chest. Her legs got weak, and she knelt down on one knee. Her breath got fast.

"Dimelo papi, watchu need?" She heard her brother's voice say.

"Get it together. Your brother needs you." She took in a breath and held it. She counted to ten, then let it out slowly. "You don't have time to have a breakdown now."

She got up by holding on to the parked car next to her. She stood up and took another breath. *I got this.* She walked towards the corner. Her brother's customer passed by her and gave her a smile. His smile made her shiver with disgust. She turned to look at her brother and she locked eyes with him. She looked down. *Don't look at him. He might recognize me."* She thought to herself.

A car turned the corner on Fort Washington, speeding up the block. By the time she looked up, she heard the shot. "Nooo!" she screamed. Time slowed... and through the driver's window, she saw him. "Kyle!"

She reached for her gun and shot at the car as it turned onto Broadway. She dropped the gun and ran toward Rodolfo.

He lay on the ground, holding his chest. "No! Not again." she yelled out. "Someone help..." She looked around but no one was there. "Rodolfo, don't give up! Wait, help is coming. Helllllp!" She yelled at the top of her lungs.

"You are so beautiful." He said, coughing up blood.

"Me?" Maria asked.

"My beautiful daughter." He breathed out and stood still.

"You have a daughter? Wait, wait, don't die. Noooo!" She buried her head in his chest and began crying hysterically.

Wailing at the top of her lungs. “Not again! No I can’t lose you again.”

The sound of sirens came closer. Some onlookers started to gather. The murmurs of the people got louder. “Who is that?” one guy said.

“That’s the son of the bodegero.” It was the woman who had given Maria the date.

One ambulance and four cop cars sped in, blocking every entrance to the block. Maria didn’t even notice them, as she was holding her brother, who was covered in blood. The paramedic approached her. “I’m sorry, miss, we must look at him.” He looked over at a uniformed officer.

“Help them.” A female police officer said as she looked at the crime scene.

“Hold on, we have check her to make sure none of this blood is hers.” He put on his gloves and looked her over. “Miss, have you been injured?”

Maria didn’t even hear him. “Rodolfo, not again, not again.” Her eyes were unfocused. He padded her chest and abdomen.

"She seems fine, but she is in shock." He said to one of the officers.

"Come help me with her. She needs to be questioned." He said to the female officer, who was walking around in the middle of the street.

"No, she needs to be evaluated. She is having a breakdown." The medic said.

"We will question her first, and if she's not a suspect, then we will bring her to the hospital.

"Wait, I have a weapon." She said taking out her gloves and putting them on.

A detective drove up to the scene and came out his car. "Bag that, please. Is she the only witness?"

"So far." The female officer said.

"No." The lady who spoke to Maria yelled out behind the yellow tape.

He waved his hand for her to come to him, and an officer lifted the tape for her to pass. "Do you know him?" He asked.

"Yes. I don't know her, but his family lives there." She

pointed to the building. She did the sign of the cross, her eyes welling up. "She asked me for the date and..." She stared at Maria, who was being pulled off his body, kicking and screaming. "She told me she was his cousin and was going to talk to him so he can stop selling that crap."

"What happened next?"

The lady was wiping her tears.

"I know it's hard, but focus on my face please."

"Ok... Then, two minutes later, I saw a car race pass me, stop in front, and shoot him. She then pulled out a gun and started shooting at the car that sped away towards downtown."

"What color was it?"

"It was red." She said, holding her forehead. She looked at Maria as they put her in the back of a police car. "Are you arresting her?" She said, raising her voice and following the police car as it left.

"Not yet. She is involved in the shooting, so we will question her first. Now, please, ma'am, whatever you can remember is important." He put a hand on her shoulder.

"Oh, my, um... I don't know what kind of car..." She

looked up to the second floor of the building. "His family lives in apartment fifty-seven of that building. Someone should tell them." She wiped her eyes.

"I will send someone now." He called over to some officers. They bagged his body and put him in the ambulance.

"I should go up there. I'm a friend of hers."

"You can't go up there now. Please tell me what you know." He pleaded with her.

***

A young black officer sat across from Maria. "Ballistics came back. This handgun is yours, isn't it?" Maria's eyes were unfocused. Her face was in a state of shock.

"I don't think she can hear you." Said his partner, a young Puerto Rican detective.

"She could be faking it." He said, studying her face.

"It's obvious she didn't shoot him. We should be sending her to the hospital." He sat next to him.

"What is your relationship to the victim?"

"Bro, look at her. She's catatonic." He pointed at Maria.

"I'm calling an ambulance."

"Fine." He said, throwing his arms up in the air.

***

Kyle drove towards the George Washington Bridge. He groaned. He swerved a few times as he came onto the bridge. *I just have to make it to the middle of the bridge*." He thought to himself.

He blinked several times and slapped himself while steering the car with one hand, pressing down on the gas pedal. As he reached to the middle of the bridge, he saw a black fog forming. He heard police sirens in the background. Once the fog engulfed the car, he saw black.

The fog dissipated, and everything went black. He blinked a few times and felt something wet and slimy on his skin. He could hear gunfire in the distance.

"There's a jeep turned over." He heard a voice. It sounded like an American accent. "He's one of ours." He felt two men grab him and pick him up. "We got you. You picked a hell of a place to lose control of your jeep."

He could hear the gunfire ringing in his ear. He blinked

and made out a young man's face. "He's been shot in the back. Get the field medic."

"I don't know when we can get a medevac." Another soldier said.

Kyle groaned. "I got you, buddy." The medic said as he turned Kyle onto his stomach to attend to his wound. "He's lost a lot of blood. We have to get him to a hospital." The medic yelled over the gunfire.

"They will be sending reinforcements to get us out of here." Another said, firing his weapon.

"There's too many Viet Cong for us to hold back." Another one said.

"We've been in worse situations. We'll get out alive." Several men moved back close to where Kyle was lying.

"Since I got to this hellhole, it's been one worse situation after another." A man said, throwing a grenade into the bushes.

The medic covered Klye with his body. Afterward, the medic patched his back up, gave him some morphine, and checked his body over. "He took a good bump to his head."

"The medevac should be here in five minutes." He had the radio next to Kyle's head to shield him.

After intense fighting, the chopper was coming in hot, firing into the bushes. An explosion went off a few yards from them. Two men who were in that area were thrown back. Something sped towards the chopper, turning it into a fireball.

"Fuck!" The radio guys yelled out.

"Vincent, watch him! I have to go attend to the other two guys."

"No worries, I will talk to him." Vincent said.

"If he gains consciousness, let me know. That will be a good sign."

Vincent lay some cover fire while it started to rain, then wiped his head and fired his M16 again. "Go!"

The medic ran and went crashing down into a nearby bush.

"Pull back, pull back." Vincent heard a voice from his left.

"Alright, buddy, we have to go." Vincent picked up Kyle and took off running deeper into the jungle. Bullets whizzed passed him. "Something up there, help me survive this hell." Vincent's heart was pounding, and his back was straining.

He arrived at the riverbank. Behind him were five other guys. "Is that it from the platoon?" Vincent said, scanning the jungle.

"Yes, sir. That puts you in charge."

"Who has the radio?" Vincent called.

"I do." A young African-American called out.

A bullet came and hit the young guy in the head. "Everyone down." Vincent crouched down and fired into the trees. "You got him, sir."

"You two, stay with him." Vincent pointed at Kyle. "You two, come with me." They ran towards the tree, and a young boy around eleven or twelve lay there, dead. Vincent covered his mouth and fell to one knee.

"Sir, you didn't know, and he killed one of our own." A soldier said, putting his hand on Vincent's shoulder.

Vincent picked up the little boy and cradled him in his arms, weeping as if it were his own. "I'm sorry, I'm so-sorry. Why?" He yelled.

The other two put their hands under his arms. “We have to go.” They dragged him to his feet.

He kicked and screamed. “Why? Oh, god, why?” Vincent wailed. They dragged him all the way back.

When they arrived, one of them had just gotten off the radio. “We have some jets coming in to bomb the area in our old location.”

Vincent shook it off. “Stand guard. The Viet Cong will be coming in.” He lay down in a defense position.

The air was stale, but a cool breeze came from the river. His eyes were peeled on the jungle. Something moved in the distance. It could’ve been an animal, but Vincent wasn’t going to wait. “Fire!” They lay down suppressing fire.

He saw the orange flash. “Incoming.” It cut through the air and exploded on his right.

Vincent covered himself. “Enough is enough.” He yelled. “If I’m going to die, I’m taking a few of them with me. Hell, I’m coming soon.” He didn’t bother to look around. He jumped up and continued firing.

“Get the fuck down.” One of his men said.

Vincent ignored him and started running into the jungle, bullets flying past him. He saw one enemy fall to the ground. "That's one! How many of you are going to hell with me?" Two jets whizzed past him, dropping their payloads to the ground, leaving a trail of explosions. Vincent fell to the side from the blast and scrambled for his rifle. He got up and continued firing. The blades roared in his ears from behind him, laying the grass flat around him. He felt someone grab his arm. He swung the butt of his rifle, stopping only inches from the head of his comrade.

"It's me." Charles said with his arms covering his face.

"I'm sorry, Charles." His face relaxed.

"Let's go, the copter is here."

Vincent looked, and they were loading the wounded men, one of them being Kyle. They dashed towards the copter and threw themselves on board. Part of Vincent wanted to stay behind. Usually, he would be so relieved at being taken out of the fighting, but this time, something had changed.

Back on base in Khe Sanh, Vincent sat in the hospital with Kyle, who blinked a few times. He groaned. "Hey, buddy, you took a hell of a beating, but you will be going home."

Kyle sat up and looked at him. “Where am I?”

“You’re in Khe Sanh Combat base. I’m Vincent. What’s your name?”

Kyle studied his face and looked around. He let out a breath of relief. “I’m Kyle.”

Vincent shook his hand. “What the hell were you doing in that godforsaken place?” He passed Kyle some water.

“I…I was…”

“The boys and me think you are on some secret mission. Why else would you be so deep in the jungle?. You lucky we found you, a few more minutes and the Vietcong would’ve got you.”

“Thank you.” Kyle said, holding his head.

“The doctor said you have a slight concussion, and they took out your bullet. A little more to the right, and you would’ve been paralyzed.”

“I’m very grateful to you.” Kyle said with a smile.

“So, where you from?” Vincent leaned in.

“I’m from…” He paused.

"Oh, yeah, before I forget, they issued you a rifle and gun." He picked it up to show him. "We are at the border, so fighting could break out at any minute. Hopefully, you won't need it."

"I hope I'm not ready to go home. Where are you from?" Kyle asked him.

"I'm from Newark, New Jersey." Vincent wiped the sweat from his forehead.

"Ok, not too far from New York City."

"Pretty close. I can take the bus into the city. After high school, I had nowhere to go and enlisted." He shook his head with regret.

Someone ran into the hospital tent. "Sir, sorry to interrupt."

Vincent stood up. "What is it?" He grabbed his weapons.

"We got orders to go back over the border, into the northern territory."

"Kyle, it was nice meeting you. Get home safe, and make sure you enjoy yourself a beer."

"I will have one for you as well."

"Have two for me." He stood by his bed, his eyes saddened. "I don't know if I will ever make it back." He walked off before Kyle could even reply.

Kyle lay back down and fell asleep.

***

He was awakened by explosions and gunfire. He jumped to his feet and grabbed his weapon. Pain shot through his left shoulder blade where he had been shot by Maria. He fumbled with his rifle, almost dropping it. He sat back on his bed. All the blood he had lost made him unsteady. "I have to get out of this time period."

A nurse ran in. "We have to get out of here! The Viet Cong are attacking the base. Can you make it to the helicopter." She said, reaching to help him up.

He waved away her help. "I can make it! Go help the other wounded. I will meet you at the heliport."

She looked him over as he got up. "Ok, see you there." She ran out of the tent.

He put on his military uniform and heard a commotion

outside. He ducked behind the bed and opened fire when he saw a Viet Cong run in. He fell to the floor, and Kyle grabbed what he could and ran out.

"I need a vehicle." He scanned the area and saw the lights of gunfire. An explosion went off to his left, and he dropped to the ground. He fired at another enemy and ran towards the vehicles that were parked next to the gas depot. He jumped in and looked for the keys. They were sitting in the ignition, so he turned the key and took off, almost hitting an American soldier. He swerved to the right, and the soldier waved for him to stop, but he kept going. The soldier went down as a group of Viet Cong approached him.

Kyle stepped on the gas and looked for the nearest exit. "I need to find the river. It shouldn't be too far from here." He turned the headlights off so he wouldn't be spotted. He went over a ridge, tapping on the gas lightly, creeping towards the river. He drove up to the bank of the river. Three Viet Cong jumped up and started firing at him, so he hit the gas pedal and drove into the river. A black fog formed around the jeep. They yelled out in fear and ran off.

CHAPTER 17

Chapter 17

"Lakisha, wake up." She jumped up in her bed.

"What's wrong?" She said, wiping her eyes.

Thomas came closer, and Mari sat up as well. "Maria is missing, look."

Her bed was empty. "Where the hell did she go?" She started changing in front of the guys.

"Give us a moment to get dress." Alien Maria said to them. They closed the door.

A few moments later, Mari and Lakisha came out the room.

"I knew she saw something in the fog that she didn't want to tell us." Lakisha said, walking towards the green fog.

"Yeah, she wasn't acting like her normal self." Thomas

said.

“Why didn’t you sense it?” Kevin said, walking behind her.

“When I’m not in the fog, I’m just like you. Wait here.” She said to them and walked into the fog. She came back out. “Fuck, she went to the day her brother died. I bet she tried to stop it from happening.”

“Isn’t that the day you met her as well?” Thomas asked.

“Yes, when she woke up, she somehow was able to reach the fog, and we became aware of her.”

“We don’t have a vehicle. Maria took it with her.” Kevin said.

“No worries.” Lakisha parted the fog, and there was a white Toyota Camry. They hoped in, and Kevin drove into the fog.

The fog dissipated and left them on the George Washington Bridge. They drove to 164th Street and Fort Washington Avenue. There was a blue barricade and a police officer in the front. It started to pour down. Thc officer waved to them to keep driving.

"We are late." Mari said.

Thomas looked at her. "Oh, wow, you guys look completely human."

"Really." She said, touching her face.

"It's just like Maria looked Pklyan on your planet." Lakisha said. Mari had light tan skin with curly hair. The other two looked Latino as well. Lakisha reached into her bag and pulled out a police radio. "Let's see if the police can give us her whereabouts." She turned it on.

"The female in question is being transferred to Columbia Presbyterian hospital for psych evaluation. Over."

"This is Detective Peterson. After I'm done here, I will pay her a visit at the hospital. Come back to the crime scene. Over."

Kevin turned on the car. "How far is the precinct from here?"

Lakisha went into her bag and pulled out a map and a siren. She put it on top of the car. "Make a U-turn." Kevin whipped the car around. "Make a right on 165th Street." He drifted the car and sped up the hill. "Turn left on Broadway and go down 169th Street."

When Kevin was about to turn, he noticed it was a one-way going the opposite direction. "It's going the wrong way."

"I know that. That's the whole point—to trap the ambulance." She yelled.

"Copy." The ambulance stopped when they saw the siren.

"Kevin, keep it running. Everyone else, let's go. She said, handing them handguns. "Don't shoot anyone. Just scare them." They jumped out of the car like bank robbers, pointing their guns at the driver.

Lakisha came around and opened the ambulance driver door. "Get out now."

"You're not police officers." He retorted, putting his hands up. "I don't have any money. I make minimum wage."

"I'm not after your money. Give us the girl." Mari made his partner lay on the ground. They opened the back, and Maria was strapped down. Her eyes were unfocused, she was jabbering something that didn't make sense, and she didn't even notice that Thomas entered the back.

"I got you, babe." He said to her.

"She needs professional help." The paramedic muttered, hands still up in the air.

Lakisha's eyes softened. "I know, that's why we are taking her. I wish you knew the whole story."

Thomas picked her up, and they piled back in the car. Maria lay on their laps. "Go back towards the bridge. They will call it in." Lakisha said to Kevin.

He backed the car up and headed towards the bridge. "Turn here on 165th street." She pointed towards the river. He sped back down the hill and got on the entrance to the bridge.

"We got company." Thomas said, looking through the back window. The sirens got louder.

Lakisha turned the siren back on. The cars moved to the side since they saw their siren lights and a bunch of police cars in pursuit. As they got towards the middle of the bridge, they could see the New Jersey police had set up a blockade.

The fog started to manifest itself around the car. They soon lost visibility of New Jersey and all the cop cars.

They arrived to the no-time zone, and Thomas picked

Maria up and sat her on the couch. “What should we do now?”

“Let’s get medical equipment from my time.” Mari said.

“No! I need to take her into the fog.” Lakisha said, picking her up.

“Won’t it make her nuts?” Kevin said, standing in her way.

“She’s already nuts. Losing your brother once is hard enough, but re-living that shit again... most people don’t come back from that. Only the fog can rewire her brain correctly.”

He moved out of her way.

Lakisha stopped right at the border of the fog. She swung back and tossed Maria into the fog.

“You’re not going in with her?” Kevin asked in a loud voice.

“No, this is one she has to do on her own. Believe it or not, there are some things the fog doesn’t want me to know.”

They paused for a second, and she sat down to wait. “How long will she be in there?” Mari asked.

“As long as it takes.” She said dryly. Everyone else was

pacing back and forth, tapping their fingers or shaking their legs.

***

Bang! Car screeching off. Her father telling them. "Rodolfo has to leave the house." *Bang!* Blood flowing from Rodolfo's body. Maria reaching for the fog. Image of her brother lying in the street. Kyle's face laughing at her. Green fog. "Bang! Bitch! Is that how your brother died?" The little fat boy laughing at Maria. "We are going to miss you." Her mother saying to her.

"Maria." She heard a voice called out to her.

Walking in the green fog. So many images fluttering through her mind. The scene of her brother dying kept repeating.

"Stop it." She yelled, falling to the floor and sobbing. She lay on her back and surrendered. "Death, come and take me."

As she lay there, hoping to die, a blue fog emanated from her pores and started to mix with the green fog. She felt herself dissolving into this fog. She smiled as she reached the end of her life.

***

Thomas was staring at the floor. “How long has it been?” He said, tapping his finger on the floor.

“Please stop tapping the floor. You are making me crazy,” Lakisha said.

“I’m worried, too, but you must relax.” Mari said, coming to his side.

Kevin and the other two aliens were playing cards. “About two hours.” Kevin said calmly.

“How can you be so calm?” Thomas said, raising his voice.

He turned to look at Thomas. “How is freaking out going to help the situation? It’s not.” He said, answering his own question. He pulled a chair and tapped on it. “Come play with us. It will help keep you distracted.”

“I don’t need distraction, I need answers.” He said, whaling his arms around.

“He’s right, you have to be patient.” Mari said, coming to his side and hugging him. She gestured for him to sit on the couch.

He put his arm around her and looked at the fog, which started to swirl around wildly. "Um, Lakisha... is that normal?"

Everyone turned to the fog. "Oh, shit." She jumped off the couch. "Grab your weapons." She yelled out.

The guys threw their chairs back and scrambled to grab any weapon. A black fog swirled forward, wiping at the green fog. It flowed around the green fog, crashing into it like a wave crashing onto the shore. The green fog opened up and crashed on to the black fog.

They went back and forth for a few moments before the black fog reached out and wrapped itself around Lakisha's neck.

***

Year 10,041 AD

"We've gathered over hundred different people for you." A young nurse said.

"And they all have the gene?" Kyle asked.

"Yes, we've double tested them." She said, looking down at the floor.

"I will transfer the money I promised to you all." She

turned around to leave. “Also... Make sure to pay all the mercenaries in their time’s currency. But...” He passed his hand around his chin. “Tell them I will pay them triple if they stay to take down one final person.”

“Yes, sir, and thank you.” She scurried off. He smiled at the sight of her being frightened of him.

He walked into the metal room, and the prisoners were chained to the floor while sitting on their knees. “Please let us go. I have a family.” One lady who was dressed in Victorian clothes cried out.

“You should all feel proud to be here. You will help me become strong enough to become time itself. The new god Cronos.” He raised his arms and started turning into a black fog. Everyone cried out and jerked on their chains as hard as possible. Some of them started bleeding from how hard they pulled on the magnetic chains.

***

Maria’s eyes opened, and she was at the playground by the Hudson River where her brother used to take her. She looked at the swings, and she could see herself as a child and her brother playing.

"Hi."

She turned around, and it was her brother. She threw herself onto him. "I missed you." She said, sobbing.

"I've missed you as well." He grabbed her arms. "I need you to do something."

"Anything." She studied his eyes.

"Become!" Everything turned back into the green fog.

She could now see the battle between the green fog and the black fog. The black fog was growing. She heard Lakisha cry out and got a sharp stomach pain as the black fog started to surround her. It latched on to her feet, making its way up her body. "Help." She cried out. The green fog surround the black fog, but the black fog consumed it. Maria fell to the ground as she felt her legs dissolving.

Then she heard her brother's voice again. "Become."

"What?" She screeched as the black fog moved up her torso. She clenched her fists, and they became a blue fog. Moving down her arm, it started seeping from her pores. It swirled around the green fog, forming a double-layer fog. Maria's body dissolved into the blue fog, pushed off the black fog, and reformed into herself again.

***

A knight came swinging a morning star at Thomas. He aimed his rifle and sprayed. The knight dropped. Kevin kicked over a chair and shot anything that came out of the black fog. Kyle had Lakisha by the neck, draining her green fog. Mari came to help her, but Kyle wrapped her in his fog and threw her clear cross the room. Different types of mercenaries from all over time piled in, attacking the group.

Thomas was tackled by a Ronin samurai. He grabbed his knife and dug into the neck of the samurai, then grabbed his gun and shot at group of Vikings who came at Kalv and Taran, hitting one of them. These Vikings were twice their size and weight. Kalv sidestepped the axe, but got backhanded, and fell to the ground. Taran had the power gloves, and he blasted him back away from Kalv. Another one kicked Taran in the back, and he fell on his face. Kevin tackled him to the ground, falling on top of him. He just kicked Kevin over him, and he landed on his tail bone. He swung the butt of his axe and hit him in the temple.

Lakisha was now on her hands and knees, and she was

starting to lose consciousness.

A blue fog started to emerge from the black fog and green fog. The green fog was being reduced by the black fog.

Maria stepped out of the fog, her body shifting, dissolving, becoming blue mist... and the whole room trembled. She was wrapping herself around the mercenaries, invading their noses and mouths, choking the life out of them. As they gasped and coughed, they fell silent onto the floor. Those who came from the future had chrono helmets on that protected them, but she picked them up and slammed them up against the floor repeatedly until they didn't squirm anymore.

The green fog was reduced to only Lakisha's body; she was now unconscious on the floor. The black fog started to enclose on the room, but Maria's blue fog swirled in around it, pushing it back. Her arms came behind Kyle and wrapped around his neck. He let go of the hold he had on Lakisha and fogged up, faded behind Maria, and began to ingest her fog.

"You are not more powerful than me, little girl! I now control time and existence." He shouted into her ear.

She bit into his arm and coughed as he tightened his grip. "I will not be subdued." She said in between breaths. She re-fogged, turned herself around, and gripped his face with her hand, sucking the black fog out of him. He rose up in a fog, and she followed suit. Their fogs crashed into each other and swirled around the room.

Thomas ran toward Lakisha's bag that lay beside her. "There has to be something to give Maria an edge." He reached into the satchel. He took out a rifle, but instead of having a barrel, it had what looked like a vacuum. He aimed it towards the black fog and began to suck in the fog.

Kyle screamed. The black fog wrapped itself around Kyle, crashing him into the floor and sending a shockwave throughout the room, pushing everything out of the no-time-zone.

CHAPTER 18

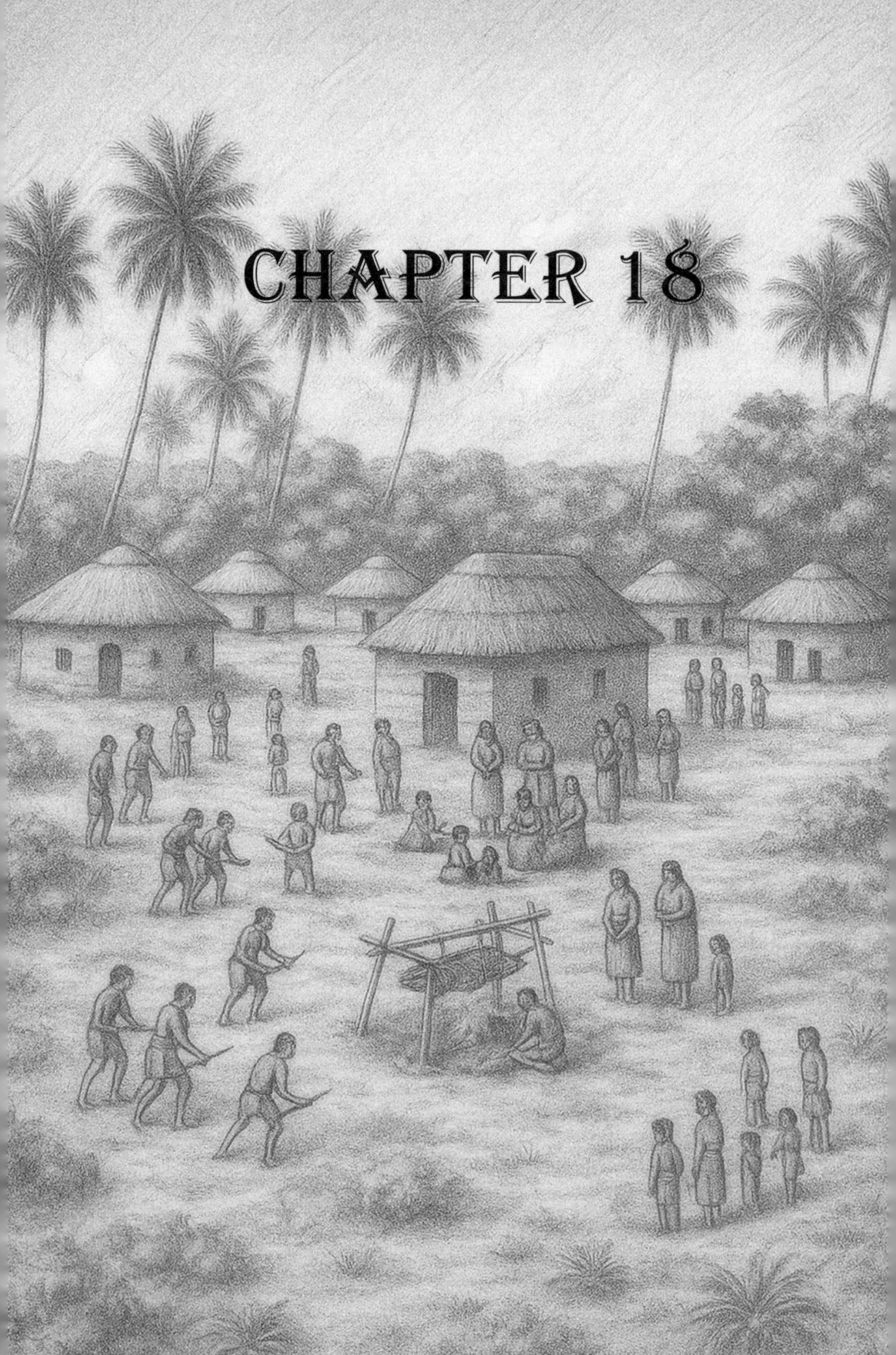

Chapter 18

Maria felt nothing. She tried to reform into her body, but it just wouldn't happen. She noticed she was neither blue fog nor human. She was clear, but not a fog.

Am I just thought? This place was devoid of light, darkness, matter, energy as we know it. Just thought.

She became aware of another thought.

I am thought." She heard in her thoughts.

"*What thought.*" She thought.

"*The thought.*" Something answered.

"The thought." It thought—her thought.

"What? What thought?" She thought Maria's confusion was overpowering any kind of understanding.

"The thought." It thought.

She felt a light, and it expanded, forming matter and pushing her out of its thought. She lost thought.

***

Maria was lying on wet ground. She felt herself being dragged. She tried to speak, but she groaned instead. When she went to open her eyes, she felt herself being dragged back to unconsciousness.

She blinked and saw the light of day coming through a hut. She looked around blinking several times. When she didn't recognize the area, she sat up.

A lady came in. She had copper skin, and was dressed only in a cotton skirt. She wore a gold necklace with shells, bare-chested, broad nose, high cheeks, straight black hair, with short bangs and a blue streak across her eyes. She walked across the hut and knelt down next to Maria. "Good morning. My name is Saoni. You are in Quisqueya. Where are you from?"

Maria looked around and rubbed her eyes. She recognized the word she used. *This must be modern-day Dominican Republic/ Haiti,* she thought to herself.

Saoni put her hand in between hers, then poured water from a jug into a wooden cup and put it to Maria's lips.

"Drink. Your body must be without water from your time at sea." Maria drank all the water, and Saoni refilled the cup. Maria gulped that down as well. Saoni's eyes were soft, and she waited patiently for her to answer.

"My name is..." She had to think of a Taino name and try to use as many of the Indigenous words as she knew. They weren't many, but she knew a few that she had learned from her reading, like tobacco and barbacoa. "Mayana. My name is Mayana." She said softly. She remembered the name from one of her books.

"Oh, that is a Taino name." She said, looking over Maria's features. "You do have our nose and cheekbones, but I'm not familiar with your skin color." She passed her finger over Maria's nose and cheekbone. Maria had much darker skin than her.

"My father was lost at sea when he was a child and landed in a land far past Borinquen, where they are very dark skin." Modern-day Puerto Rico.

There was something familiar about Saoni; she felt like home. Maria's shoulders relaxed, and she took several deep breaths. *This must be precolonial, the only time the air feels this clean*, she thought.

Her thoughts were disrupted. "I've heard of legends of people who are darker skin and people who are lighter skin as well, but those are legends from long ago." She touched her hair. "No worries. Consider yourself home. What we have is also yours."

"Thank you." Maria got a shiver down her spine, knowing what would happen to this part of her culture. "I came to learn from you. I thought I wouldn't make it past that great ocean. Is this your Bohio?" Maria remembered another Taino word used in modern times.

"No, this is your Bohio, and you can use it as long as you stay with us." Maria grabbed her hand and put it next to her heart. That was when she realized she was bare-chested as well. She pushed aside the feeling of being so naked. "Thank you."

"Let's go meet everyone in the tribe. They are eager to meet you." She grabbed her by the hand and led her outside.

The tribe were gathering outside. An older man around 5'7" stepped forward. "My name is Cacique Biautex." He greeted Maria with a slight bow. His hair was tied up on top of his head, and it stood over his feathers crown that he wore. The feathers were short and colorful.

“I am Mayana.” She lowered her head to show respect. She felt some sweat beads going past her chest. That was when she remembered she was bare chested like the other women. She fought the urge to cover herself, and her arms fumbled a bit. Some young children came up to her and touched her skin. She crouched down, and they touched her hair. Maria’s hair was very curly, unlike their jet-black hair.

“Why have you come to our land?” The Cacique said.

She looked up and smiled. “My mai is from the black lands on the other side of the great waters, past Borinque. My taita was lost at sea when he was a child, and he told me of his homeland. After he passed, I promised I would come here to learn of my culture.” She was breathing all the sites and people.

He walked up to her, and the children stepped back. She stood up and he examined her nose and face. “You are darker skin than us, but I can see some of our features in your face. I heard from my grandfather about other tribes that look very different than us.” He smile. “We welcome you home.” The tribe cheered. Saoni came to her and hugged her.

Her nose smelled something good. She looked around and saw a barbeque made of wood. The wood frame was made of small logs with a small fire underneath. A wet blanket was draped over the meats, trapping in the smoke.

"Have you ever had barbacoa before?" He asked.

"Not like this. I would be honored to have some." Her stomach growled loud enough for Saoni to laugh.

He looked at Saoni, and she grabbed Maria by the hand and brought her over to the barbacoa. Some of the other woman came over and placed a banana leaf on the floor, and Saoni tore some meat off a pheasant and placed it on the leaf with some casabe, a bread Maria was very familiar with, made of yuca, that Dominicans still ate to this day. Maria held her hand back. "Please eat." She broke off a piece of casabe and placed a piece of meat on it.

After lunch, Saoni showed her around their village, and they did some chores together. At nighttime, after dinner, the Cacique told her and the children the origin stories of their people. After he was done telling several, he looked at Saoni. "I think it's time."

Saoni brought her into the main bohio where they

would have meetings. At the smell of the small fire, Maria's shoulders relaxed, and she smiled. A breeze entered through one of the windows. Saoni sat her down and held her arm. "We will open a portal to the spirit world so you may contact your ancestors to guide you, and they may tell us how we can help you."

Maria looked around, and several elders came in holding instruments and flutes. As they began to play, Maria saw a Y-shaped wooden pipe was passed to the Cacique. A young lady loaded it up with a light brown powder.

She had expected him to light it, but he placed it on his left nostril, covered his right nostril, and inhaled it.

Maria's heart started to thump; she had seen people sniff coke, and the saliva in her mouth made her feel nauseous. Her stomach muscles tensed up.

Saoni placed a hand on her lap. "Don't worry. This won't harm you, and I will be right next to you to guide your quest. This will show us and you what you seek."

Maria took a deep breath. She wanted to explain, but modern-day cocaine would not be invented for several hundred years. "Okay, if you are here, I will try."

"It will make you feel better but that is not the point. It's to guide you to find what you seek. Focus on that." Saoni said, rubbing her back.

My friends, Maria thought to herself. They passed the pipe to Saoni, and she loaded it up with the powder, then placed it on Maria's nostrils.

"Breathe in deep and picture yourself exhaling the negative." Maria breathed in. "Hold it in. Good. Now, breathe out, and inhale the jobo powder." She inhaled, her face tightened, and she held her nose. She felt as if someone had raked the inside of her nose.

Saoni prayed and was swiping her hand over Maria's body and head. With each swipe, Maria could feel her wiping away the dirt off her aura. She smiled, and her pupils dilated. The vibrations of the flutes and drums penetrated her skin. Her stomach turned, and she threw up into a bowl that a woman was holding for her. Saoni held her hair while she kept singing, and once she was done, she wiped her mouth and gave her water. Saoni wiped her face and back of the neck with the water. She moved down to her back and chest. Maria felt herself swerving round and round. Saoni continued to wipe Maria until her toes. Each drumbeat felt like a step that was carrying her off. Saoni drenched Maria's hair in the water, and she couldn't feel it. She looked at Saoni's face, and it morphed into another woman's face then another and another. They were starting to look more mixed until she recognized her mother's grandmother, then her grandmother, her mother and finally her face in Saoni's face.

"Great, great grandmother." Maria cried out. She hugged Saoni, and tears of joy streamed down her face.

"I was right." Saoni said and kissed her forehead. She felt her third eye open as Saoni kissed her in the same spot. She saw Thomas, Kevin, Mari and her two friends. She looked at her hand, and it started to turn into the blue fog. Saoni and the rest of the tribe jumped back, and the music stopped, but she continued to morph in the fog. She dissipated and felt herself become one with the universe.

"Oh, it's you again." She said to the thought. "What are you?"

"I am thought, and you are my thought with your own thought."

"What am I?"

"You are my thought, you are your own thought, I am

your thought, which creates your own life and destiny."

"Why am I here?"

"To be, and to know."

She felt her fog flow away like a stream flowing through different time points. At the seam where **green** and **black** collided, Maria's **blue** surged through like a flood.

Green had shrunk to a faint halo clinging to Lakisha's unconscious body. **Black** coiled over her, pulling the last threads away. Maria ripped through, slammed Kyle back, cocooned Lakisha inside her **blue fog,** and left Kyle's no-time zone.

When she opened a new pocket of no-time, she picked up Lakisha and put her in her blue fog. Lakisha's fog was barely keeping her alive; it had mostly been absorbed by Kyle. Maria put her hand on her neck, and her pulse almost nonexistent "My blue fog will nourish you while I go find the others who are lost throughout time."

She turned to fog and felt herself being pulled to one time period.

Her body began to solidify; she felt her fingers and

legs. She looked around and sa that she was next to a pond in a jungle. By the pond, the **black fog** solidified—Kyle's arms locked her waist and slammed her into the mud, knocking the air from her lungs. His body formed above her.

"You think you can hang with me, little girl?" Two hard shots broke her nose and split her lips; blood and tears mingled. "I made you." He hissed. "And I'll feed on your **chrono genes**." He gave her a few more shots to the face.

Suddenly, a spear flew into his hip; he screeched, headed towards the pond, and turned into the black fog—and his fog dissipated.

"Maria, are you okay? Don't move."

"Thomas..." She groaned.

"Don't talk. I think your jaw is dislocated." She could only see out of one eye, as the other was shut closed. Her cheek was swollen, and the bleeding ran like a stream. "I have a mule. Can you create the fog?"

She nodded. He picked her up and placed her on it. The fog started to swirl around her, and they went back into her no-time zone.

She pointed with her finger, and he placed her inside, avoiding contact with the fog. Thomas pulled the couch and faced it towards the blue fog. He was holding his hands and tapping his foot. After five minutes, Maria limped out of the fog, holding her ribs. Thomas jumped up to his feet. "Are you ok?" He said, coming up to her and scanning her injuries. "It looks a little better, but you still need to heal."

She waved her hand. "Don't... worry about my injuries." She winced as she spoke the words. "I need you to..." She took a deep breath and held her ribs tighter. "Go find the others; they are lost throughout time." She waved her hand, and a car appeared. On top of the car was a satchel. "Anything you need from that time period will be in the bag."

"What about you?" He stepped forward and held her hands.

"I'm... fine. I will go back to the fog to heal." She turned and took one step at a time, wincing with each step.

"Maria, wait..." She turned around. "I've seen you take on many enemies? Why did you let Kyle beat you so bad?"

She looked down and waved her hand. "Now is not the time to talk. Go, they need you."

He jumped in the car and sped off into the fog.

CHAPTER 19

Chapter 19

With Lakisha and Maria being out of commission, Thomas was on his own. As the fog covered the car, he squeezed his hands and wiped his mouth. His heart pounded and his stomach turned. "You don't have time for this. Your friends are waiting for you. Let's do this." He took several deep breaths.

The fog thinned... Thomas sat astride a horse, cold air cutting his face, rifle resting across his lap, breath turning white. A frozen forest opened around him, snow muffling the ground, a stream whispering behind. "Smells like home," he murmured, tightening his grip on the reins. He looked at the trees. "Yes, this must be Canada." He looked down at his chest. "I must be near my people's native home." He was dressed in his tribe's native clothes. He wore an elk skin shirt and pants.

Thomas wrestled to take off his bag and open it, and

there was a mirror. His left eye and cheekbone were covered in black paint and his right cheek and jaw. He put the mirror back in the bag. He straightened his back and stuck out his chest. He heard a rustle to his left, so he jumped off his horse, crouched down, and held his rifle. He stepped with his left foot, placing the left ridge of his foot on the ground.

Two men wearing buckskin were dragging a native girl behind them. *Is that Maria Alien? Her face is the same, but she looks more native now*, h." He thought to himself. *As much as I want to help, I have to make sure. I can't afford to change the timeline.* He stepped again.

She turned her head and met his gaze. He stood up and aimed his rifle at the man with a scraggly beard to his left. They both reached for their revolvers. "Don't." Thomas warned, rifle steady. "Or you'll meet your Christian god today."

"You can't take us both out before we kill you." The other man said, twitching his finger. He had a couple of teeth missing.

"Is that a bet you want to make?" Thomas said, relaxing his shoulders.

"Let her go." The other one said. "She's not worth your

life, at least not mine." His partner dropped the rope, and Maria Alien ran over to Thomas.

He pulled her behind him and stepped back. "Smart choice. Now, get going."

The man with scraggly beard nodded. "How do I know you won't shoot me in the back?" He spat on the ground.

"You don't, but I'm not you. Go before I change my mind." They rode off. He kept his gun aimed at them until he felt they were at safe distance. She hugged him.

"Your people... so violent. I look human, yet they see me as something beneath them." Her eyes dimmed.

"I know. It's a long, disgusting history." Thomas said with a sigh. "But we should really get going. They'll come back with friends." They walked over to the horse, and he lifted her onto it.

"Where are the others?" She asked.

He got on the horse and turned to face her. "Maria and Lakisha are recovering. Maria was beaten pretty badly by Kyle. Luckily, I was in a jungle hunting when I heard the fighting, and I was able to injure him. And Lakisha lost most of her fog.

As far as the others, I don't know. I hope we can easily find them. Maria's fog is guiding us."

"I hope we don't run into any more of your disgusting history." Her gaze stayed hard, unblinking.

"Me too." He led the horse into the stream, and the blue fog enveloped them.

***

The fog began clearing up, and they were in a Kei-car crossing a bridge. "This must be Japan." Thomas said as he looked at a sign that was written both in hiragana and kanji.

"Can you tell who is in this timeline?" Mari asked.

He looked at her face. "Your race changed again. Now, you look more Hispanic."

"Oh, I wonder why my face keeps changing?" She said, touching it.

"I have no idea, but to answer your question, I don't have the slightest idea." He said. Looking at the dashboard, he could see the date. "Oh, it's 1992. I wonder what part of Japan we are in." He looked around and saw a Seven-Eleven. "Let's stop here." There were some old men smoking cigarettes by an ashtray in the front. They stared at Mari.

"Why are they staring? Am I doing something wrong?" She asked.

"No, they just don't see people who look like us that often."

Around the corner from the Seven-Eleven, Thomas could hear a commotion. He walked around and saw two police officers yelling at Klav and Taran. One officer was holding Taran by his belt loop. Taran looked like he was going to pop him. "Visa?" The older officer barked, fingers curling around the weighted baton at his side. Klav and Taran seemed stumped.

Thomas and Mari understood them. Thomas stepped forward. They stepped back when they saw his height. "Excuse me, officer, I have both their visa here." He said in Japanese.

Both officers seem to be jumpy as he reached into the satchel. He handed all four passports, one Canadian and three from Chile. "Your Japanese is very good." The older officer said, taking the passport.

Thomas waved his hand and bowed his head. "No, no, no, it's not good at all. We are all here studying Japanese; they just started, so still can't speak well. Sorry for the bother." He said, bowing.

The older officer waved his hand. "It's no bother, they just need to carry their visa at all times."

"I will make sure they do." Thomas said, moving away from them.

"Please wait one minute. Can we check your bag?" He pointed to the bag.

Thomas's face became stern. "Only if you have a warrant. Do you have one?" He puffed his chest out.

The officer's face became red, and he looked down. "It's ok, please have a great day."

"Thank you, and please be careful." He bowed again. They turned the corner.

Both officers followed them. "Excuse me, is that your car?"

Thomas turned around with a blank look. "Yes, it is. Here is my license and papers to the car." He reached into the bag and passed it to the officer. This time, he stared at him, and the officers seem to shrink.

"Oh, perfect." He passed it back to him. "Thank you. How did you pay for the car?"

Thomas took in a deep breath and tightened his face. "That is not your concern. Anything else?" He waited for him.

"Oh, no, no, you may go."

"Thank you. Excuse me for bothering you." Thomas said, bowing again.

They jumped in the car and drove off. "He sure asked a lot of questions." Mari said.

"Yeah, in this time period they do that. My grandfather lived out here for a couple of years teaching English, and he told me all about how the police would sometimes harass foreigners. But at least they are not as bad as the American police." He said, turning on the car.

"Why were they asking you so many questions?" Mari asked.

"All we did was ask where we were." Taran said.

"I didn't know we could not ask questions." Klav said.

"Yeah, why is your planet so violent?" She said.

“Your planet doesn’t have war?” Thomas turned to her, and she was looking out the window.

“It does, but not like your planet. People are so ready to kill. I’ve never been on a planet that I was so scared of.”

“Yeah, Earth is pretty messed up, but we are trying.” He let out a sigh. “We are at the bridge. Hopefully, we can find Kevin in a peaceful time period.”

The blue fog surrounded them and started changing into a long boat. Thomas shivered and looked at the others, who were wearing seal skin. The fog cleared up. “Where the hell are we?” He saw a giant ice wall. In the distance, their were other boats—different types of long canoes carrying twenty to thirty people each. As he got closer, he saw Aboriginals, Maori, Africans, and South Americans. “No way.” He said.

“What is it?” She asked.

“I think this is a meeting in Antarctica.” The sun was in mid-setting or rising; he wasn’t sure.

“What so special about that?” Taran asked.

“It’s just... I never heard about this in our history.” Thomas answered. “I wonder what time period this is? Keep rowing towards the boats and follow them." He grabbed his bag and checked for a map. "It is Antarctica, and according to this map it's 2300 BCE." They follow the other boats into an inlet. As they reached a rocky shore, men came out to pull their boat in. All sorts of people waved at them. Some of them men were building ice structures similar to igloos.

"Thomas, over here." Thomas looked over, and it was Kevin.

Kevin ran over and picked him up. "Oh, my god, I've never been so happy to see you guys." He hugged everyone. "I thought I might have to take a journey back with one of the tribes."

"This is incredible, there are Maori, Aboriginals, Africans, and South Americans here. What the f..." Thomas said, looking around.

"There are also some Polynesians as well." He pointed.

"This rewrites our entire history." He was almost jumping up and down with excitement.

"I know. According to some of the elder south Americans, they do this once every ten years, but he said it has become harder and harder. They are able to trade with the different people. But I'm the first white man they've seen in centuries."

"Wait, what?" Thomas' eyes widen.

"I will introduce him to you, he said there used to be some tall redhead people that use to come here. It only lasted for two weeks, and then they headed home to make it back before the sun starts to fully set." He pointed to the sun, which had started to rise again, so it never fully set.

"Should we get going?" Thomas asked.

"I think we should stick around for a bit. This is a once in a lifetime, and it's something forgotten to history."

"I agree with you, but..." He rubbed his chin. "Maria is in bad shape, and Lakisha is on the edge of death trying to recover her fog. She lost almost all of it." Thomas showed concern in his eyes.

"What? I'm sorry, I didn't know. Let's go." Kevin said with urgency.

They started walking towards their boat, and an old man from the Selk'nam tribe in modern-day southern Chile came up to Kevin. "Are you leaving so soon?" He placed his hands on Kevin's arms.

"Yes, unfortunately, we have to go back to the northern lands. Something has happened in our tribe."

"I see." He looked down for a few breaths. "I have something for you and your group but not here, follow me." They dug about one meter down from his group's shelter.

From the satchel, the elder pulled a dagger. Its blade shimmered faintly, flecks of crystal embedded like trapped stars. "Long ago," He said softly, "Twelve beings came to us. They gave this to my great-grandfather... and said one day, it would find its owners." Who are the ones who supposedly contacted all the different people who you see here today." He handed it over to Kevin.

"It's gorgeous. I can't take this; it's a family heirloom." He said, handing it over back to him.

"No, this belongs to your group. My grandfather said that I should give it to the group that comes here with mixes of people of different nations. That is your group. I was also told you will need it to stop a black fog." They all looked at each other.

"Who are the twelve men you refer to?" Thomas asked.

"Not much was known about them, except they were made of twelve men who all came from different nations, and some of them had complexions that my great grandfather has never seen."

"Let me see it." Taran said. Kevin passed it to him. "Yes, it makes sense." He stared at the blade.

"What do you mean?" Kevin asked.

"You see that crystal dust imbedded into the blade?"

"Yes, it's what gives it the sparkles." Thomas answered.

"These aren't just minerals," Taran whispered, eyes wide. "They're **time crystals**... a quantum structure that folds reality in repeating loops."

"Time what?" Kevin asked.

"A time crystal is a quantum system of particles that are in a state of repetitive motion, and this motion is periodic in time. They are used mostly in quantum computers. But how did they get it in this blade? That's too advanced, even for my time." Taran said.

"Be careful not to cut yourself with it." he old man said, putting up both his hands as caution. "It turns you into light, as I understood it from the stories passed down."

"Now it makes sense why we came here. Thank you but we really need to head back." Thomas said.

"Yes, thank you for everything, I wish we could stay longer and learn about everyone's culture." Kevin said to him.

"Be safe, and may you prosper." He said, hugging Kevin.

"Thank you." Kevin said, leaving the shelter of ice.

As they walked outside, some men passed by them carrying penguins. Thomas frowned. "Are they going to eat that?"

"Yup, I wasn't too thrilled about eating penguin. I'm sure glad it's illegal in our time."

They all stared at it and continued to their canoe. They jumped in and started rowing.

As soon as they were far enough the blue fog came in.

CHAPTER 20

Chapter 20

Maria was sitting there with a somber look. She had her hands on her head. Mari and Kevin got out the car and ran over to her and hugged her.

"I missed you." She squeezed her tight, yet Maria's face remained the same.

"I'm sorry, Mari, I need to be alone." Maria said to Mari. She got up, ran to the room, and shut the door behind her. She threw herself on the floor and dug her face into her hands.

"Did I say something wrong?" Mari asked the humans.

"No, not at all." Kevin said, hugging her. "What the hell happened?" He asked Thomas.

"Kyle beat the hell out of her, but something else happened before that. I'm almost sure it has something to do with reliving her brother's death. I'm going to find out." He walked towards the door and knocked a couple times. "It's me, Thomas, I'm coming in."

He didn't wait for a response and walked in. Maria was lying on the floor, sobbing. "Leave me alone, please." She said through the tears.

"I will, but please tell me—what did he do?" Thomas said, walking towards her and crouching down next to her.

She sat up and wiped her face with the back of her hand. "He..." She dug her face back into her hands.

He rubbed her back. "Who's he, and what did he do?"

She looked up. "He killed my brother." She let out with a scream.

"What?" He stood up. "Are you talking about Kyle?"

"Yes." She wiped her nose with her sleeve and lay back down. "He murdered my brother." She yelled out.

"Get up. Let's go and get him." His eyes were stricken with fire. He was trying to pull her up by one arm.

"No, I can't." She dropped her weight. "I can't beat him. I don't have the power Lakisha gave me." She faced the ground and sobbed.

He stepped back. "You what? Are you going to give up." He yelled down at her.

"Leave me alone." She yelled back at him.

"Is that why you let him beat your ass?" He said, raising his voice.

"He's too strong! I can't do it." She sat up, her eyes red and puffy. "I'm not a warrior like you."

He stepped back. "Bitch, get up." He commanded. She paused and looked at him. "You heard me, bitch. Get up."

She winced. "Why are you talking to me like that?"

"Him taking your brother like this is not your fault, but you wallowing in pain instead of doing something is on you. So, stop acting like a little bitch, and get up." He commanded again.

Her face became red. "Who the... fuck do you think you are talking to?" She started getting up.

"I'm talking to you, bitch. What, are you going to do something about it, or are you going to be a little bitch?" He put his hands up and waved her forward.

She threw a left hook, then a right hook. He dodged

left, then right. She threw a front kick. He leaned to the right and slapped her foot and grabbed her in a bear hug from behind.

"I love you." He whispered into her ear.

Her body went limp. She turned around and stared into his eyes for a few seconds, then grabbed his head and kissed him. They stood there intertwined. She unbuttoned his pants and got a handful.

He stood back and held her by the arms. "What are you doing?"

"I need this. I need you to make me a woman."

"What?" The blood drained from his face.

She walked towards her bed. "Yes." She took her pants, then her panties off, threw them at him, and jumped into bed. She fogged up the door. "Now, no one can disrupt us."

She called him with her finger as she took off her shirt, revealing the rest of herself to him.

He stood there for second, then shook it off and dove towards the bed.

***

Maria got up and was putting on her pants. "My coochie still hurts." She said, stretching her legs and giggling in a silly manner.

"I'm sorry." He said, getting up.

"Don't be." She leaned over and kissed him. "I needed that. Now, let's go get that mother fucker." She cracked her knuckles.

"Wait."

She turned around to look at him. "What is it?"

"We got something from Antarctica. I didn't even have a chance to tell you about our last trip, where Kevin was at." He said, putting his shirt on.

"You guys went to Antarctica?" She walked back towards him.

"Yes, and there were different tribes there from South America, New Zealand, Australia, South Africa, and even Polynesia."

"What, are you serious? How is that possible?" She asked.

"Yes, it was about two thousand years ago. Kevin became friends with an old man that gave us something we can use."

"Where is it?" She gestured.

"Kevin has it." He pointed at the fog.

"Oh." She un-fogged the door.

Thomas was walking behind her, and she turned around and kissed him again. "What was that for?"

"Because I want more of you later." She said, grabbing his crotch.

"Behave, young lady." He said, jerking back.

She just winked at him. She fluffed up her hair and composed herself by fixing her shirt, then cleared her throat and opened the door.

Everyone got up from the couch and walked over to them. They studied her face. She walked over to Mari, kissed her, and dipped her back. Mari's skin glittered.

"What the hell did you say to her?" Kevin whispered to Thomas, who just shrugged.

"Kevin, show her the knife." Thomas pointed to a bag

that was on a chair.

Kevin reached for the bag, pulled out the knife, and handed it to her.

"Wow, that is beautiful. How were you able to bring it through the fog?"

"That's just it. I don't think it operates under the same laws. That's why I think this can kill Kyle. But check this out: his great grandfather had passed down the story that it was given to him by twelve men, and some of them didn't look human."

She unsheathed the dagger and passed her finger over the blade. "It has crystal dust in it."

"Don't do that?" Thomas screamed, and she jerked back her finger. "Be careful. If that can kill Kyle, it can kill you and Lakisha."

"Oh!" She held it at a distance from her body.

"Yeah, Taran thinks they are time crystals, and that's why we were able to bring it through the fog. Also, they told his great grandfather that it can kill the black fog." He said.

"If true, this changes everything." She said, sheathing

the knife, putting it in her waist, and pulling her shirt over it.

"We have to be careful it doesn't fall into his hands." Kevin said.

She looked at him in the eye with a stern face and the vein in her neck throbbing. "He won't get the chance. Let's go make a plan to get him. Alright, everyone, we need a plan to get Kyle, and thanks to you, Kevin, we have a weapon than can kill him." She said, tapping her waist and sitting down with her back straight.

"The biggest question is, how to find him?" Thomas asked, grabbing a chair from the table, turning it around, and sitting down.

"That's easy. We have to figure out how he finds us and do the same." Kevin said, looking towards the fog. "Speaking of, how is Lakisha doing? We could really use her help."

"Not sure, but what I do know is that she needs a lot more recovery time. It wasn't like last time. This time, he consumed almost hundred percent of the green fog that sustains her. As you can see, there is barely any green fog."

"What if we go to his no-time zone?" Mari asked.

"From what I've noticed, he is a lot more vulnerable outside of the no-time zone. Both me and Maria were able to injure him." Thomas said.

"What does he want the most right now? We could use that as bait." Kalv said.

"Me." Maria got up and paced around the room. "And... I think I know how to draw him out. We have to pick a time period and place that gives us the edge." She stared at the fog.

"What I don't understand—and it's many things with this—is... what's the end game? I mean, he is really powerful now, and he hasn't changed time at all."

She turned around. "I know. I don't even think he knows what is the point either, other than becoming powerful. What the fog does is it controls the tick of time like a gigantic cog controlling all the smaller cogs around our 3D dimension. But we are still bound by 3D rules. I went to a place when I was looking for you guys. All I could call it is the thought dimension; it lacked anything except thought—no color, no light, no darkness, just clear."

"What do you mean? I can't picture that. When I close my eyes, I see darkness and I'm able to have a thought." Kevin said, scratching his head.

"That's right, but you only see darkness because your eyelids are closed. Separate that from the thought, and what do you have?" She asked him.

"Thought." Taran said.

"Are you talking about god?" Kevin asked.

"I'm not sure. All I know is that is where all thoughts originate from, because without the thought, you can't have creation. Thought has a thought and creation manifest. Don't ask me to explain, because I don't get it, but as our thought expands, so do we, that's all I know."

"That's it." Thomas said, jumping up.

"What's it?" Mari asked.

Maria pointed to her eyes and then to his. "We force him to go there."

"How the fuck do we do that?" Kevin asked.

"That's the million-dollar question." Thomas said. Mari, Klav, and Taran had a blank look on their faces.

"My question is, if we take him to the Thought, as you

call it, then why do we need the knife?" Thomas asked.

"I'm not sure it would take care of him, but it might level him out, or may not, but it's worth a try, and if it doesn't work, then I'll jig his ass." Maria did an action with her hand.

"Again, I have to repeat the question: How do we get him there?" Kevin asked.

"I'll let him get a taste of me." She pointed to herself.

"You mean you'll let him get some poon-poon?" Kevin laughed.

"*No!* Stupid, I will let him take a little of my fog, and he will follow me anywhere afterwards. His thirst for power is insatiable."

"Ohhh." He still was laughing.

"Ok, now, that we know that part, where and when?" Thomas asked.

"As we know, he has way too many allies in my time." Taran said.

"I think the past—a place with little water." Thomas said.

“I think the Nevada desert in precolonial times would be perfect.” Kevin said, looking like he was thinking out loud.

“That makes a good spot, and we can hide in the distance.” Thomas said.

“How will we get him there?” Mari asked.

“Don’t worry about that. He’ll come... once he senses my fog, he won’t be able to resist.” Maria said, standing up. “Let’s go, then.” She commanded, and they all stood up.

They walked over to the car and got in. Thomas drove into the fog.

CHAPTER 21

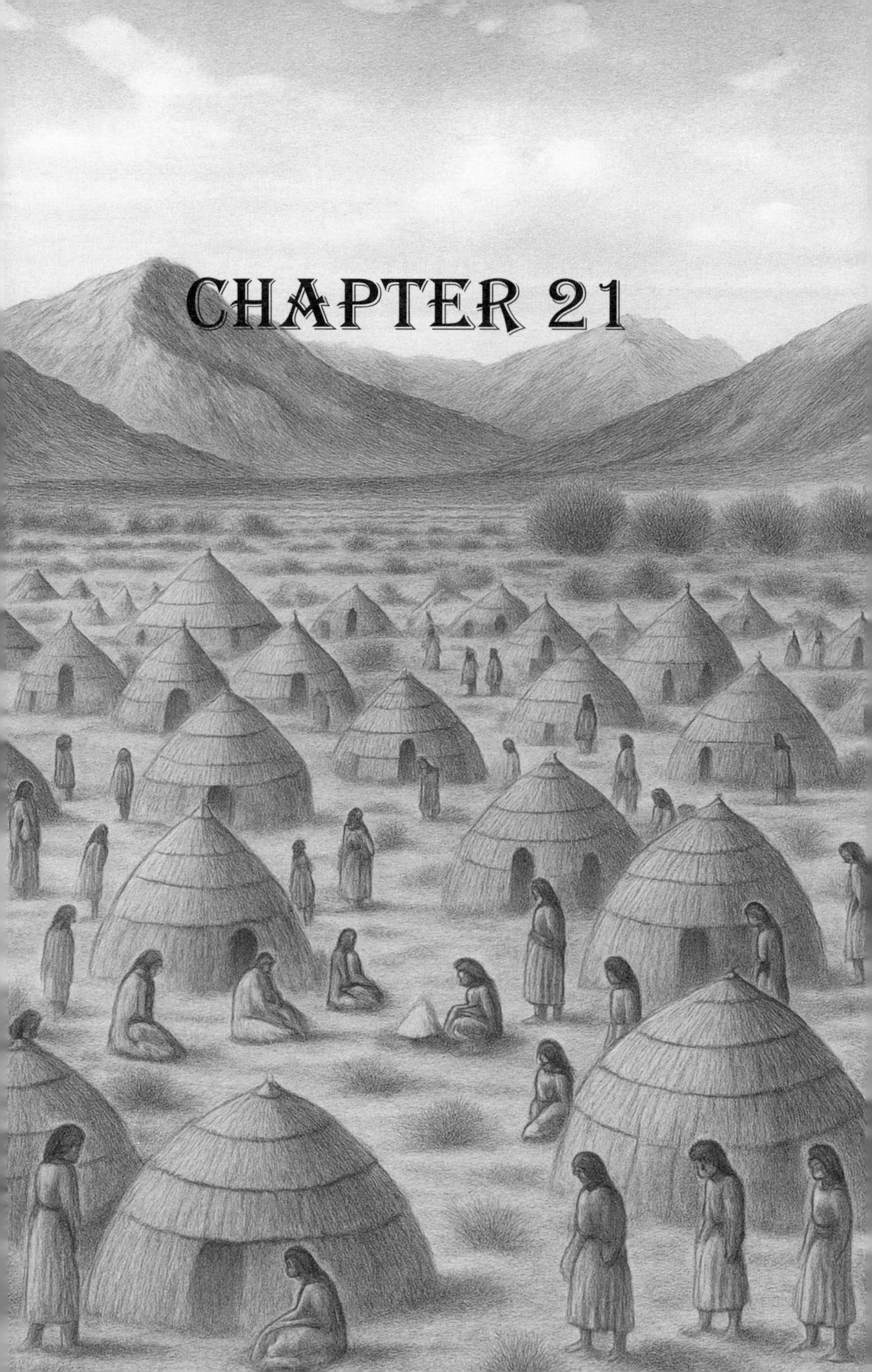

Chapter 21

As the fog cleared, they were back on a bison. This time, Maria could feel it didn't have as much fur as before. She had a spear on her back, a tomahawk hanging from her belt, and was wearing antelope skin.

She looked at the lake in front of them. When she looked over to her right, she saw Thomas admiring his tomahawk. "You know you can't keep that, right?" She said, smiling.

He looked up at her. "I know, but I can still appreciate it."

She smiled at him. "Let's check the map." She went into her satchel and pulled out a map. "This is modern-day Walker Lake, in Nevada." She got off her bison, and everyone else followed suit.

"What's the plan now?" Kevin asked.

"I'm going to flood the basin. He'll feel me... he always

does. Everyone else... hide." She sat in front of the lake and closed her eyes. She felt the fog oozing out of her skin. After a few minutes, it covered the landscape, giving it an eerie look as it spread over the desert and the lake shore.

She opened her eyes, and her skin was still producing the fog. She stared at it for a second and got up, then went into her satchel, and as she reached in, she could see from the corner her eyes a black fog beginning to form.

Her heart jumped a bit, and she dropped her bag. As she scrambled to grab it, a spear came flying through the air; she moved her hand from the bag, and the spear stuck the bag to the floor. She rolled away from it.

Kyle and a few mercenaries disembarked from a canoe. A spear hit one of Kyle's men between the neck and shoulder. Maria's friends ran out from hiding. Kyle threw his lance at Thomas, who rolled to the side, throwing his tomahawk. Kyle dodged to the right, and the tomahawk planted itself in another man's forehead. Kyle waved the men to retreat back to the canoe. Three of them pulled the canoe back. Mari helped Maria up. She pulled the spear out of the bag as Kevin launched his spear and missed the canoe. Kyle's fog began to surround the canoe.

"¡Mamaguevo... te voy a matar!" Maria yelled out in Spanish. She ran towards the water, splashing as she ran. Her legs vaporized to blue fog, and she skimmed the water, tomahawk raised. Kyle's eyes widened, and he grabbed his tomahawk.

"Fucking shit." Kevin said, and they all took off running into the water.

Thomas grabbed a tomahawk from Mari's waist and took off ahead of everyone.

Maria reached Kyle, swinging her weapon at his head. He deflected it with his weapon, knocking her tomahawk out of her hand. She swirled behind him, put him in a choke hold, and bit into his shoulder. He yelled out in agony. One of his men grabbed Maria by the hair. She released Kyle, and the man holding her picked up his weapon to bring it down onto her head. Thomas threw his tomahawk and hit him in the shoulder, dropping him into the water.

Taran threw his javelin at Kyle, who deflected it with his tomahawk and pushed Maria into the water. The fog covered the canoe, and they were gone.

Thomas swam out to Maria, and they swam back. "You

ok?" He scanned her with his eyes.

"I'm fine." She said with an attitude.

"What the fuck was that?" He asked, matching her attitude.

"What the fuck was what?" She stopped and looked at him.

"That's the kind of move that gets you killed." He paused for second "And the rest of us." His temper raised a bit.

She grinned at him. "I left him a nice beauty mark on his shoulder."

They came out the water. "Be that as it may, that was stupid. Don't you think so?" He held her arm.

"What?" She raised her voice. She took a deep breath and trembled a bit. "Look. I had a chance to kill him, and I took it."

"Yes, and almost got yourself scalped. If it wasn't..."

She cut him off. "Thank you, but that's the kind of risk I must take to kill that bastard. Or did you forget? He's the hijo de puta that killed my brother in some sick game to get at me. And you guys never noticed how fucked-up he is."

The others were quiet and standing a little distance from them. He winced at her comment. "You're right, but..." He held both of her hands and looked into her eyes. "You are not doing this alone. You have a team; we all want to get him. For Christ's sake, we all want to get him. This is bigger than us. How many people has he killed just to become stronger?"

She looked down for a second. "You're right. We need a better plan and need to use our individual strengths together."

"That's my girl." He pushed her hair back. "Can you get us new clothes? I'm freezing."

She checked herself. "Where's my bag?"

They both looked around. "What's wrong?" Kevin asked.

"She lost her bag," Thomas answered.

"It's over there." Mari said, pointing to an area a few yards from where Maria and Thomas were standing in the water.

"I got it." Thomas said. He ran deeper into the water and swam towards it, grabbing it and swimming back, holding it in his hand and shaking. He passed it to her, and they came out of the water.

“Please tell me that you still have the dagger.” Kevin asked.

She looked into the bag. “Yes, it’s here.” She held it up, and it shone in the sun.

“That’s a relief.” Thomas said. “Can I get some clothes?”

“Oh, yeah, who else needs clothes?” She looked at the group. Every hand went up. She took out some clothes and handed them to Thomas; they were made of buckskin, with leather leggings. They had bead designs. “These are traditional clothes of my people.” Thomas smiled from ear to ear.

“I guess you like it. Do you mind if I give the others the same clothes?”

“No, not at all. It’s better if we appear to be all from the same tribe.” Thomas smiled; he was almost glowing. “This reminds me of my grandmother. She would dress me up in these clothes. I used to hate it. It wasn’t until I got older that I saw the importance of learning about your roots.” He stared at the clothes, and his eyes lit up. “Can you get me one more thing?”

“Yeah, just think about it and reach in.” Maria passed

him the bag.

He closed his eyes and reached in. He pulled out something that was rolled up and almost looked like a yoga mat, but it was made of buffalo hide. He unrolled it, and it hardened to the shape of a rectangle shield. “That’s it. It’s just like the one my grandfather had.” It had the head of an eagle on it. He knocked on it a few times. “Get one for everyone. It protects against arrows and tomahawks.”

“I wish you would have thought of that before the battle.” Maria teased.

“Sorry.” He said, raising his shoulders.

She went to the others in the group and gave them similar clothes.

“Are we back to square one?” Thomas asked.

“Don’t worry; we will figure it out.” Mari said.

“I’m not sure where to go next.” Maria said, looking at the others for ideas.

“The good thing is, he doesn’t know about the knife. We have to draw him back here. I’m ready for him this time.” Thomas hit his shield with confidence.

“I have a question.” Mari said.

“What is it?” Kevin asked.

“I think we are here for a reason.” Mari said with a child-like look.

“The fog is part of me, but at the same time, it has a mind of its own. So, you could be right.” Maria answered.

“Then shouldn’t we explore it?” Mari said.

“What are we looking for?” Kevin asked.

“I don’t know, but I don’t think it’s an accident that we are here. Just like it wasn’t an accident that you came to my planet.”

“Good point.” Maria said. “Lead the way.” She gestured to Mari.

They got on their bison and headed northeast. After an hour, they reached the north of the lake. “Let’s take a short break.” Thomas said, dismounting his bison. He led his bison towards the lake so it can take a drink. The others follow suit. He looked at Mari. “Which direction from here?”

She looked at the lake. “I guess we continue to follow the lake until we find a river, then follow it.”

“Why do you think we should follow the water?” Kevin asked.

“From what I observed, it’s the source of Maria’s powers, at least in this reality, but when we are in the no-time zone, the fog is all around her, so she doesn’t need the moisture.” She said, petting her bison.

“But that means that is also the source of Kyle’s power as well.” Thomas said.

“Yes, that’s true, but Maria’s powers came naturally, where Kyle’s powers comes from consuming the chrono gene.” Mari answered.

“We should be able to exploit that,” Taran said, staring at his ride.

“The question is, how?” Maria asked letting out a sigh.

“Don’t worry. It will come to us when the time is right. If not, another way will. We keep going. What else is there to do?” Thomas said, getting back on his bison. “Let’s see what we find.”

They all got on and continued their journey.

From a distance, they could see people fishing at the

mouth of the river. A young man in his teen spotted them and announced it to the others. They all stood up and kept them in sight. "Now, remember, when we are in spear-throwing distance, get off your buffalo, and put your weapons on the floor." Thomas said.

"We know the routine, and this is before colonialism, so I won't cause a bad reaction from them." Kevin said, putting down his weapons.

They waited for the group of men to walk to them. It took them a few minutes. An elder man led the group. Thomas reached over for Maria's bag as they approached. He took out a woven blanket and placed down dry buffalo meat and arrowheads.

The men stopped ten feet from them. "Who are you?" The elder man with white hair and wrinkle cheeks asked.

"We are from the Piikani Nation. We are looking for somewhere to rest. We brought food and arrowheads as gifts."

The man crouched to study what Thomas placed down.

Thomas also crouched down, tore a piece of dried buffalo, ate it, and handed it over to the man, who looked at his eyes for a second, then the piece of buffalo. He smelled it and placed it in his mouth. He bit down hard and chew on it. Then he smiled. “This is good. I have never had it before.”

“This is from my homeland, north of here about two moon cycles.” Thomas said.

“I see.” He stared at Maria and Thomas. “Are they from the same tribe?”

“No, she is of mixed tribe, and he is from past the ocean on the other side.”

He got up and came closer to them, studying their features. “We welcome you. Please follow us.” He gestured for the young men to pick up the food and arrowheads. The young men couldn’t take their eye off the bison.

The youngest of all asked Thomas. “What are these beasts?”

“My people call them iinnii. They are hard to tame, but make great meat.” Thomas held him by the lead. “Would you like to pet him?”

“Absolutely.” His eyes lit up.

“Slowly pass your hand over his forehead.” Thomas showed him.

His hand shook a bit, but once he felt the bison's fur, his shoulder relaxed, and a smile came across his face. "They are beautiful."

"That, they definitely are. They are so majestic. Go ahead, get on." Thomas stopped and helped him on. "Be careful with your heels; if you kick his sides, he will run off."

"I will." He lay on the bison's back and hugged his side. "He is so soft."

They reached the village, their eyes filled with wonder at the sight of all of the tipis. "These shelters are beautiful." Mari said to Maria.

"I know." Maria answered.

All the kids in the village came running towards them. They were excited about Maria, Kevin, and the buffaloes. A few of the young girls wanted to touch Maria's hair, as they'd never seen curly hair. She had so many little fingers in her hair and all sorts of questions.

But she wasn't the only one getting the attention. The boys of the tribe wanted to play with Thomas' shield. "Let me show you how it's used." As Thomas held his shield and took a fighting stance, a smile came over his face. He caught the eye of Maria, blushed, and looked down.

"I've never seen him look so proud." Mari whispered to Maria.

"Right, that must bring back memories for him." Maria answered.

The old man came over and invited them into a tipi. They walked in, and the women of the village brought cooked fish. They all sat in a circle. The smoke rise from the fire rose out the hole at the top of the tipi. Maria listened to the crackling of the wood in the fire.

As the flames danced around the log, her stare was interrupted by the chief. "The kids really enjoy your presence. Thank you for your patience and taking the time to play with them." He said with a smile as he poked the fire.

"No need to thank us. We all really enjoy it. It's how they learn, and they will be telling this story for generations to come." Thomas answered.

"So, I have to ask, why are you here?" His face was stern, but with a slight smile.

"We are just passing through; we are looking for something, but we are not sure what. We are going on the hunch of my friend here." Thomas said, pointing at Mari.

"I see. You are letting nature show you the way." He replied.

"Yes, you could say that. Were you in battle?" He asked.

"How do you know?" Maria asked.

"I've lived many moons and learned to see patterns. Her face tells me of revenge, and also the small bruise on the side of your face." He pointed to her face.

Maria touched the side of her face. She winced a bit. "Yes, we are fighting a black fog and man who has become evil by absorbing people's..." She thought about how to word it to match the time period. "Time's energy, and he killed my brother many moons ago."

"You also have this, but you gained it differently from him. Yours grew naturally." He said to her.

"How do you know?" Thomas asked.

"My young warrior, you are not using all your eyes." He tapped his forehead. "Watch nature, and it answers, but only when your mind is quiet. That's when you realize there are no boundaries between us and nature. When we learn to open ourselves, our thoughts become those of nature and the animals. Right now, you are like a young hunter who tries to rush towards the deer, and the deer leaves before he is close enough, and he goes hungry."

Maria sat up straight and focused her ears on his voice.

"He hunts you, and you are like a cornered buck who attacks when he comes. Listen to the dirt, the sky, and the birds. Nature is like water; it flows, and now, you are stagnant. Like water sitting in a puddle with nowhere to go." He paused for a second and looked at Maria's eyes. "Enough talk. We must nourish ourselves." He grabbed the fish and distributed it to the group.

Maria put small pieces of fish in her mouth, but the words of the chief rang in her ears. She ran his words over and over in her mind.

After dinner, they sat outside and played with the kids, and they heard stories about this tribe. The wife of the chief showed them where they could sleep, and they had their own tipi. Maria sat outside with a blanket over her. She looked at her breath and touched the ground, looking for some insight.

Thomas stepped out. “He gave you a shitload to think about, didn’t he?” He smiled and sat next to her, putting his arm around her.

“You think?” Her voice raised a bit. She turned her face to look at him. “His words drilled into my mind.” She picked up some sand and let it fall from her fingertips.

“He’s right. You rushed forward without looking at what was going on.” Thomas said, looking at the stars.

“I know.” She looked down to play with the sand. “All I want to do is destroy him at any cost.”

“And therein lies the problem. Don’t let him turn you into him.” He squeezed her a bit.

Some tears trailed down her cheeks, and she wiped them.

Kevin walked out the tipi. He looked at them. “Sorry, guys. Nature calls.” He walked behind the tipi.

“Make sure you wash your hands.” Maria yelled out.

“Sure, after I take a nice hot shower.” He answered back.

“What should I do?” She held Thomas’s hand.

"First and most important is to work together. Use our strengths. Each one of our weaknesses is strengthened by the other." He looked at her.

"I understand, and you're right. I do need to put more trust in others. Let's head to bed. I'm sure the village wakes up as soon as the sun comes up." She stood up, holding his hand.

"No internet, no tv—that, they definitely do." He said, laughing.

***

Her eyes opened to the sound of footsteps. It was twilight.

She had a weird feeling in her stomach, so she elbowed Thomas and put her hand on his mouth, pointing outside. She made a gesture with her fingers of people walking outside. She grabbed her bag and weapons. Then she and Thomas tiptoed over to the others and woke them up.

They gathered on either side of the entrance. It was quite a few.

"I think it's a warring party." Thomas whispered. He reached out to Maria to pass him the bag, grabbed some war paint, and put it on his face, then passed it to the others. Black on the upper left and white on the lower left.

Once they all had the paint on, he gestured for himself and Kevin to go out first. He held up his shield and they stormed out in a line. As he ran out, he saw one, startling him. He wound up and crashed in with his shield, dropped him, and finished with a crown strike, then called out a war cry, warning the others.

Kevin was blocking the attacks of another; he gave him a front kick, knocking him off balance. He came down with all his might on his shoulder, then finished him off with a blow to his crown.

Maria faced one, but it seemed he wanted to take her. She swept him off his feet and brought her tomahawk down on his chest. Taran ducked at a weapon being swung over his head. He hooked his tomahawk under his armpit, threw him over his back, and finished him off.

The young boy came out his tipi and was facing a man twice his weight. His weapon shook in his hand, and his opponent laughed at him and swung at his head. He blocked the blow, but the hit send him back a few steps. The man kicked him square in the chest. He flew back and rolled onto his knees. The man came at him, swinging his weapon down at his head.

Thomas crashed into him using his shield. He stepped back a few steps and came back at his head, but Thomas blocked it and countered towards his ribs. He jumped back and went for Thomas's head, but he rolled to the side into a crouch with his shield and rushed forward, hitting him in the face and busting his lip. Thomas swung; he countered and kick him in the leg, and Thomas fell and rolled forward. The young teen swung his weapon, and he jumped back and punched him in the back of the head, sending him into a face plant.

Thomas rushed forward, crashing their weapons together, then headbutted him and hit him with the butt of the weapon on the cheek. When the teen came forwards, he gave him a side kick to the stomach. Thomas shot towards his knee, knocking him down and bringing his tomahawk into his face.

Another guy rushed forward, but a hatchet struck him in the side of the head. When Thomas looked, the teen had killed him.

Maria was facing two opponents; she was being pushed

back. She huffed and puffed. Mari came in with a flying kick to one man's side and did a spinning roundhouse, knocking the other guy onto the ground. The guy got up, but one of the young warriors hit him in the back of the head. Maria looked around and saw him. "What the fuck?"

Their eyes met, and Maria tapped Mari on the shoulder. "Let's get him!" Mari screamed. She rushed forward, and Maria took off behind her.

Kyle dodged to one side and grabbed Mari by the neck, slamming her onto the floor. Maria threw her hatchet at him, and he blocked it with his. She went into her bag, grabbed the knife, and unsheathed it. Kyle looked at it with curiosity as Maria rushed forward. "Die, you piece of shit." She yelled out with spit coming out her mouth. She slashed towards his chest, but he jumped back.

"You can't kill me, you little bitch." As he spoke, he punched her in the face, knocking her down to the floor. He grabbed her by the hair and started to drag her. He lifted his left hand and started gathering dew. His right hand fogged up, and he started to feed on her. Part of her hair turned into blue fog, and it was being sucked up into his hand. She yelled out in agony, then grabbed his hand with her left and was able to give him a small cut.

He let go and screamed, dropping his weapon. “What is that?” The cut turned black, then white. He took off running.

Maria got up and started running behind him. “Who’s the bitch now?” She screamed.

A guy tackled her, and as she was falling, she thrust the knife into his abdomen, and he burst into blue fog, which went into the knife, then into her. She felt stronger. Her eyes widened, and she dropped the knife.

Mari came and helped her up. “Are you ok?” She asked.

“I—I—I... don’t know.” She said, shaking a bit.

Mari picked up the knife, and the rest of the enemies were retreating back, being chase by the warriors of the tribe. She handed it over to Maria. “What was that?”

“I absorbed his energy.” Maria looked at the knife. “This knife is dangerous... and it *pulls*.” Her face was pale, and the knife was shaking in her hand. “I want to do it again.” She looked at Mari, face stricken by fear.

“Maria, hand me the knife.” She reached for the knife.

“Yes, that’s a good idea.” She handed it to her, and Mari

put the knife in the satchel. "I never want to experience that again."

"That's what Kyle felt. I've never seen him scared." Mari paused. "Well, he will think twice before attacking us again."

Thomas came up. "Are you guys ok?" He looked at Mari's face. "Did you see a ghost?" He asked Maria.

"It's the knife." Maria answered. "It can absorbs people's energies and turn them into fog."

"You should have seen how scared Kyle looked." Mari said to him.

"Kyle! He was here. Why didn't anyone call me." He said, swinging a punch into the air.

"I think because we were a little busy fighting for our lives." Maria said, twisting her lips at him.

"Oh, yeah." He said, rubbing his head.

The chief had a cut on his arm, and his wife was wrapping it. They walked up to Thomas. "I'm sorry we brought this battle to your village. We will leave as soon as possible."

"Nonsense. Those are the Klamath; they are our enemies, and we've had many battles with them. The white man with them—was that your enemy?" His wife looked up and asked.

"Yes, they've must have gotten together to attack your village," Maria said.

"I hear from Niyol that you are fierce warrior and that you alerted the tribe of the raid."

"Yes." Thomas smiled.

"Niyol said you saved him."

"He also saved me; he is the brave warrior, not me. Even though his opponents were bigger, stronger, more experienced, faster, and he was so scared his weapon shook in his hand, he still fought bravely, despite all the things he had going against him. That is the making of a great warrior." Thomas said, smiling, looking straight into the chief's eyes.

"As a father, I thank you for those words. He is my son, and the truth is, he was reflecting what he saw from you." The chief put his hand on his shoulder. "We now consider you part of our tribe. Only nature knows how many warriors we would have lost if you and your people were not here." He said, wiping his eyes. "Nature always brings you what you need when you are open to it like a tree, growing in all directions. We only see how tall the tree grows, but we never pay attention to how deep the tree's roots grow. Live by this, and no storm can knock you down."

Thomas stood back with his eyes watery, and mouth open, then hugged him. "You have given me more than any other man has ever given me."

Maria stepped forward. "I agree. Thank you. We found what we were looking for."

Kevin appeared, holding his arm. Blood was seeping through his fingers. The chief pointed to his wound. His wife rushed towards him. "Please sit." She pointed to a log near the tipi.

Kevin grunted, and his face contorted.

"What happened?" Both Maria and Thomas asked.

"You should see the other guy." He laughed and winced as the chief's wife added a cream to his wound to stop the bleeding. Taran and Klav showed up. Taran had a black eye, and Klav's nose was bleeding. Mari started to take care of him by holding his nose back and pinching the bridge of the nose.

"Please stay as long as you want." The chief said to

Thomas.

"Thank you for your hospitality, but we must leave as soon as the others are ready to travel." Thomas answered.

"Then please come back soon." The chief said.

"We will try." Thomas said. The chief hugged him again. "Do you think we can go?" He asked Kevin.

"It still hurts, but it stopped bleeding. I'm good as long as we don't get in another battle." He said, giggling at his own joke.

After an hour or so, they left the village. As they were riding out, Niyol ran after them to say goodbye to Thomas.

Thomas got off his bison. "Thank you."

"No, I'm the one who should be saying thank you."

"Well, we saved each other's life. You keep this." Thomas handed his shield and tomahawk over to Niyol. "Protect your village."

"I will. Thank you." Thomas mounted the buffalo, and they rode back towards the delta.

Once they were far enough, Kevin said. "I have a peculiar question. Didn't we change the timeline?"

"That's a good question." Thomas added.

They all looked at Maria. "Why are you looking at me?"

"Well, you're the closest thing we have to an expert," Kevin said.

"I'm not sure. I'm still a novice to all of this, but I guess we will find out when we arrive to our own timelines."

"OK, so where to now? What's the plan?" Klav asked.

"Ask our new general." Maria said, smiling at Thomas.

"Me?" Thomas retorted.

"It make sense. You have the most battle experience, and you outrank me." Kevin answered.

"Alright, then let's head back to the n- time zone and regroup." Thomas said with a grin.

CHAPTER 22

Chapter 22

They arrived and dropped all their gear off. "I'm going to take a shower and get some sleep. If that's ok with you general?" Maria asked, smiling.

"That sounds like a plan. We should all get some sleep." He said, heading towards the men's room.

Maria walked into the room, and Mari was right behind her. "Do you mind if I take a shower first?"

Mari was back to her alien form. "Not at all."

As she undressed, Mari came up behind her, hands sliding up to cup her breasts with slow, deliberate pressure. Maria froze for a breath, stunned—then a low shiver ran through her as heat pooled in her chest. "Oh... what are you doing?" She froze... and wanted more...

Mari's skin glimmered as she kissed her. She gave into her desires, pulling her into the shower.

***

When Maria woke up, Mari had her arm around her. She turned around and Mari open her crystal eyes and kissed her. “Good morning.” Mari said, placing her hand between her legs, caressing her. Maria’s moisture flooded Mari’s hand.

“Oh, this is a nice way to wake up.” Maria said, kissing her back.

***

“We need to get out of bed.” Maria said to her.

“Why? I can go again.” Mari said, and her skin glimmered.

“I love when your skin does that, it turns me on, but we have to see if Thomas came up with a plan.” She passed her fingers over her shoulder and shook her head. “We really must get up.”

“Ok, if we must. But I’ve wanted to hold you like this for a long time.” Mari sat up and held her hand.

Maria got lost in her eyes for a moment. “I must tell you, me and Thomas also...”

Mari interjected. “I know, I can tell. Why, should we

invite him next time?" She said, passing her lips over Maria's chest.

"Ooo, girl, you bad." Maria bit her lips.

Mari sat up straight. "You think I'm a bad person?" Her eyes filled with tears.

Maria sat next to her. "No, no, no, I meant I like how you think. But we really have to concentrate on getting Kyle." She said, wiping Mari's face.

Mari stood up. "Yes, right, we have to stop him. Who knows what kind of damage he can do." She said, putting on her clothes. "We should also check on Lakisha to see how she is doing. How much longer before she recovers?"

"I'm not sure, but I will check on her." Maria fixed her hair. "Are you ready?"

"Yes." She said, stealing a kiss from her.

They walked out the door. Kevin was cooking breakfast, and the guys were sitting on the couch. Thomas was sitting at the table, making a list. "What are you working on?" Maria passed a hand over his shoulder.

"I'm making a list of things we know about him." He

said, putting his hand on hers.

"You guys served with him for five years. You two know him better than anybody else." Maria looked at both of them.

"He's disciplined." Kevin interjected.

"That he is." Thomas agreed.

"How so?" Mari asked, coming towards the table.

"He would be the first one up in our unit to train." Kevin said.

"Yup, he would go over weapons training several times, until he mastered it." Thomas added.

"And how did the war break out, again?" Taran asked.

Kevin rubbed the back of his neck. "Officially, border disputes. Unofficially... something doesn't add up."

"But someone was moving the borders. It's a little complicated, but it started a whole mess of problems. The US wanted to take over a library where the front is in the US and the back is in Canada. Then, they said the town of Almonte belonged to them because of Mexico's help over almost two hundred years ago." Thomas added.

"Taran, are you thinking what I'm thinking?" Maria asked.

"If you mean that he has been manipulating history to have the outcomes that benefit him, then yes. Well... he killed..." He stopped to look at her with compassion. "He killed your brother to help you gain power."

Maria took a deep breath and wiped her tear. "But... how would he know Lakisha's fog would make contact?"

"We need Lakisha, I feel she can answer a lot of questions." Kevin interjected.

"I will go check on her." Maria turn around and walked into the fog.

"I think what we have to figure out is what's his endgame, and then we could know what he's missing, and we will know his next move." Klav said.

"You're right. So... if he's after power, the question is, what for?" Thomas said.

"To manipulate time?" Mari added.

"Ok, but why? There has to be a deep need," Taran said, getting up to pace.

"Kevin, did he ever talk about his past?" Thomas asked.

"No, he always deflected the conversation. All he ever said was that he moved around a lot." Kevin answered.

"That's true. He never talked about his childhood at all. So, is he from our past or our future? I don't think he's from our time period." He said to Kevin.

Kevin's eyes lit up. "Eighteen hundreds." He said, raising a finger.

"What makes you say that?" Thomas said, looking at him.

"Think about what time period he talked most about and knew the most about." Kevin said.

"You are right. He always said he just liked to read about that period, but... if I put it into context, the things he knew could only come from someone who lived that life." Thomas rubbed his chin.

"Spot on. But I didn't even believe in time travel until Maria showed up. So why would I think he was anything else than a history buff?" Kevin said, grabbing a seat.

"Ok, so what happened to him?" Thomas asked.

"Death!" Kevin paused and looked around. "Look at how it changed Maria's trajectory." He whispered to them.

"Yes! If he controls time, then he could change the death of a loved one. Nothing is a bigger driver than that. Even Maria might do that." Thomas lowered his voice. "I know I would. Who wouldn't?" He stood up to pace.

"Then, if we know who and when, he would visit quite often to see them." Kevin said.

Thomas stopped and came closer to him. "Yes, that's it."

At that moment, Maria and Lakisha came out. Lakisha was leaning on Maria for support.

"Oh, my god, Lakisha." Kevin ran over and kissed her.

"Oh, I see someone missed me." She blushed.

"Sorry, I don't know what came over me. Did I cross a line?" He asked, stepping back.

"No, not at all." She smiled and winked at him.

Maria smiled and then turned her attention to Thomas. "Any progress?"

"Yes!" He raised his voice. "But we need your help."

Lakisha sat on the couch, and Maria raised her legs.

The team caught them up. “It makes a lot of sense, but the only issue I found is that he blocks us from tracking him.” Lakisha breathed in heavily.

“I agree with her. I’ve tried many times.” Maria said.

“Yes, but there is one resource that Maria has that we are not using.” Thomas said.

“Which resource is that?” Maria asked.

“Really?” Thomas asked in disappointment. Maria looked lost. “Thought!”

“Thought?” Lakisha asked.

“Oh, shit, you’re right. Thought was this place I went to where only thought existed, and I met the grand thought, as I call it.” Maria explained.

“You mean God?” Lakisha sat up straight.

“I don’t know, but it’s our thoughts and its own thought, yet it’s the wellspring of all ideas and thoughts.”

“Can you take us there, Maria?” Klav interjected.

“I don’t know how.” Maria looked at Lakisha.

"I think you can if you use me as an anchor." Lakisha said.

"You mean the way you used me as an anchor in the shower?" Maria asked.

"Exactly. You can't take them physically, but... you can take them consciously."

"How am I going to do that?" She asked and her heart sped up a bit.

"Don't worry. I will guide you." Lakisha said.

"Then it's settled. Let's get started." Thomas said, clapping.

"How did you guys get to him being from the eighteen hundreds?" Maria asked to take her mind off the task ahead of her.

"He always talked about it as if he had been there more than any other time period." Thomas answered.

"Makes sense." Lakisha said.

"Ok, everyone, lay down on the floor here." Lakisha stood up with the help of Kevin.

“Are you sure you’re up to it?” Maria asked with a weary smile.

“My part is easy. I just have to stay grounded to help bring them back. You’re the one that has to worry about not frying their brains.”

“What?” She raised her voice, then lowered it. “No pressure, right?”

“None at all. You know I got you.” Lakisha winked at her. “Say what you want to say about me, but I was always there since the day your brother died. You didn’t know what I was, but I was there. And when I almost died, you became you. So, this is easy.” She said with confidence.

Maria took a deep breath. “Let’s do this.” The group lay down next to each other. She knelt down next to their feet and sat on her heels. She rubbed her hands together. “Ready, baby girl?” She asked Lakisha.

“You know it.” Lakisha took a deep breath.

Maria reached out, facing her palms at their feet. “Grab both my ankles.” Lakisha followed her instruction. “Everyone follow my voice. Take a deep breath, hold it, release, let out all the stress. Hold, take a deep breath. You are so comfortable, you only hear the sound of my voice. You find yourself at the beach, feeling the warmth of the sun on the bottom of your feet."

From her knees to her chest, she turned into the blue fog, swirling around them. "You feel the warm water coming around your body, slowly carrying you. You are more relaxed. Ten, nine, more relaxed as the water carry you off. Eight, seven, six, you feel this river carrying you up. You never felt so relaxed. Five, four, three, you see stars, galaxies passing by you. Two, one, you've arrived in a place with no color, light or form. All you are is thought. Open your eyes. We have arrived."

Thomas felt different thoughts from Kevin. "I wonder if Lakisha likes me. I'm crazy about her."

"Kevin, we can all hear your thoughts, she now knows." Thomas said.

Before they he could answer, he was saved. "Welcome home." The thought said.

"I don't remember." Mari said.

"But I do, and I am your thoughts, and you are mines." It said.

"We need to find someone," Thomas interjected.

"He is you and you are him." The thought answered.

"Then why hurt us?" Maria asked.

"Because he hurts and all he knows is hurt." It said with calm.

"We want to stop the hurt." Thomas said.

"By hurting him, that does not stop the hurt but perpetuates the hurt. Do you understand?" It answered.

"I think so, but we can't let him continue." Maria said, feeling her thoughts becoming jagged.

"But this is not a thought for now. Just be where he be." It said.

"Just be where he be." Thomas thoughts became the predominant thoughts, and the others' infused into his. Maria's thoughts smoothed out. They felt their thoughts riding the river flowing through time and space, passing quasars, alien civilizations, flowing through England. It was like they were part of wind flowing through the alleys and over the cobblestone.

They came up to a boy and his mother.

"That's him." Thomas thought to the others.

Kyle was around eight years of age. "Mummy, do you have to go again tonight? Can't you stay with me?" He pleaded.

She crouched down next to him. "My dear boy, I wish I could stay with you, but mummy has to go and make money for us to eat and our landlord. Now, listen to your mother and run back to our flat, and I will be there later on tonight. I will make you your favorite breakfast." She kissed him on the cheek and gave him gentle slap on the bottom. "Now go." He looked back, drooped his shoulder, and hung his head. When he turned the corner, he stopped, hid, and waited for his mom to keep walking and then he followed her.

She walked into an area where other women were standing. He stood far enough where he couldn't hear what she was talking about with the other women. Men came by and would take some of the other women to the rooms above.

It was getting late, and he hid in an alley and took a nap. He awoke and ran back to the spot to see his mother. She was there by herself. A man with long dark coat with fur-trimmed collar and cuffs, light waistcoat, dark trousers, dark felt hat, button boots, gaiters with white buttons, and a black tie with a horseshoe pin came up to her.

The scene pulled back, and they were able to see from many different angles. Adult Kyle ran towards them, and he hit an invisible barrier, then turned back into black fog and dissipated. Then another version came from a different angle, and he also dissipated. Then another and another hundreds of versions.

The man grabbed her and slit her throat. Young Kyle screamed and ran off. One of the adult Kyles waited for him he followed the man. The man noticed and ran. Kyle chased him through the Gunthorpe Street. The man fell, and Kyle picked him up by the neck. "Jack the Ripper, you will never kill again."

It started to drizzle. Jack went to stab him in the chest, but Kyle's chest turned to fog. His hand that was holding him fogged up and went into his nose, eyes, and ears, ripping him apart from the inside disintegrating his entire body.

Maria's group flowed back to the house, where young Kyle was frantically crying. He closed his eyes, and the room filled with a small portion of green fog, but as it got closer to him, it started to turn black and went into the pores of his body. The boy jumped up and ran outside; when the rain hit him, he fogged up and dissipated.

They flowed through time right behind Kyle, where he landed ten thousand years into the future. They saw a sped-up version of Kyle growing up with a woman who had adopted him when she met him on the streets where he was crying. But the black fog was with him. One day, he was thinking about his mother, and that was when he first attempted to stop his mother's murder. He came back distraught and ran to his adopted mother. She was holding him. He saw her chrono genes lighting up and he pulled her being into his fog. He stood up and was able to use his fog more easily. He went back to try again, but failed. Then he traveled through time to find another and another.

They were pulled out, went back into the river of thought, and they were back with thought. "You've seen what you need." They flowed back on the river and were brought back to the no-time zone.

Maria stood up. "What the fuck?"

Thomas sat up. "That makes total sense." He walked over to Maria, who was still crouched down. "We have to get the last version of him."

"Boy, that is a lot to take in." Kevin said.

"Right." Lakisha stood up. "I don't remember that happening."

"His chrono gene must be just as strong as Maria's, but when you came to Maria, she didn't know yet that her brother was dead. He saw his mother being murdered, so the little bit of fog that came through was transmuted into darkness." Thomas helped Maria up and sat her down on the couch. "That's why you don't remember—because it broke off from your fog and became its own. Maria's fog didn't develop until much later." He said.

"How will we know the latest version?" Lakisha asked.

"He will have the scar from the chrono-blade." Thomas replied.

"I don't think it will heal as a normal cut would." Mari said.

"I agree. That knife was made to hurt people like you, so he will most likely be in pain and wearing a glove." Taran said.

"Ok, then let's go and get him." Maria stood up, walking towards the fog. "Lakisha, do you feel strong enough to join us?"

"Yes, but give me a second." She walked into the fog and green fog started mixing in with Maria's blue fog. She walked back out. "Now I feel a hundred percent."

"I think I can take us there without the use of a vehicle."

"Really?" Lakisha asked. "I can't even do that."

"Yes, especially now that our fogs are combined. Everyone, stand together." A cyan color came about and circled them.

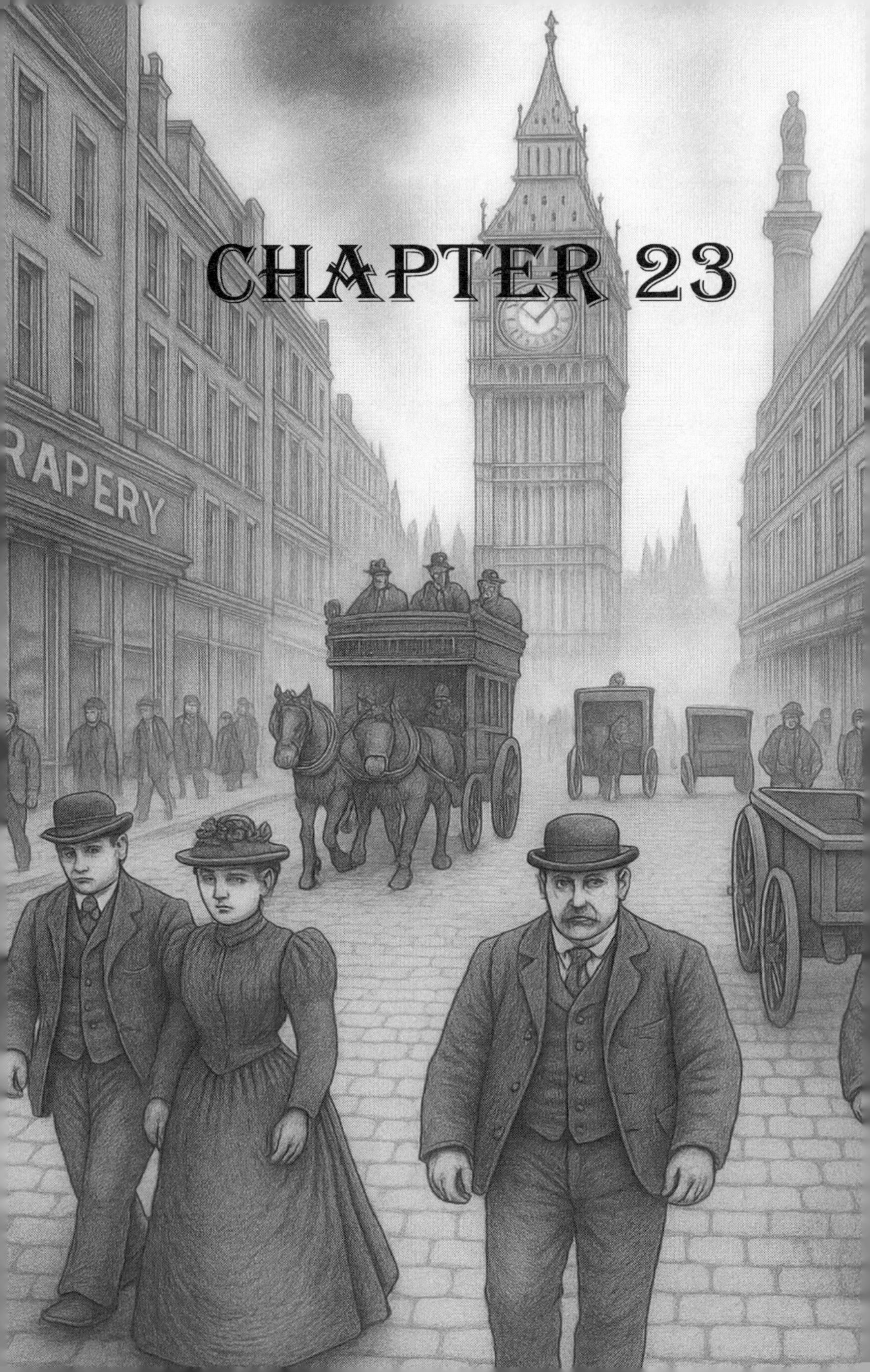
CHAPTER 23
RAPERY

Chapter 23

Thomas felt a cold cobblestone floor. He sat up and looked around. The wind blew into his neck, and he shivered. The rest sat up.

"You did it, Maria." Kevin said, dusting himself off.

"Everyone, keep your eyes peeled." Thomas ordered. They were standing in an alley. "Check for weapons." They checked their pockets and waists.

Kevin saw a revolver on his waist, and he had brass knuckles in his jacket pocket, better known as knuckle dusters in Victorian England. "I don't think you should use that unless you really have to." Thomas pointed to the gun.

"Why not?" Kevin asked, almost looking offended.

"Because we don't want unwanted attention." Thomas said.

"Agree." Lakisha said, adjusting her red-and-black Victorian dress.

"Then I'll use this." He said with a big smile, holding up the brass knuckles.

"I think our faces and accents will attract attention." Maria said.

"They might attract weird looks, but not the police." Kevin said, putting away his new toys.

"Ok, agreed, then." Thomas said, and everyone nodded.

Maria tucked her special quantum-blade in her bustier. "Follow me." They walked towards the main street. As they got to the main street, many people stared at them.

"There goes the young Kyle with his mother." Klav pointed with his eyes.

"Great, look around. There should be different versions of Kyle. Look for the glove or scar." Thomas ordered.

"There goes one version, but it's not him. That looks like a version before he joined the Canadian military." Kevin said. Kyle was reading the newspaper in a far corner, taking quick glances at the boy.

"Why not just kill that version?" Maria said, tapping the

knife on her chest.

"Hold on, tiger." Thomas squeezed her hand. "I have a theory if we kill the wrong version, it won't stop our version."

"Why not?" She said with an attitude.

"I don't have time to explain. Let's just say it's a hunch." He stared at her eyes with compassion.

"Fine." She sucked her teeth.

The mom pushed the boy towards home, and they followed her towards the alley where she worked. She took several men up to a room, and they waited outside. It was getting late.

"Where is he?" Maria asked, tapping her foot.

"He's not going to want to relive this part, so he will show up right before he kills her."

They saw several different versions of Kyle.

"That's him." Lakisha said.

"Everyone spread out. Me and Kevin will attack first. Klav and Taran, you're second wave. Mari, keep an eye out for the police, and Maria and Lakisha next. Lakisha, you will hold him down, and Maria, you finish him off."

Kyle was dressed as a beggar, and they could barely make out his face. Thomas pulled out his knife. Kevin pulled out his knuckle duster, and he was approaching him from the opposite side, focused on the alleyway where his mother stood.

Thomas thrusted his knife towards his chest, but Kyle kicked his leg from under him. Kyle guided the knife towards the floor. He rolled over Thomas's body and stood up.

Kevin swung the brass knuckle at his head, but Kyle ducked, grabbed his arm, kneed him in the stomach several times, and tossed him onto the floor.

Taran kicked at his head, and he parried to the left and gave a right hook to the chin. Klav went for a front kick, but Kyle stepped to the left, then crouched down picked him up by his pants using his shoulder and arm and slammed him on the floor.

Kyle pulled out a billy club that was nestled in his waist on the back. Thomas came with the knife, but Kyle stood in a fighting stance and hit his wrist and then his head. As Kevin came in, he hit him on the head and kicked him in the back.

Lakisha's hand fogged up and grabbed his wrist. He dropped his billy club and fogged up his hand, countering her fog. Maria came from the side and grabbed his other arm, fogging up both her arms. Lakisha swung over to his back and wrapped her fog around his neck and started to suck his fog. Maria thrusted her fogged hand into his chest, and he screamed.

"How did you... get... here?" He breathed heavily to get the words out.

She tore the Quantum Blade from her bustier, its edge catching the last flare of the setting sun. "You are done!" Maria screamed at him with saliva coming out of her mouth.

"No... not yet! If I can fix time, I can save her. I can stop my mother from being murdered! Once I do that, it will all go back. Your brother will be alive, and I will never have come to any of your futures. Isn't that what you want?" He pleaded with Maria, throwing his hands up.

Maria held the knife high up. "That's never going to work. How many times have you tried already and failed?"

"I wasn't strong enough. That's why I need your fog and hers. Why do you think I've guided Lakisha to you and help you become what you are." He said, sobbing.

"Maldito, look at you. The best thing I can do for you

is to take you out of your misery, you sorry piece of mierda." Maria said in Spanish.

"No, Maria, if you love your brother, you won't do this. You will help me become and override reality."

"That's not how it works! Are you trying to become god? I will not let you." Her eyes were red with fury.

"Kill him already!" Lakisha scream.

Her grip tightened on the Quantum Blade—ready to drive it down.

"I'm your thought and you are mine." The thought whispered to her in her head, and she was there with it.

"Why have you brought me here?" She screamed.

"Because you want another way." It answered in a calm voice.

"I never said that. Now, put me back so I can finish him off." She demanded at the top of her thoughts. Her thoughts became jagged and incoherent.

"See from my thought, as I see you." It said to her.

She felt Kyle's jagged thoughts slam into hers, sharp

edges scraping against her mind until their pain tangled, multiplying, spreading—bleeding into the fabric of reality itself. Each thought fractured, splintering outward like cracks in glass, infecting everything it touched.

She was back in the park near the Hudson River, playing on the swing, her laughter rising as her brother pushed her higher. The sun filtered through the trees, and for a moment, she was weightless. Then the scene shifted—she was watching her ten-year-old self. The girl smiled, her chest glowing with a warm golden light, pure and innocent.

In an instant, everything snapped to London. Shadows swallowed the streets as her younger self drove a knife into Kyle's chest. Blood darkened the scene. She turned toward the older Maria, whose chest was now black, her grin twisted and oozing with evil. Maria looked down at her own arms—the once-blue fog had turned pitch black.

"Maria… **kill him**!" Lakisha's voice cut through the chaos, snapping her back into herself.

Maria's chest heaved. Her vision blurred. Her grip faltered, and the **Quantum Blade** slipped from her trembling hand, clattering against the cobblestones with a sharp ring.

Her throat locked. She swallowed hard, forcing the words through ragged breath. "No..." Her voice cracked. "No, there's another way."

She wiped her face with the back of her hand, tears burning down her cheeks. She stared at Kyle, broken, desperate, and something shifted deep inside her.

"I..." Her voice wavered, then steadied. "**I forgive you.**"

And in that moment, it felt as though the weight of the world lifted off her shoulders. Years of pain, vengeance, and rage slipped away like smoke in the wind, carried with each tear splashed on the cobblestone.

The **Quantum Blade**, lying between them, began to hum. A deep, resonant tone spilled into the alley, pure, alien, vibrating the stone beneath their feet. The sound grew louder, higher, until it was almost unbearable. Everyone clutched their ears as the blade dissolved... blue fog first, then white, then brilliant gold. The golden mist coiled upward and plunged into Kyle's chest.

His body convulsed, as if the weight of a thousand lifetimes collapsed onto him at once. He sobbed, raw, unrestrained, as though centuries of grief were unraveling. His black fog shredded, turning gray... then white... before flaring into blinding gold.

Kyle looked at Maria, tears streaking his face. His voice broke.

“Thank you.”

And then he burst into **pure light**.

Time **shattered**.

The world outside the alley fell silent. Horses froze mid-breath. People hung mid-step, mouths caught half-open. A flock of pigeons hovered, wings suspended, trapped between beats. The air itself stood still.

Only Maria and her group could move.

Thomas turned to her, awe and terror twisting his face. “What the **hell** did you just do?”

“I freed him of his burden by forgiving him.” Before anyone else said anything, time started to go backwards.

“Follow it.”

Maria chased the ball of light that was now Kyle. People and the horses and carriages were going backwards. They arrived back at the corner with young Kyle and his mother. The ball of light entered his chest, and time resumed forward.

His mother pushed him off, and he split into two. One version ran away, and the other turned around and hugged her. “Mummy, I love you more than anything else in the world.”

Her eyes filled with tears. “My dear son, I love you more than that.” They stayed in the embrace. She split into two. One walked away as the other stayed with her son. They stood like that for about five minutes.

“Excuse me, is your name Mary?” Asked a man about in his thirties, dressed as rich merchant.

“Yes.” She looked up to study his face.

“You don’t remember me?”

“Danny, is that you?” She stood up.

“You do remember me.” He said hugging her.

“How could I forget you?” She said, hugging him back and giving him a kiss.

“Mummy, who is this?”

The man crouched down next to young Kyle. “I’m your

father."

He looked at his mother. "Yes, he is." She turned his attention to Danny. "I was told you were dead, your whole ship disappeared in the new world."

"For a while, I thought I was dead, but I survived, and was finally able to make back to England. People told me that I would find you here. I own land in America, and I came to find you and my son."

Maria turned to Lakisha. "What the hell is happening?" She whispered.

"I think... we just created a ***Mandela Effect***." Thomas said.

"What's a Mandela Effect?" Mari asked.

"Nelson Mandela was or is or will be one of the main people who brought the end of apartheid to South Africa. Many people remember him dying, but he was still alive. So basically, when two timelines exist at the same time." Kevin answered.

"I think you're absolutely right." Lakisha said.

Time sped up, and they turned in thought and then

moved to America. This version of Kyle grew up, got married, and had a family.

Their thoughts flowed through time and space, and they ended up back in the n- time zone.

They were lying on the floor, and Maria stood up first. “Holy shit. Is it really over?”

Mari was touching her face and arms. “I think it’s really over.”

“We need to celebrate.” Kevin jumped up and down.

“My friend, I think you are right.” Taran said.

“How did you know to forgive him?” Lakisha asked.

“When I was going to stab him, the thought brought me back to his realm and showed me my thought being all jagged and sporadic and how it combined and amplified other people’s jagged thoughts. Like when you play music through a music plate and create different patterns. I didn’t want to be that, so I chose a path that created the opposite. My question to you is, why did you listen to me when I told you to let him go? I expected you to fight me on it.”

“I don’t know. I just knew it was the right thing to do.”

Lakisha answered.

"Hey, Maria, pass me your bag. We need some tequila." She passed Thomas the bag, and he pulled out a bottle of tequila, opened it up, and took a swig, then passed it along.

They drank and talked for a few hours. Maria was feeling tipsy when she felt someone grab her from behind. She turned around, and it was Thomas. "Oh, do you want some?" She pressed her butt up against him.

"Let's disappear somewhere." He said, holding her waist.

By this time, Taran and Klav had passed out on the couch. Lakisha grabbed Kevin and created a new room, which they disappeared into. Maria grabbed Thomas's hand and was walking towards another room when she looked at Mari, whose skin lit up for a few seconds, and she looked down. "Hold on." She wobbled a bit and grabbed Mari's hand and pulled them both into the room.

"Really?" Thomas asked with a smile from ear to ear.

"It was her idea, but you can stay if you're not interested." Maria said.

"I will be quiet now." He answered.

***

In the morning, Thomas was cooking and preparing his supposedly famous hangover drink that he learned from his grandfather. That afternoon, they were getting ready for each of them to head back to the right timelines.

"Is everyone ready?" Maria asked.

"I will never drink human alcohol again." Klav said, still holding his head.

"I think that is a good idea." Kevin answered.

"We all say that, but somehow, we end up drinking again." Thomas said.

They gathered around Maria, she fogged up, and they dropped off Klav, Taran, and Mari.

They then headed towards Thomas and Kevin's timeline. They appeared near a barracks away from the border war. "What will you two do now?" Maria asked.

"Now that we know how the war started, we will try to stop it." Thomas answered.

if they succeed, your entire existence will vanish." He said in a low, **thunderous** voice, then looked at his hand. "I promise we will explain everything in my dimension. I promise I won't hurt you."

"I know you." She said louder than she wanted to. "You gave an ancient tribal elder the quantum blade in Antarctica."

"Yes. We have to go." He waited.

Maria took a deep breath. "Well, I did travel through time. So this can't surprise me."

She took his hand, and they fazed out of reality.

To be continued in

United Earth, Book Four:

Ashes of Tomorrow

R.M. ALMONTE
UNITED
EARTH
BOOK FOUR
ASHES OF TOMORROW

About the Author

In 2002, after reading The Alchemist by Paulo Coelho, R.M. Almonte felt a pull he couldn't explain. With only $800 in his pocket, he spent three months in Japan — no plan, no safety net, just a feeling. That leap reshaped the course of his life.

Upon returning to the United States, Almonte began writing with intent — not to impress, but to make sense of his dreams, lived experiences, and the connections that shaped him. Influenced by his research into ufology and his lifelong love of science fiction television (Star Trek: Deep Space Nine, Stargate SG-1, and others), he realized he was walking the path that had been calling to him all along.

The next twelve years brought him back to Japan, this time as a foreigner navigating a new culture. That chapter expanded his worldview and gave him the discipline to forge a literary path. Along the way, he skydived, earned his Open Water Diver certification, became fluent in three languages, taught himself blind touch typing at 45, learned to drive at 47, and traveled to more than seven countries. He co-hosted The Hundredth Monkey radio program, spoke at the ECETI Conference, and connected with communities drawn to extraordinary experiences.

Today, Ramon Manuel Almonte — publishing as R.M. Almonte — is an author, speaker, father, and founder of R.M. Almonte Publishing/Media, a traditional publishing house focused on metaphysical and science fiction. His work blends the imagination of genre fiction with the rawness of lived truth, weaving dream phenomena, contact experiences, and personal transformation into compelling narratives.

He is the author of the United Earth series, including:

- •Scratching the Cosmic Conscious
- •United Earth: Rough Beginning
- •United Earth: Exile
- •United Earth: Dvespair & Hope
- •Fogs of Time — his newest release

His writing has gained national attention, including features on Coast to Coast AM and Paranormal 60 with Dave Schrader, where his story and ideas resonated with audiences eager for the extraordinary.

R.M. Almonte continues to build a publishing vision rooted in resilience, wonder, and the unknown.

www.rmalmonte.com

R.M. ALMONTE
UNITED
EARTH
SCRATCHING
COSMIC
CONSCIOUS
R.M. ALMONTE
R.M. ALMONTE
UNITED
EARTH
R.M. ALMONTE
UNITED
EARTH
BOOK TWO
EXILED